I0538387

The President's Agent

Red Sky Morning

Greg Marion

Red Sky Morning
Copyright © 2011 by Greg Marion
CS5 SP
All rights reserved.
Except for brief passages quoted by a reviewer in a newspaper or magazine or as permitted
under the U.S. Copyright Act of 1976, no part of this book may be reproduced, distributed, or
transmitted in any form or by any means, or stored in a database or retrieval system without the
prior written permission of the author. This book is a work of fiction. Names, characters,
places, and incidents are the product of the author's imagination or are used fictitiously. Any
resemblance to actual events, locals, or persons, living or dead, is coincidental. Thank you for
respecting the author's rights.
ISBN-13: 9780991414109
ISBN-10: 0991414101
Cover of *Red Sky Morning* by Greg Marion – Copyright © 2013. All rights reserved.
Author's website: gregmarion.com
Email: gregmarion@outlook.com
The author is not responsible for websites not owned by the author.

Other novels by Greg Marion:

Paper Tiger

White Sands

Dedication

To my wife Rose, who is my biggest fan.
She's also my biggest critic, which keeps things interesting.

"And in the morning, *It will be* foul weather to day: for the sky is red and lowring.

O *ye* hypocrites, ye can discern the face of the sky; but can ye not *discern* the signs of the times?"

~Jesus, to the Sadducees and Pharisees, Matthew 16:2-3

-PROLOGUE-

Sunday, October 6, 1963

La Ascención, Nuevo Leon, Mexico

Change is the law of life. And those who look only to the past or present are certain to miss the future."
~President John F. Kennedy

In his mirror, he saw only a cloud of dust while ahead was a bleak, windswept landscape, and beyond that the unknown. Clayton Donovan knew, however, that even the most desolate places are often filled with interesting possibilities.

His vehicle, an inconspicuous '54 Chevy pickup, had a strong engine, an automatic transmission, and was fitted with a custom camper shell. With one hand on the wheel, he glanced back and forth between the dirt road ahead and the radio dial as he searched carefully for a signal. The fourth game of the World Series was well under way and Donovan was having trouble picking up a broadcast this far from a major city.

He turned the dial slowly, passing over a few Spanish music stations until he found it, then turned the volume up and listened intently. This year's World Series featured the New York Yankees playing against the Dodgers, who had famously moved out of Brooklyn a few years ago to Los Angeles. Most New Yorkers, Clayton Donovan included, were still having trouble accepting that.

The announcer reported the score was still 0-1 with the Yankees behind at the top of the seventh inning. The signal was fading in and out, but he could understand that the Dodger pitcher, Sandy Koufax, had just delivered a fastball to the Yankee batter, Mickey Mantle. Mantle swung and connected with the ball. Donovan heard the roar of the crowd as it almost drowned out the voice of the announcer: *"It's a hit...a deep hit out between center and left field!"* he yelled. *"It's going...going..."*

At that moment, the signal faded out and was gone; despite Donovan's frantic attempts to tune the station back in. After a minute or two, he let out a deep breath and turned the radio off, focusing his thoughts back on the mission that lay ahead. In a few minutes, he'd be arriving at La Ascención, a small, secluded village known to the locals as *La Chona*.

While keeping one eye on the road, Donovan reached down and pulled up his left pant leg and took a moment to adjust the top strap of his aluminum leg brace. Almost at once, he felt a sharp pain coming from a second wound located just under his right ribcage. He pressed his hand over the site as he exited Mexican Federal Highway 61 and headed to the center of the small village.

Upon reaching the town plaza, he noticed a group of teenage boys gathered around the park benches. He stopped the truck and placed his cowboy hat on his head, then rolled down his window and called to them, *"Señor Ignacio Soto?"*

They gazed at him curiously, having never seen a gringo in their village before. One of the boys seemed to understand. He walked over to Donovan and asked, *"Señor Soto?"*

In Spanish, Donovan replied, "Yes, the house of Ignacio Soto, please."

The boy muttered a few words, then walked out in front of the truck, waving for Donovan to follow. After two blocks, he pointed to a tiny home at the end of a dirt street.

"Muchas gracias," Donovan said. He pulled out a few Mexican centavos and handed them to the boy before continuing down the street, parking his vehicle close to Sato's home. The late afternoon sun cast his shadow long as he walked carefully to the front door. So far, his fractured left leg had been healing well and he was hoping not to aggravate the injury.

He knocked and waited. Before long, a woman came to the door, opening it only a few inches. She appeared to be about fifty or so, with long, greying hair and weary eyes. Almost at once, Donovan detected the aroma of wood-fired cooking and homemade tortillas, which reminded him of his empty stomach. He tipped his hat and addressed her, *"Buenas noches Señora."*

The woman eyed at him from head to toe. *"Buenas noches,"* she replied, leaving out the *Señor*.

Donovan was far from fluent, but he could speak and understand Spanish well enough to suit his needs. He explained that he was an American working as an official for the Mexican government in Nuevo Leon and asked the woman if she knew the whereabouts of Ignacio.

She seemed apprehensive, but finally explained that her husband was a cattle rancher and would be returning home after sunset.

Using Spanish, he asked, "He found a machine?"

"Si," she replied. The woman explained that her husband had discovered a strange contraption buried in the hills behind his ranch and had reported the find to the officials.

"¿Dónde está la máquina?" Where is the machine?

Señora Soto led him around the outside of the house to the rear of the small property. To the east, the low mountains rose up from the desert floor and extended north and south for miles. She pointed out the location of her husband's cattle ranch. She also described where Ignacio had found the machine, directing his attention to a narrow ridge above the ranchland.

That was all Donovan needed.

After taking a moment to study the topography of the ridge and its surrounding features, Donovan thanked the woman for her help. He also explained that he and his assistants would be back soon to check on the find and warned that everyone stay far away from it until the officials have inspected it.

As he began to leave, a neighbor, a rail-thin man of about forty, approached him. The man seemed to object to Donovan's presence and began making threatening statements while pointing at him and shouting.

From what Donovan could tell, the neighbor didn't like seeing an outsider, especially a gringo, appearing at a woman's home while the husband was away. At first, Donovan wasn't too concerned, noticing he was about a foot taller and probably a hundred pounds heavier than the man. Nonetheless, the neighbor's shouting continued and Donovan began to worry that this would turn into a scene.

The man stepped closer to Donovan and began to repeat himself when Soto's wife finally cut him off. *"Cállate, estúpido!"* Shut up, stupid!

Ignoring that, the man began to shout insults and accusations at her as well.

Having heard enough, Donovan grabbed the neighbor by the collar and lifted him from the ground with one hand. He looked him in the eye. *"Cállate, Sí?"*

The man trembled with fear.

Donovan released his grip and pointed to a nearby chair. "Sit!"

He sat.

Donovan thanked the woman once again, then tipped his hat and left. While heading to his truck, he kept one eye on the house to be sure that Estúpido didn't run home to grab his gun and do something…stupid.

Donovan drove out of the village, turning left onto the highway. After a few hundred yards, he pulled over and parked. There, he used his binoculars to study the mountains and trails around Soto's ranch while waiting until he felt certain that Ignacio had headed home. The sun was low on the horizon and he watched the desert sky as it changed from blue to yellow, then to orange and finally to a deep crimson. Soon, the stars began to appear in the east while a cool breeze carried with it the smoke of dozens of wood fires from the village.

Donovan checked his watch and saw it was now 6:40 p.m. He started the truck and drove up the road until he spotted a rocky mule trail heading toward the mountains. He turned there and maneuvered the truck carefully over the bumpy path. Before long, he spotted a barbed-wire fence which marked the perimeter of Ignacio's small ranch. Thanks to Soto's wife, he knew the *máquina* would be located high up on the ridge directly behind the ranch.

The distinct smell of manure came to him as he made his way up the foothill of the mountain. He shifted into low gear and proceeded slowly and cautiously, aware that the narrow ridge dropped off sharply on each side. Skillfully, Donovan steered the truck around numerous rocks and ledges and over small desert bushes that scratched noisily along the undercarriage.

It soon became too dangerous to drive. Donovan stopped and reached under the seat for his handgun and holster, then stepped out of the cab. After fastening the holster to his belt he went to the back of the truck and retrieved a small kerosene lantern and his digging equipment. He lit the lantern and held it out while studying the ground for clues.

Before long, he spotted mule prints in the soil and began following them. After a few minutes, he needed to catch his breath. Just as he stopped, he heard the unsettling sound of a rattle coming from behind him. Turning slowly, he held out the lantern and saw a huge diamondback wound in a tight coil only six feet away. Hissing wickedly, it shook its tail in warning.

Without hesitation, Donovan flipped open the strap of his holster and drew his .45 automatic. He aimed the barrel at the serpent's head while it displayed its fangs and glared at him with piercing eyes. He pulled the trigger and fired. Instantly, the serpent's head exploded from its body while the sound of the gunshot echoed through the mountains, sending bats and birds flying wildly in all directions.

He returned the gun to its holster and continued up the hill.

After another hundred feet or so he noticed human footprints on the trail. He followed the footprints down from the crest of the ridge and along a precariously narrow ledge. After about fifty feet, he spotted something unusual. Holding his lantern high, he saw an object resting upon a large flat stone, buried partially into the steep hillside.

A wheel.

From the ledge, Donovan climbed up onto the stone and set the lantern beside the find. Now that he was close, he could see there were two bright alloy wheels, each about eleven inches in diameter. The metal itself showed little evidence of corrosion or wear, while the hubs appeared to be connected to a main body, which was mostly buried.

Donovan paused briefly to take it all in. From the looks of it, he could tell the device had been buried for hundreds, perhaps thousands of years. He recognized that this was a moment of great historical and scientific importance. Regardless of that, he knew he would be one of few individuals who would ever lay eyes on it.

Using his digging equipment, he began to unearth the machine. With a small pick, he gently poked away at the small rocks imbedded above it, then used a pointed shovel to remove the dirt from around the body. Once the dirt and rocks were removed, he grasped the machine with both arms and moved it from its burial site onto an opened tarp. After wrapping it tightly, he carried it to the truck, securing it with rope to the inside the bed.

Donovan was ready to leave. After closing the tailgate, he felt the pain at his side worsen. He pressed his hand over the wound as he took a moment to study the terrain behind him. He would have to reverse down the hill for at least a few hundred feet before the path would be wide enough to turn around.

He climbed in and released the parking brake, then began to back slowly down the dark, precarious slope. To see the path behind him more clearly, he opened the door and hung his upper body out of the cab. Almost at once, a sharp pain shot from his side. To Donovan, it felt as though he'd been knifed all over again.

Quickly, he pulled himself back into the cab and grabbed onto the steering wheel with both hands. At the same time, he hit the brakes too hard, causing the truck to career sideways in the loose dirt. He turned the wheel sharply, though the truck continued to skid across the rocky path until it lunged headlong over the edge. The vehicle went airborne for a few seconds before landing with a loud crash, then began barreling down the steep, rocky hillside.

After bounding over countless rocks, ledges, and bushes, the vehicle finally reached the bottom of the dark ravine where it rolled to a stop. After the noise and dust had settled, Donovan grabbed a flashlight from the glove box and climbed out of the vehicle while holding his hand firmly over his aching wound. He walked slowly around the vehicle checking for gas leaks and damage. A cursory look under the hood revealed only heavy dust and some cactus debris. Underneath, he saw the oil pan had been dented, though it appeared to be otherwise intact.

After that, Donovan lifted his shirt and used the flashlight to study his knife wound. There was no blood or discharge to be seen, though he realized he could be bleeding internally.

Clayton Donovan understood well the risks and dangers his job presented, especially lately. Nonetheless, he felt tonight's discovery would make it all worthwhile—provided he could get himself and the machine over the border.

After several tries, the motor started, coughing a few times while a cloud of heavy smoke poured out of the tailpipe. He revved the engine until it smoothed out, then began to drive out of the ravine. Before long, he came to the highway where he turned right.

Once he was under way, he took a moment to consider what to name the machine. After some thought, he came up with the name *Rueda*, a Spanish word meaning wheel. Satisfied with that, he sat back and prepared himself for the long trip ahead.

In the city of Monterrey, he had a Chevrolet panel van parked and waiting. After the vehicle swap, he planned to transport the machine over the border at Laredo and continue on to Dallas. There, it would be stored in a secured facility until it was decided how and where it would be studied, and by who. He knew his employer would be in Dallas for a campaign trip on November 22, and could inspect the machine himself if he chose to.

In the meantime, Clayton Donovan would focus on recuperating until his next mission as the President's Agent.

-PART I-

Sixty-six years later

Cape Canaveral, Florida

"If men were angels, no government would be necessary."
~President James Madison

Chapter 1

Early Saturday, June 16, 2029

A bolt of lightning struck, followed closely by a crack of thunder which shook the building and Ellis Lacorde's nerves as well. He could hear the rain pouring down and wondered how his three associates were holding out. Two of them were waiting atop an abandoned launch tower while another, a new female recruit, was positioned on the roof of a nearby office building.

Carrying his toolbox, Lacorde stepped to the center of the main hangar deck where he stopped and gazed up at Praxis II. Surrounded by spotlights, the towering white launch vehicle stood glistening. Its construction was completed and the work crews had removed the last of the scaffolding.

Though he'd been servicing the hangar's fire prevention systems for the past three weekends, this was his first good look at the finished rocket. After the successful trial of Praxis I, the test model, the Praxis II would soon be put to use with some minor modifications. Wright Aerospace had specifically designed this new vehicle for their upcoming unmanned projects, including the much-anticipated Venus Missions.

Lacorde glanced at his watch and saw it was almost two a.m. He gave the gleaming white spacecraft one final look before heading to a nearby welding equipment storage room.

Ellis Lacorde wasn't interested in space missions. Tonight, he and his three accomplices had a mission of their own. One they had spent endless hours planning and rehearsing.

After learning that this particular hangar housed a secret and secured information storage room, Lucas Richter, the group's leader, along with Derrick Haut, a computer expert and industrial spy, devised a plan to steal the data.

Richter and Haut took great care putting together the details of their plan, knowing the data stored there had cost years and billions of dollars to gather. Together, they developed a specialized computer virus specifically designed to alter the facility's central security system. Lacorde, posing as a fire systems expert, had assisted with the upload of the virus. Tonight, it would be put to the test.

If all went as planned, they would gain invaluable information while at the same time dealing a crushing blow to Wright Aerospace.

While planning their scheme, Derrick Haut discovered that Wright had divided the stored information into two separate data archives. Half of the records would need to be downloaded physically at the source, while the second half required a special wireless receiver. This way, the stored information could only be obtained if downloaded in unison, thus making data theft impossible.

Almost impossible.

Tonight's mission required a significant diversion, and the success of that depended largely on Ellis Lacorde. Hours earlier, as part of what appeared to be regular maintenance, Lacorde had removed most of the high-expansion foam chemical from the building's fire suppression system. The storage tanks were then carefully refilled, though with a highly flammable liquid, Cyclopentane.

Lacorde walked across the main hanger to the welding equipment storage room and went in, closing the door behind him. From his tool bag, he retrieved a small electronic detonator and set the timer for 2:30 a.m., then placed the device on a shelf where it would be out-of-sight. After that, he cracked open the valves on a few acetylene tanks and exited the room.

From there, he strode across the deck of the hangar, this time ignoring the massive rocket as he headed straight to the data storage room.

Across the street, the Wright Aerospace administration building stood dark and quiet. On the roof, Safire lay motionless upon a long window-cleaning scaffold which was covered with heavy canvas. Her arsenal for tonight's job consisted of an EL-5 Cheetah, a specialized weapon designed to launch custom-built 38 mm plastic explosive capsules. She also kept a small, silenced handgun at her side.

She had dressed appropriately for the occasion, wearing a black, weather-resistant cat suit which clung tightly over her slender body, along with boots, a rappelling vest, and a black mask. On the west end of the roof, she'd fastened a length of climbing rope to a bracket and coiled it neatly.

Patiently, she waited while rehearsing in her mind her important part in tonight's mission.

Chapter 2

Two miles away, high atop SLC-40, a retired launch tower, Lucas Richter and Derrick Haut waited for their moment. Though dressed head to toe in raingear, they were nonetheless tormented by the heavy downpour along with the gusting winds and the violent lightning storm that surrounded them.

The two men had their electronic equipment ready in preparation for tonight's operation. This included a small dish receiver which would be used to intercept the transmission of stolen data which Lacorde would soon be sending.

At precisely 2:20 a.m., Richter's phone alarm chimed, signaling that the appointed time had arrived. He gave Haut a nod and used his phone to send a coded text to both Ellis Lacorde and Safire, informing them that tonight's plan was on.

After receiving the text, Safire climbed out from under the canvas and set the bipod of her weapon on the ledge of the roof. She aimed carefully using the launcher's laser sighting and fired one capsule. The shot hit the target, the hangar's main communication enclosure, and stuck solidly. She aimed again and fired a second shot of the plastic explosive which affixed itself about two feet below the first.

After that, she targeted two junction boxes, one of which housed the wiring for the hangar's security system and the other the circuitry for the Halon fire-control system. After that, she flipped open a cover on the rifle's stock exposing a small red button. When pushed, this would transmit a signal detonating all of the explosives simultaneously.

Inside the hangar, Ellis Lacorde approached the door of the data storage room and swiped his card-key across the reader. This, he knew, would activate the computer virus, thus allowing only his card to operate the door. At once, the magnetic solenoids inside the door clicked, allowing him to enter with a turn of the knob.

Lacorde counted four holes on the steel doorjamb, two on each side. From his toolbox, he selected four plastic plugs and inserted one into each hole. This would ensure that the door would not become bolt-locked by the security system while he was inside.

After closing the door behind him, he set his toolbox down and examined the mainframe for a moment. At once, he was able to quickly identify the hard drive unit, an external device in a steel enclosure the size of a shoebox.

He removed his snub .38 revolver from his toolbox and set it to the side, then used a Torx screwdriver to remove four small mounting screws on the enclosure. Following that, he removed the cover and connected a specialized transmitter which had been fitted into the bottom of his toolbox to the proper port on the mainframe. Once that was done, he plugged the transmitter into a simple wall receptacle and flipped the switch.

He knew that at this point, if everything was going as planned, Haut and Richter would be receiving the first part of the data through their dish on the launch platform two miles away.

He placed his revolver into his ankle holster and exited the room, making his way to the main building where he climbed the ladder leading up to the overhead bridge crane.

The bridge crane spanned the width of the hangar and moved along a fixed railway the length of the building. The main hoist ran from one side of the crane to the other and was fitted with a remote-controlled fire hose. Lacorde knew the system was designed to direct the foam extinguishing agent in almost any direction.

The crane operator, Marvin Hadley, was seated at the controls. He was a thickset man in his mid-fifties. Beads of sweat rolled down his face as he attempted to adjust his communication radio. He turned and recognized Lacorde. "Hey, it's the fire extinguisher guy. What brings you to this neck of the woods?"

Lacorde smiled. "Fire drill."

Marvin managed a laugh. "You're kiddin' me, right?"

"Relax," Lacorde replied. "I'll be out of here in a minute or two."

Marvin nodded and turned his attention back to his radio.

Earlier, Lacorde had carried a full set of fire-fighter's gear up to the crane deck. He removed his revolver from his ankle holster and set it aside along with his card-key. He then began dressing himself into the gear starting with the pants and jacket, followed by the rubber boots and helmet, keeping the full-face respirator aside for later.

Marvin turned again and saw Lacorde dressed in the gear. "Hey…what's going on?"

Lacorde stared at his wristwatch and made no reply.

"What's with the suit?" Marvin asked. "Are you expecting a fire or something?"

Lacorde reached for his revolver.

Marvin was shocked. "Hey—what are you, crazy? You can't have a gun in here!"

Lacorde glanced up from his watch for a moment, taking note of Marvin's body mass. "Sit over there," he said, pointing to a spot on the deck.

"What are you talking about? You're gonna be fired for this, you idiot."

Lacorde chuckled at that, then pointed the revolver at Marvin's face. At once, the man moved out of his chair and sat himself on the deck.

"What are you staring at your watch for?" Marvin asked. "What's gonna happen?"

Lacorde held up his index finger, then began to count down, "Twenty-five…twenty-four… twenty-three…"

"And what's with the countdown?" Marvin asked. He began to stand up. "That's it. I'm calling security!"

Lacorde looked up. Without hesitation, he aimed his gun and fired a shot directly at the man's face. The bullet shattered through the left lens of his glasses, entering his head through his eyeball. At once, Marvin's massive body dropped to the deck.

Lacorde placed his gun and card-key into his pocket, then continued his countdown, "Three… two… one…"

Right then, a deafening explosion shook the building as the acetylene gas ignited. In an instant, the welding room door blew from its hinges, followed by a huge ball of fire and flying debris.

At the same moment, Safire pressed the button on her launcher and watched as the plastic explosives detonated all at once. Wasting no time, she aimed and fired more of the capsules onto the same boxes and hit the red button again. After that second wave of explosions, she gathered her gear into a long black bag and slung it over her back and darted out from under the canvas to the coil of rope. After securing the rope to her harness, she leaped over the side of the building and rappelled the nine stories to the ground.

Lacorde sat himself in the crane operator's chair and flipped the power switch to activate the fire control panel. Using the joystick, he pointed the fire hose nozzle away from the welding supply room and turned on the pump. At once, a stream of liquid foam shot out. He aimed the chemical toward the entrance of the fire brigade room, thus making the floor slippery at that spot.

After a few seconds, he could see that the flammable cyclopentane solution had begun spraying out, replacing the liquid foam. He turned off the pump for a moment and threw the crane lever marked BR forward, moving the entire crane platform closer to the Praxis II rocket.

Once Lacorde felt he was close enough, he stopped the crane and began spraying the chemical over the surface of the rocket and its platform. After that, he pulled back on the crane lever, sending the bridge in reverse.

Due to the threat of lightning, several liquid fuel storage tanks had been moved into the hangar from outside. Lacorde knew about this and made sure to douse the tanks thoroughly with the flammable liquid.

Once the crane had returned to the west end of the hangar, he sprayed a trail of the solution connecting from Praxis II to the liquid fuel tanks and finally to the fire itself.

At that, he jumped up from his seat and ran to the ladder where he descended to the ground floor. On the way down, he noticed a group of workers had dragged a fire hose from a station in an attempt to save the rocket. He watched as the group aimed the spray at the base of the fire only to discover that the liquid was fueling the flames. Frantic and screaming for help, they became devoured in fire themselves.

Once on the ground, Lacorde ran straight to the data storage room. Using his card-key, he entered the room and grabbed the hard-drive unit while unplugging it from the mainframe. At once, the room's security alarm triggered, sounding a loud alert while activating the solenoids in the entry door. The plastic plugs, however, prevented them from locking the door.

With the hard drive in one hand and his revolver in the other, he kicked open the door and ran out.

Outside, a guard was directing the workers as they ran from the burning building. He noticed Ellis Lacorde, who was still holding his revolver in his hand.

The guard held his hand up. "Hold it right there, Mister!"

Ignoring the order, Lacorde continued toward the street.

Without hesitation, the guard pulled out his Taser and aimed it at Lacorde's back. "Stop and put the gun down or I'll Taser you right here!"

Lacorde stopped.

"Put the gun down—right now!"

Lacorde held the revolver away from his body. "Listen," he said, "I'm a firefighter—"

"Put the gun down on the pavement, *then* we'll talk."

"But I—"

"You have exactly two seconds to comply!"

"Okay!" Slowly, Lacorde bent down. As he placed the gun on the asphalt he heard the guard make a strange sound. He turned slowly, only to find the man lying on his back with a small bullet hole in his forehead.

He then heard the toot of a horn and looked to see Safire waiting in a nearby car.

Just then, another powerful explosion ripped through the building. With the hard drive still tucked under his arm, he grabbed his revolver from the pavement and headed to the vehicle.

"Nice shot," he said to Safire as he climbed in.

She glared at him. "You fool! Why did you have your gun out like that?"

"It doesn't matter now. Just go."

She hit the gas and pulled away from the curb. Once they were under way, she glanced over at him. "I should have let him Taser you."

Lacorde held up his .38. "Don't piss me off, lady, or—"

Before he could finish his sentence, Safire's right hand flashed through the air and chopped him in the wrist. In that same instant, she grabbed the gun from his hand and held it against his head.

She looked ahead at the road again and asked, "You were saying…?"

Lacorde let out a sigh.

The worst of the storm had passed and the rain had slowed to a drizzle. Derrick Haut and Lucas Richter rode the launch platform elevator down to the ground level. As they stepped out and prepared to exit the property, Haut turned to look at the Praxis II hangar one last time. A thick pillar of smoke was rising up from the building. In the distance, he could hear sirens and saw lights flashing from emergency vehicles as they hurried to the scene.

"Do you think Lacorde is okay?" Haut asked.

Richter wondered about that, seeing the destruction was much greater than he'd expected. "Ellis always enjoyed playing with fire," he replied, "and when—"

Just then, an enormous explosion shook the ground. The two men were startled and stopped in their tracks. Inside the hangar, the liquid fuel tanks had finally ignited, erupting all at once. Stunned, Richter and Haut watched as a ball of fire mushroomed upward from the east end of the structure.

Richter drew a deep breath, then glanced over at Haut and finished his reply: "When you play with fire long enough, you eventually get burned."

-PART II-

Friday, November 7, 2031

Washington, D.C.

"I don't know whether it's the finest public housing in America or the crown jewel of the American penal system."
~President Bill Clinton, on the White House.

Chapter 3

I stood from my chair and stretched for a moment before stepping over to the bulletproof window. Outside, it was drizzling while gusts of wind blew late autumn leaves across the White House lawn. Inside, it was warm and dry, but I couldn't say I felt entirely comfortable. Over the years I've become accustomed to the warmer weather of coastal Florida. Nonetheless, I knew I could adapt to living here in D.C. All that, of course, would depend on how well this morning's job interview goes.

As I thought about this, a voice came to me from behind. "Michael Brennan, I presume?"

I turned around and was surprised to see the White House Chief of Staff, who I recognized from photographs and television. "That's correct," I replied. "And you must be Daniel Morris."

He smiled.

As we shook hands I told him, "I thought I'd be meeting with your assistant—"

"I decided it would be better if I handled this a different way. If you don't mind, that is."

"Of course not. It's just unexpected."

Just then, a secret service agent entered the room and approached us. He was a big fellow and looked more like a well-dressed weightlifter than an agent. His suit was tailored to fit his physique, which gave him an odd appearance.

"Excuse me, gentlemen," he said. "The President is ready to meet with you."

I looked over at Morris. "The President?"

"Yes, Michael. He lives here, you know."

"Right. Was that his underwear I saw on the clothesline?"

The agent heard that and held back a grin. Wasting no further time, he led Morris and me to an unmarked door at the east side of the room. There, we entered a small office where we walked past a secretary who seemed not to notice us before we arrived at a second door. The agent typed in a password and mumbled something into his microphone. After a few seconds, the door buzzed and he opened it. Daniel Morris entered first, followed by me, while the agent stayed behind.

I looked around for a few seconds before realizing I was standing in the Oval Office.

To my surprise, I saw the Vice-President, Mark Westfall, was there. He stood from a chair and gave me a wave. After returning the gesture, I looked over to the windows and saw the President himself seated at his desk. He stood and walked over to greet us. I noticed he was dressed casually, wearing khaki pants, topsider shoes, and a navy blue polo shirt.

After Morris had introduced me, the President shook my hand. "Thank you for coming all this way to meet with us," he told me. "I've heard good things about you." After that, he directed me to a pair of couches in the midst of the room.

He remained standing while Morris and I sat on one couch and Westfall sat facing us on the other.

The President smiled at me. "You probably didn't expect to find yourself in the Oval Office this morning, did you Mike?"

"This is certainly a surprise, sir, to say the least."

"I'll get to the point," he said. "The job position of…of…" He looked over at Daniel for help.

"It's a research position," Morris reminded him, "working in the office of the Deputy Security Advisor."

"Right." He turned back to me and continued, "As it turns out, another position has opened up that we think would better suit your particular skillset. I believe you'd find it far more interesting than research projects."

"Who would I be working under?" I asked.

Morris answered that one. "You'd be working directly under the President, Michael."

"So, I'd be here in Washington?"

"Actually, no. In fact, you could be anywhere in the world, but never here."

I nodded.

The Chief of Staff continued, "Your assignments would be of an extremely sensitive nature and would therefore be performed in complete secrecy. The position we're offering requires total anonymity on your part. It also necessitates complete deniability on ours."

I'm no Sherlock Holmes, but what he'd just described sounded in every way like a specialized espionage job. "I'm going out on a limb here," I said, "but it sounds like you're looking for a President's Agent."

None of them replied to that, which said a lot. I noticed my mention of the term 'President's Agent' had brought an air of tension over the room and I felt I'd hit the nail on the head. If so, it was important for them to know that I was looking to *leave* the spy business—not to be promoted.

The President moved from his standing position and sat next to Westfall. After a long, awkward silence, he said to me, "It's interesting that you should bring that up, Mike. Tell us what you know about the President's Agent."

I shrugged. "Only rumors, really. I've never been sure whether they were factual stories or just tall tales. To most people, the President's Agent is more of an urban legend. I'm sure it's a popular topic for all the conspiracy theorists. According to the stories I've heard, the agent is a personal spy working directly for the U.S. President—though off the books, so to speak. Supposedly, the agents are assigned to missions considered too politically sensitive for any of the three-letter agencies to handle. The kind of stuff that, if it were found out, would cause a lot of trouble for all involved."

No one had a comment, so I went on, "Supposedly, the agents are expected to work solo, operating independently without assistance from anyone or any organization. This would be necessary in order to maintain the highest level of secrecy. In fact, the term 'agent' would be a misnomer since they aren't part of an agency at all. They're more like contract spies."

I noticed that all three men made a subtle nod.

I continued, "According to the rumors, mostly all of the Presidents have at one time or another employed a special agent, and always for the specific purpose of handling delicate assignments. The facts, of course, are few since there is no record keeping and everything about it is taken to the grave. All I know is what has been passed on by gossipers, political theorists, and other people's imaginations." I looked over at The President. "Am I close?"

He glanced over at Morris, who gave him a nod. He then turned back to me and said something surprising. "A few weeks ago," he told me, "my agent went missing."

Then it's true.

"Last Wednesday, after an exhaustive manhunt, he was finally found."

"By 'found,' you mean…?"

"I mean to say his body was found."

I shook my head. "I'm sorry to hear that, sir."

The President acknowledged that and continued, "The man was a true patriot, Mike, and a great asset to this office." He looked me in the eye. "We need someone to replace him. Someone with experience in the field of espionage. Someone who can handle tough assignments without the need of supervision or assistance. From what I'm told, you're just the man we need."

Okay. So they know I'm a spy.

He went on, "I'm offering you the position of President's Agent, Mike, and I'd like you to start today." He put on a grin and added, "If you like, we can change the job title to President's 'Spy.'"

I smiled politely in return and took the opportunity to remind them, "The only reason I came here today was to interview for a research job. You need to understand that I'm looking to get out of the spy business altogether."

Mark Westfall leaned forward and asked me, "Why quit something that you are apparently quite good at?"

"For one," I replied, "it's a risky business; especially with all the rewards being offered these days for the arrest and conviction of a spy. As you know, we now have the death penalty in place for anyone convicted of espionage in this country."

The President surprised me by saying, "You wouldn't have to worry about that."

"So…I'd be operating above the law?"

He shrugged. "I'll put it to you this way, Mike: you would be exempt from any prosecution. In ways, it would compare to diplomatic immunity. No matter what, we'd have you covered."

I let that sink in and then asked, "What else can you tell me about the job?"

The President and Vice President both looked at Daniel Morris, who was apparently the expert on the subject. In a calm, steady voice, Morris told me, "Right now, Michael, your country needs you. We're offering you an opportunity to serve this nation in a way in which you are well suited and for which you will be well rewarded." He explained, "You'd be provided with almost unlimited access to vast informational and financial resources. You'd have no agency watching over your shoulder telling you what you can or cannot do. You'd be virtually independent. I think you'd enjoy that kind of freedom, wouldn't you?"

I found myself nodding in agreement.

He went on, "We have the technology to contact you, discretely, no matter where you are. The President would use special communication tools to contact you only for occasional reports and to provide you with new assignments. From there, it's up to you to decide how to accomplish each mission. You'd design your own protocols and game plans and do things your way. All we ask is that you provide results and never disclose who it is you work for. For example, you would never admit to having been here in the oval office this morning or having ever met any of us. Under no circumstance would you ever attempt to contact us."

"What if I decide to decline the offer?"

A brief silence came over the room before Morris cleared his throat and advised me, "I *strongly* recommend you accept."

I felt my heart twitch as I realized what he was saying. Obviously, these three men, polite as they were, were willing to use their knowledge of my being a spy to railroad me.

I turned to the President. "What happens when your term in office is over?"

Morris answered that one, too. "After a President's terms are completed, their agents usually go on to become men of great power and influence. As a reward for their service, these men are often placed into high positions in government, industry, or finance." He paused for effect and then added, "You'd be surprised, Michael, how many of America's leaders had once served as agents." He turned to the President and tapped at his watch.

The President noticed that and told me. "This is a one-time chance, Mike. We're inviting you to become part of a great legacy." He looked me in the eye. "So, what's the verdict? Are you in or out?"

I took a moment to consider my answer. Though a lot went unsaid, I knew they had enough information on me to cause problems. Big problems. Somehow, they knew I was a professional spy and therefore had that on me. I had no doubt they could concoct enough evidence to put me in the Greybar Hotel for a hundred years.

The job would be dangerous. If the stories I'd heard were even half true, most of the President's agents died from on-the-job accidents. Usually from lead poisoning. Other times, apparently, they were just 'found'.

I considered another fact: I had been made aware by the ultimate source that the President's Agent story was no fairy tale. And that knowledge alone made me a dangerous person in their eyes.

Tension filled the room once again and you could cut it with a knife. Finally, Daniel Morris interrupted my thoughts. "I'm afraid we'll need an answer now, Michael." He repeated the President's question, "Are you in or out?"

My heart was still divided. I felt like a pawn on a chessboard surrounded by a king, a knight, and a rook. Any of them could checkmate me in one move. I thought about my plans for a simple job in research and my dream of, for once, living a normal life.

Those plans and dreams effectively vanished while I looked first at Morris, then Westfall, and finally the President. My words, though few, felt heavy on my tongue as I answered.

"I'm in."

-PART III-

Five months later.

Cape Canaveral, Florida.

"The only man who makes no mistake is the man who does nothing."
~Theodore Roosevelt

Chapter 4

Tuesday, April 20, 2032

The spy business isn't all it's built up to be, and I believe Hollywood is largely to blame for that. Movie spies are usually played by handsome actors who are ever so eloquent and mannerly. They dress perfectly and drive expensive sports cars. They hook up with exotic women in exotic places. Plus, they always have exactly the hi-tech gear they need right when they need it. Sounds exciting, right?

The real world of espionage is a different story altogether. Not to brag, but as the President's Agent, I'm probably considered one of the top spies in the world. Despite that, I'd never make it as an actor or model. I'm not what you'd call eloquent or mannerly, either. Right now, my exotic location is a seat positioned in front of a low-tech computer screen in my office at Cronus Aerospace in Cape Canaveral. The view from my window is a bleak landscape of two abandoned launch towers rusting silently in the distance. I've been stuck here for the past two months trying to appear as though I'm performing my duties as Director of Security.

This is my first mission from the President, and his instructions were vague to say the least. Apparently, he had reason to suspect that Cronus was up to something since my instructions were to simply look for any incriminating evidence within their Venus Mission Project. When done, I am to send an encoded report of my findings to a remote server accessible only to the President, the Vice-President, and the White House Chief of Staff.

After that, I would wait to receive my next mission orders, which would be a recorded message sent to my implanted communication device, or ICD, which had been placed in my right ear. This electronic gadget is smaller than a grain of rice and inserted just under the auditory canal. With the device, I can receive communications and also record voice messages and conversations to the remote server. To operate it, I was given a special gold and platinum ring. One side of the ring is designed to activate the recorder while the opposite side, which has an inlay of gold, deactivates it. I was also given a transdermal charger, which I use now and then to keep the batteries full.

Besides the ICD, I also received a welcome package. Inside were a few citizen cards, some very authentic-looking passports, a stack of cash, and a tablet. I was also given the login and security codes for a Swiss bank account. Apparently, the money is there to cover my job expenses and incidentals, though that left a lot up to interpretation.

So far, I've received only one message on my ICD, and that was over five months ago when the President assigned me to this mission. I'm starting to think he's forgotten me.

Anyway, I've been spending most of my time data mining and cracking files, though I've found nothing of importance to submit to the remote server. Until this morning, that is. That's when I discovered my first major piece of evidence. After all these months, I'm finally beginning to understand the President's interest in this.

While I was contemplating all this, one of the receptionists, Trinity, spotted me and stepped into my office.

"Good morning, Mike."

I returned the greeting and gave her a quick look over. As usual, she was dressed like a professional. And that would be true if she was a prostitute. Or, if it was ladies night and this was a nightclub instead of an office building.

She strolled over to my desk and leaned forward. "So…are you going to miss me?"

"Why? Are you going somewhere?"

She slapped me on the arm. "I'm sure you know Madison is back. That means today is my last day."

Just so you know, Trinity had been brought in from a temp agency to cover while Madison was away on vacation. During that time, Trinity and I had dinner once or twice. If I recall correctly, one of those dinners may have led to a sleepover.

As I was thinking of something to say, Madison appeared at the door.

"Oh, there you are," she said.

Trinity turned. "Oh… Hi Madison. I was just letting Mike know you're back."

Madison stepped inside and glanced around. "Well, well. Nice office, Mike." She turned to me. "So, what happened to Teri?"

That would be Teri Dunne, my predecessor here at Cronus. To be truthful, I may have initiated a chain of events which led to her being canned. But the official story was that—

"I heard she was arrested," Madison said.

I shrugged. "All I know is that Teri Dunne resigned for personal reasons. I was asked to take over her position." That's the only way I'd have access to all the files I needed without someone hovering over me.

In a low voice, Madison added, "Well, nobody liked her anyway."

I made no verbal reply, but I may have nodded in agreement. Personally, I didn't care for Teri Dunne either and I was glad she was…done.

Madison, however, wasn't done yet. "So," she asked, "what else went down while I was away?" She glanced over at Trinity.

Uh-oh. "There's been another step-up in security," I replied. "In case you weren't informed we are now at level four."

"What's that all about? Are we worried about terrorists or—"

"We're mostly worried about spies," I said. "They're our worst enemy. Also, our planetary rover will be landing on the surface of Venus tonight, so we have additional security concerns involving that." Mostly, I was concerned how well the secret transmitter I'd placed into the project's mainframe would be able to record things.

Madison grinned and asked me, "So, are you starting to wish you'd stayed at Wright Aerospace?"

I shook my head. "I guess part of me sometimes—" Just then, I looked and saw the Mission Director, Lucas Richter, standing at my door.

Richter realized he'd been spotted, so he stepped in and joined us. This place was starting to get crowded.

He smiled at each of us, then told me, "It's okay, Mike, please go on."

"To be honest," I said, "though I like it here at Cronus, I do miss my old job sometimes. But after the accident there—"

"When Praxis II was destroyed?" Richter asked.

"Right," I said. "That was also when twelve people perished. After that, Wright began to fall behind in the area of fusion research, which is something I believe in. Cronus has now become the leader in that field and I want to be part of it."

Richter seemed to study me for a moment before he informed us, "For tonight's landing, I've been told everything is going as planned. We're expecting Rhea to touchdown at around 9:27 p.m."

Madison asked, "What do you hope to find?"

He shrugged. "This will be the first planetary rover ever to explore Venus. Who knows what we'll discover." He looked over at me. "You'll be here for the landing, right?"

"I wouldn't miss it."

"Good. Now why don't we all go grab some lunch. I'm buying."

"Go on without me," I said. "I've got a few things I need to check on."

No one argued with that and the three of them headed off to the lunchroom. Thank goodness, too, since I really did have some work ahead of me. After five months of digging I finally had something to report to my real boss.

And it was big.

Chapter 5

Tonight was the big night for Cronus Aerospace. Everyone involved with the Venus mission project was here at the control center. The center itself was a vast, six-sided domed room painted black from floor to ceiling. For effect, the place was kept essentially dark with the only lighting provided by the individual workstations and the five mammoth video screens surrounding us. Each screen was about eighty feet wide and capable of displaying any combination of data, maps, transmissions, or live video. It would be the perfect spot for a Super Bowl party.

The secured and windowless primary control room was situated at the rear of the center. The room was off limits to most everyone except the project's four senior operators and the Control Room Director, Glenn Hosato. They were all in there right now and no doubt busy with the final details and preparations for the rover's landing. Or maybe they were just playing video games.

Through the crowd I spotted two of my friends, Kaui and Kekoa Hamilton. Their workstations were located just outside the primary control room and I headed there. So you know, Kaui and Kekoa are identical twin brothers from Honolulu and classic examples of the modern beta male. By their appearance and disposition it's hard to believe they're both Ph.D. engineers with MIT diplomas on their walls.

Unlike me, Kaui and Kekoa seem to thrive on complex and incomprehensible things. Together, they've contributed much to the project, including a way to equip the rover's drive wheels with automated retractable traction spikes. They also designed and helped program the control room's mainframe—the same mainframe into which I recently planted a spy transmitter.

The twins and I are neighbors at the same apartment complex in Cocoa Beach where they enjoy keeping me company, especially when I'm grilling something. They also find it convenient to travel to and from work with me since neither of them own a car.

I soon reached their workstations and asked Kekoa, "So, what are the odds of this rover landing in one piece?"

He glanced around for a moment and then replied, "Maybe one out of four."

That surprised me. "Why do you say that?"

He shrugged. "If we weren't talking about *Venus*, I guess I'd be more optimistic."

"So, landing on Venus is more complicated?"

They both rolled their eyes at that, which answered my question. Kekoa explained, "The other rover missions, the ones to Mars and the Moon, were simple compared to this."

Kaui broke in. "The place is a blast furnace. The temperature there is around nine-hundred degrees along with a surface pressure one hundred times that of Earth. That, plus the whole planet is surrounded with clouds made of sulfuric acid. In addition, the planet is host to hundreds of huge active volcanoes and almost endless sandstorms."

"Sounds bad," I said. "Do you think the rover can handle it?"

Kaui leaned close and whispered, "If it manages to land perfectly, then *maybe*, though I wouldn't bet the farm on it."

I don't actually own a farm. If I did, I'd take his advice.

"It's insane how much the whole project cost," Kaui added. "But all that money doesn't mean much when it's millions of miles away."

He was right. That's why I keep my money in Switzerland.

Just then, Raquel Richards, who was a member of the team and close friend of the twins, came over and joined us. I thought Raquel was an interesting young lady and I was quietly hoping she'd stop by. From her file, which I *may* have glanced at, I knew Raquel was employed as an astronautical engineer and propulsion specialist. Whatever that is. I also knew that she was only five foot, weighed a whole ninety-seven pounds, and was thirty-four years-old, although she looks even younger than that. Oh, and she's single.

Raquel greeted Kaui and Kekoa, then turned to me. "Hi Mike," she said. "Where have you been hiding?"

I shrugged. "They only let me out when there's a full moon," I said, immediately regretting it.

She smiled politely. "The full moon isn't until the 25th."

"Should I head back to my cage?"

She seemed to think about that. "You can stay," she told me, "but only because tonight is special."

At that moment, the control room door opened and Derrick Haut, one of the senior operators, exited. As he strutted across the complex, he glanced over and spotted Raquel. In a loud voice he over called to her, "You should be at your work station, Richards." I noticed his eyes shifted over to me and our eyes locked for a moment. He then turned away continued across the room.

Raquel mumbled something, which sounded a lot like an obscenity. I couldn't tell whether Haut heard her or not, but I was sure a few people around us did.

After that there was an awkward silence, so I asked, "Where did the name *Rhea* come from, anyway?"

"Have you forgotten what you learned in Greek Mythology?"

"I must have skipped that class."

"Well, Rhea was the sister of one of the Greek gods"

"And they owned a restaurant, right?"

She giggled. "She was the sister of Cronus."

"That's right. Now I remember."

"Good. Then I'm sure you also remember that she and Cronus became husband and wife. Their son Zeus later overthrew his father to claim heaven for himself."

I nodded. "That's why they warn people about inbreeding."

She giggled again.

I looked around the room for a moment and changed subjects again. "I notice your whole group seems to be cut off from what's happening inside the control room. Why do they allow only five people inside there?"

"You'll have to ask Lucas Richter about that," she replied. "It was his idea." She explained, "Each of the senior operators are assigned at least two assistants out here to help with things such as problem solving and calculations. The twins and I work under Derrick Haut."

"Lucky you."

"Right. He has anger issues, that's for sure, but the real problem with Derrick is that he doesn't let us in on what's happening most of the time. It seems to be the same story with all the senior operators. Supposedly, all the secrecy is meant to protect the mission from spies. Personally, I think it's a recipe for disaster."

Well, I think I'd discovered the real reason for all the secrecy, but trying to protect a place like this against spies can be an exercise in futility. I'm clear proof of that.

While Raquel and I talked further, she described to me what to expect tonight. "The transit module carrying Rhea will begin a planetary orbit soon," she said. "Our goal is to land the rover in the west upper quadrant of Aphrodite Terra."

"Another Greek god?"

"Goddess," she corrected. "From the orbital position, Rhea will detach from the module and begin her descent at about sixteen thousand miles per hour. For me, that's when things start to get scary."

"Me too."

She continued, "On the way down, Rhea will shed her aeroshell and use chutes and descent motors to slow down to about five miles per hour before finally touching down on the surface."

"And then it sends us a signal, like, 'Hey, I made it.' Right?"

"It will actually be more complex than that," she said. "Rhea's computer and communication systems are highly advanced. She's the smartest object anyone has ever sent into space."

"If she's so smart, she should turn around now and come back to Earth."

She giggled at that one and told me, "Once the diagnostics are complete, she can begin preparing for her mission almost at once."

"And her mission is...?"

"You don't know?"

I shrugged. "They keep me caged in my office, remember?"

She nodded. "Well, part of Rhea's mission will be exploration, like gathering samples and collecting scientific data about Venus. But her main purpose is fusion energy research." She explained, "First, Rhea will search for an appropriate landing site for Zeus, then serve as a locator beacon and provide guidance and data such as wind and weather conditions to assist with coordinating Zeus's landing."

"I'm told there are sandstorms there."

"Windstorms, mostly," she said. "It can be an extremely hostile environment—"

"Like working with Derrick Haut?"

She glanced around. "Speaking of which, I'd better head back to my station before he has a stroke."

"Let's talk later, okay?"

She nodded. "I'll explain more about Zeus then."

While Raquel headed back to her workstation, I looked up at one of the huge monitors mounted across one of the walls. For now, the monitor was filled only with indecipherable readouts and figures. Soon, however, its screen would display a video feed transmitted from the surface of a faraway planet. To me, the whole project seemed too risky and complex to actually work. Besides that, I had discovered something interesting about this mission; a secret I was sure few people knew about.

Meanwhile, Rhea was fast approaching her final destination and preparing to enter the mother of all hostile environments.

Venus.

Chapter 6

It was approaching zero hour for the landing, and I found myself strolling around the crowded room. The staff, which was comprised of mostly scientists and technicians, appeared eager and anxious. For them, this was the big evening, the culmination of years of hard work and long, strenuous hours. And tonight it would all pay off.

For me, the whole thing was a big Maybe with a capital M, and I wasn't betting anybody's farm on anything.

Anyway, I was on my own personal mission and had just found what I needed. There, to the side of the primary control room, I spotted the self-service coffee bar. And the line looked short.

I glanced at my watch. It was 8:44 p.m. and kind of late for coffee, but I figured a shot of caffeine would help me appear more excited about what was happening.

After pouring a cup, I took a whiff and savored the aroma for a moment before taking a long sip. Cronus Aerospace may have some idiotic projects going, like this one, but they know how to provide good coffee. I made a mental note to mention this to my old boss, Craig Van Essen. I remember that the coffee at Wright tasted like—

"Hi Mike."

I turned around and was not completely surprised to see Raquel Richards standing in line at the same coffee bar. She smiled and waved at me, so I waved back and waited for her. After she'd filled her cup she came over and made a suggestion, "Why don't you come sit with the twins and me? You've probably been on your feet for hours."

"Good idea."

As we approached the workstation, I mentioned, "I hope your buddy Derrick Haut is behaving himself. Has he calmed down?"

"He never really calms down," she replied. "But at least he's back inside his hole."

"The control room?"

She nodded. "He's been quiet for the last twenty minutes." She lowered her voice and mentioned, "Derrick's a smart guy, I have to admit, but sometimes he can be a real turd in the punchbowl, if you know what I mean."

"I do. That's why I stick to coffee."

She smiled at that, then pointed to a chair beside a small table. "Have a seat."

I sat.

Kaui and Kekoa seemed busy with their computers. I took another sip of my coffee while Raquel put on her headset. She then turned and faced me, then leaned back and crossed her legs. I'm not the most perceptive guy, but I thought I detected some electricity flying around between us.

"Isn't this a busy time for you?" I asked. "I don't want to interrupt your work."

"It's only busy if Derrick contacts us for something," she said. "Right now, it's quiet. Besides, you're not interrupting." She smiled at me in a sweet way while playing with a braid of hair.

My electric meter was spinning.

She looked into my eyes and I thought I heard her ask, "Would you like to take my shirt off of me?"

Huh? There was a lot of background noise, so I leaned forward and asked, "What was that?"

"I asked if you'd like to take more sugar for your coffee. There's some right there on the table."

Just then, Lucas Richter, the Mission Director, walked over and stopped to speak with the twins while Raquel uncrossed her legs and sat up in her chair.

Like me, Richter had thought to wear a business suit for tonight's occasion. According to his file he was my age, forty-four, and stood at six feet. He weighed around two-hundred pounds, though he appeared lighter. I knew he used the facility's workout center and the jogging trail every morning. Judging by the hours he put in, he was also the most dedicated Director I'd ever heard of. Richter literally lived here at the facility. He had a couch with a foldout bed in his office and a dog pen on the grounds for his pet Doberman. From what I'd observed, he seldom left the facility except on business. Where do they find these guys?

Richter chatted it up with Kaui and Kekoa for a few minutes before turning his attention to Raquel. "How's everything going here?" he asked her.

"Good, I guess. It's been quiet."

"Well, things should pick up soon." He leaned close and advised her, "Be sure to keep your headset on and don't wander off. You know how Derrick is about that."

She nodded.

Once Richter was gone, Raquel folded her arms and fumed. "Derrick must have said something to him about me."

"I wouldn't sweat it," I told her. "In the end, guys like Derrick Haut always get what's coming to them."

Raquel took a sip of her coffee and said to me, "I wanted to finish telling you about Zeus, remember?"

"Right. I'm interested in hearing about that," I lied.

"Okay. So after Zeus lands on Venus, Rhea will load the ship's cargo bay with a variety of rocks and soil samples she'd collected. Once that's completed, Zeus will launch from the surface, then rendezvous with its transit module and return to Earth."

"With the rocks."

"Right. Those samples will be the first extraterrestrial items brought to the U.S. since the Apollo missions—"

"And the first samples ever from another planet," I added.

"Correct. But there's more to this mission than just that." She explained, "What most people outside this room don't realize is this: we know with some certainty that a large solar flare will occur soon—and we think solar flares are the key to understanding fusion energy."

About then, Kaui and Kekoa scooted their chairs back and began listening in.

Raquel continued, "According to our current data, the flare is likely to occur on the part of the sun's surface directly facing Venus."

Kekoa broke in, "Once Zeus is positioned on Venus it will wait until the right time to launch three test probes from its cargo bay. These will be aimed at the spot where we predict the flare will occur."

"At the sun?"

Kaui answered that one. "Sort of, but the probes will vaporize before they can get close."

Rachel explained, "Before they disintegrate, the probes will send information to us: one probe before the flare, the second one during, and the third one after. Each contains a different chemical payload. As the probes vaporize, the two transit modules orbiting Venus will study what happens to each chemical using spectrometers and—"

"If it works," Kekoa interrupted, "we should have the final pieces of the puzzle we need to understand fusion energy. That, of course, would—"

"That would change the world," I said, completing his statement, "while making Cronus the wealthiest corporation on Earth."

He and Raquel both nodded in agreement.

I could now see the President's interest in this. However, there was one small thing that I was sure even *he* didn't know about. While cracking files this morning, I discovered a nicely hidden secret: I learned that the probes being launched from Zeus will actually be long-range ultrasonic ballistic missiles. Most alarmingly, I discovered that each missile would be armed with multiple warheads. The nuclear kind.

If I had to guess, I'd say someone high up at Cronus had figured out that the spectral analysis would require more than just a few probes filled with inert chemicals. Something with a bigger bang was required. The problem is international law strictly prohibits the detonation of nuclear weapons in space.

Secrecy must be the first order of business for whoever is behind this. If the details of this plan ever leaked out, the public outcry would quickly put an end to Cronus Aerospace altogether.

Until the President tells me otherwise, my plan is to keep snooping. In my position as Director of Security I can do that without arousing much suspicion. In the world of espionage, you always want to be the last one anyone suspects. If you do your job correctly, no one will know what happened other than that a series of unfortunate coincidences had somehow unfolded.

I was starting to like this job.

Chapter 7

Before long, things in the Command Complex began to pick up. Raquel and the twins were busy checking readouts and making calculations. Kekoa looked unhappy while speaking to someone on his microphone, so I figured it was probably Derrick Haut on the other end.

Raquel glanced over her shoulder and let me know, "Looks like Rhea has begun her descent."

"Here comes the moment of truth," I said. "How much longer?"

"It's already close," she replied, "but because of the distance to Earth there is a delay of two-minutes, fourteen seconds each way." She turned back to her screen.

I scooted my chair closer to Raquel and saw she was working on some kind of calculation. Just then, something caused her to be alarmed. While pressing her headphone to her ear she turned quickly to Kaui. "Did you hear that?"

"We're on it," he replied.

All at once, the three of them began clicking away at their keyboards. Within seconds, Kaui jumped up from his chair and shouted to Raquel, "Tell Haut he needs to use the category DM prompt."

Using her keyboard, she entered that.

He went on, "Have him increase the thrust on the descent motor by eight percent at two-thousand feet." He repeated that and added, "Have him send the prompt right now."

Raquel typed frantically while speaking into her microphone. Once done, she nodded to the twins and fell back in her chair. Kaui wiped his forehead and took a few breaths, then turned to me and explained, "Rhea indicated that the deployment of the parachutes occurred about six seconds later than expected."

"That was just what I figured."

Kekoa stopped clicking at his keyboard and directed Kaui's attention to a map on his screen. The two of them discussed things while a small crowd began to form behind our workstation. After a minute or so, Kaui turned to everyone and explained, "Due to the chute delay, the landing will probably occur about five hundred miles east of the planned site, but that's still within the target radius."

There were sighs of relief and some light applause from the crowd while Kekoa clicked at a few more keys. Seconds later, a map indicating the new landing site appeared on one of the huge overhead monitors. I could hear some murmuring going around, but most people were just holding their breath.

Raquel checked her screen and assured those of us nearby, "The control room team sent the prompt as recommended." She paused for a moment. "We have more data coming in now."

The crowd stared up at the monitors and waited anxiously. Over the next four minutes hundreds of messages from Rhea poured in and were quickly deciphered. Everyone seemed particularly interested in the descent speed and altitude. Finally, at 9:28 p.m., the message was received: the chutes and descent motors had functioned correctly and the craft had touched down, upright and apparently intact.

Rhea had landed.

Chapter 8

The drive home was when I did my best thinking, and tonight was no exception. It was after eleven o'clock already and traffic was almost nonexistent. Raquel Richards had agreed to drive the twins home once the celebration winds down, which would probably be another hour or two.

Personally, I was glad the thing landed in one piece, though in this business it's a good idea not to count your chickens too soon. By the time I left for home, Rhea was only beginning her pre-startup self-diagnostic check. For all anyone knew, she might be sitting inside a volcano.

Anyway, I had a few things to think about. One item that stood out in my mind was the unexplained six-second parachute delay. No one seemed too concerned about it, but that small malfunction was enough to land Rhea hundreds of miles off course. Was it just a glitch—or something else? I made a mental note to talk to my old boss, Craig Van Essen, about that. While I'm at it, I'll also try to find out what landing sites Wright Aerospace had planned on before the Praxis II disaster.

I also took a moment to think about young Raquel Richards. I'm not good at navigation, but I could tell we were on each other's radar screens. The thing is, this mission will be over soon, and I'll be gone. Knowing that, I didn't want to start anything I'd later regret with someone I didn't want to hurt. In my line of work there was no room for the sweet or the innocent. Besides, there were plenty of not-so-sweet and innocents out there just waiting to be hurt.

I parked and walked to the door of my apartment where I looked up at my surveillance camera and waved. After using my card key, I went in and was immediately hit with a foul odor. I didn't recall leaving a dead body behind, so I flipped on the lights and soon traced the smell to the kitchen sink where I'd left some dishes laying out with unfinished food. Dozens of maggots were creeping everywhere, which was disgusting, so I quickly scraped them and the food into the garbage disposal and hit 'frappe.' Once that mess was cleaned I opened the kitchen window to air things out. From there, I headed to the shower and then straight to bed.

I figured by morning the rover would be operational and ready to begin a survey of the landing site. Thanks to the transmitter I'd secretly placed inside the control room's mainframe, I'd have full access to the live video of that while downloading all of the data arriving from Rhea.

If it was still functioning, that is.

Chapter 9

Wednesday, April 21, 2032

The next morning I got out of bed and stumbled through the debris field of underwear and socks on my way to the bathroom. After that, I threw on some clothes and ventured out to the kitchen. I noticed an unpleasant odor still lingering from the rotten food I'd come home to, so I opened the front door and a few more windows to help clear the air.

After that, I made a pot of coffee and headed to the living room where I nestled into my new recliner. I fired up my tablet and took a moment to put my ICD charger in place just below my ear.

I was curious to see how well my secret transmitter worked, so I logged in to my remote server. Once in, I noticed it had already downloaded a lot more data than I'd expected. I switched to Rhea's live video mode and was surprised to find the rover had already detached from her landing skirt and had begun exploring. The planet's surface was a bleak, windswept, and barren place. There were rocks everywhere, most of which were flat and more imbedded into the surface than those found on the moon or Mars. The horizon appeared hazy, but I could see the outline of high rolling hills in the distance, shimmering under a brilliant white sky.

Rhea seemed to be working perfectly and so was my transmitter. I could lean back and watch it all from the comfort of my living room. Most modern espionage work is done this way, with the spy alone behind closed doors, staring into a computer screen.

Rhea was moving along remarkably well and seemed unbothered by the intense heat and pressure. I watched as she maneuvered herself easily around a large jagged ledge and moved steadily across the treacherous terrain. After a few minutes, the rover stopped at the side of a narrow slope beside a rugged ridge. Seconds later, she turned ninety degrees to the right and began moving again. From what I could tell, she was heading directly for an unusual-looking rock formation in the distance. The rocks, which were lined up high along a hillcrest, jutted out of the surface in a way that resembled dozens of monstrous teeth arranged like a train wreck.

By design, Rhea could plot her own course and follow it if given a destination. She was programmed to self-navigate around obstacles and dangerous terrain. Over longer distances, this was safer and more efficient than being guided every inch of the way by the team back on Earth.

I soon began to realize how distant and enormous the odd rock formation was. Each stone slab appeared larger than a football field and cast a dark shadow over the cavernous space below. I'm no scientist, but I knew the shaded area below it had to be significantly cooler than the broad daylight.

Several minutes later, the rover entered the shaded surface under the teeth and stopped. I assumed the team wanted Rhea's temperature to stabilize before going further. I removed my ICD charger and stood to stretch. It was close to 8:30 already and the twins and I would be expected back at the facility in another hour or so.

I decided to check Cronus's Venus Mission website, which was open to the public. The site featured the same video I was watching, though delayed by ten minutes. Of course, no one knew I also had access to the live, uncensored version of this. In fact, everything coming from Venus and the control room was being downloaded not only by Cronus, but by my remote server as well. Ironically, that's exactly what Cronus had hired me to prevent.

It's people like me that make it hard for me to trust people.

Soon, Rhea began moving again, now using her headlight. She began exploring the dark cavern, steering around scattered rocks and over sand and gravel. After a minute, the rover came to an abrupt and unexpected stop before slowly reversing. A maneuver like this meant either the team had decided on a new route or they'd spotted something of interest and wanted a second look. After the rover had reversed about ten feet, she stopped while her camera panned slowly to the right. After a few seconds, Rhea adjusted her view angle to the left then zoomed in. I could see dust and gravel spread about the cavern floor, but nothing unusual.

Minutes passed until her camera finally aimed further up and more to the left. There, on the cavern floor, I spotted a blurred pair of horizontal lines. The control room team made camera adjustments until the image became clearer. At once, I realized what it was. I sat up in my chair and watched in shock as Rhea's lights revealed a set of indentations forming a distinct pattern across the powdery surface of the cavern floor. The pair of markings, running parallel, had been pressed into the surface with a recognizable footprint almost beyond belief.

Tracks. From *another* rover.

Chapter 10

I nside the primary control room, the five senior operators stared in silent awe at the image on the large monitor before them. Glenn Hosato, the team leader, turned to the other four and asked, "Is everyone seeing this?"

Without taking his eyes off the screen, Jason MacQuaid answered, "Yeah, we're seeing it, but not quite believing—"

"No, I mean, *everyone*..." Glenn made a gesture indicating the outside world.

Derrick Haut spoke up, "No one has seen it but us, Glenn. There's a two-minute video delay to the team outside and a ten-minute delay to the—"

"Shut it off."

"You mean except for *us*, right?"

"Yes!" Glenn snapped. "Shut down everything outside this room—and do it quickly."

"Okay, got it." While Derrick worked on that, the rest of the team exchanged glances.

Keri Jenkins, the team's optical engineer, was surprised at Glenn's decision. "Why should we hide this from anyone?" she asked. "This is an amazing find."

Glenn ignored that as he lifted his glasses and squinted to study the image closer.

In his thick Russian accent, Viktor Ivanov, the robotics engineer, told Keri, "It's just another security thing. Cronus loves to keep everything a beeg secret. You know this, yes?"

"Believe me, Viktor, I know this," Keri replied. She turned to the others and asked, "Does anyone have any idea how those tracks got there? They have to be from another rover, right?"

"They certainly do," Glenn answered. "But we are all aware that no one has sent a rover to Venus until now."

"Maybe it's not from Earth," Jason suggested.

Viktor crumpled a piece of paper and threw it at Jason, hitting him in the head. "You watch too many stupeed movies," Viktor told him.

Derrick Haut shook his head and told Glenn. "I should contact the Mission Director about this."

Glenn nodded in agreement. "Use the secure line."

The rest of the team went back to studying the image while Derrick contacted Lucas Richter. After a brief conversation, Derrick ended the call and informed everyone "The Mission Director is on his way here."

"Oh, wonderful," Keri said, rolling her eyes.

Derrick continued, "After Richter gets here, we'll go into full lockdown. That means no calls, no texts, and nobody enters or leaves this room. Period."

Glenn spun around. "Lockdown? Why?"

"That's just what I was told. I didn't argue with the man, okay?"

Glenn shook his head. "Seriously? They'll evacuate the whole building except us and—"

"Except us and security, I know," Derrick said. "You can discuss it with Richter when he arrives. And good luck with *that.*"

Moments later, the door buzzed. Glenn glanced over at the security monitor and saw Lucas Richter standing outside the entrance. He took a deep breath and pressed the button for the door, unlocking it. Richter entered and went straight to the monitor. After looking at the image on the screen for a long moment, he told Derrick Haut, "Initiate the lockdown."

He then turned to Glenn and asked, "All the data and video feeds are off, correct?"

"Everything but this room," Glenn replied. In a low voice, he told Richter, "A Code Red lockdown seems excessive. Are you sure that's—"

"These tracks you found," Richter interrupted, "they could only be from another rover. Right?"

Glenn shrugged. "It would appear so. But we both know that's impossible since—"

Just then, an announcement came over the speaker system:

"Attention all personnel. This is not a test. The security alert system has been activated. This is a Code Red alert. Please evacuate at once to the nearest exit..."

Derrick lowered the room's speaker volume as the announcement continued.

Richter turned to the team and asked, "Are we certain these tracks are not from Rhea herself?"

Jason answered, "Rhea had just entered the cavern and hadn't been anywhere near the spot where the tracks were found, so..."

"Then someone has been there before us?"

"Something," Jason said correctly.

Viktor spoke up, "We should follow the tracks and see where they lead. That way we'll know what we're dealing with."

"Right," Richter said. "Let's see where the tracks go. With luck, we can find whatever it was that made them. In the meantime, not a word to *anyone.* No calls and no one other than me leaves or enters this room for any reason. Understand?"

Everyone acknowledged that except Keri, who shook her head. Richter noticed this and asked, "Do you have a problem with that, Miss Jenkins?"

She looked up at him. "I just...I don't understand why the rest of the team can't—"

"The rest of the team can wait," he said. "You understand that this company has invested billions of dollars into this project. Right?"

"Yes, I do, but—"

Richter leaned down in front of her. "And they expect us to follow orders. Right?"

"Yes."

In a raised voice he asked, "Do you understand how to follow orders Jenkins?"

She made no reply.

"Answer my question."

At this point Keri was trembling. "No—I mean yes. I just—"

"Enough!" Richter shouted. He stood and glanced over at Jason and Viktor, who both appeared shocked. He then turned to Glenn and told him, "If anyone here can't follow orders, I want them fired."

Glenn said nothing, but nodded in agreement.

Richter took one more look at the screen, then told the group, "Congratulations on your discovery. I'll bring some food for all of you when I come back. Until then, I need you all to focus on finding where these tracks lead and make sure Rhea doesn't become stuck in there. We don't want any screw-ups."

Without further comment, Richter pressed the door release button and exited the control room, closing the door behind him.

There was a brief moment of silence, which was soon broken by Keri, "What a complete ass."

That was followed by a burst of laughter from the rest of the team, who then leaned back in their chairs, exasperated.

"I'm sorry, Keri," Glenn told her, shaking his head in regret. "I should have stopped him."

"Don't worry about it," she replied. "I'm fine."

Jason turned in his chair and asked the group, "I wonder what kind of story Richter will come up with for the rest of the team, or the public for that matter?"

"The public?" Viktor asked. "How will they know anything about this?"

"We're evacuating the facility," Jason replied. "That would make the news, wouldn't it?"

Glenn leaned back in his chair and told the group, "Let's all take a break. I know we can't leave, but I want everyone to relax for a few minutes and decompress."

Viktor pointed up at the ceiling mounted camera. "What about the all-seeing eye?"

"It's deactivated during a lockdown." Derrick told him. "Don't you ever read any of those security—?"

"Take five already!" Glenn called out.

"Ja Kommandant," Viktor replied.

Keri tried closing her eyes, but couldn't keep herself from looking up at the monitor. After a few minutes, she found herself reaching for her control pad and adjusting the resolution.

Viktor sat up in his chair, then leaned toward Keri and whispered, "Which way do you think the tracks are heading?"

She zoomed the image back out and thought for a moment. "The way the dust is packed, I'd say that whatever made them was heading…north."

Glenn heard that and sat up. He rubbed his eyes and looked up at the screen. "North, huh? Let's find out."

Before long, Rhea was maneuvering through the powdery silt, following the tracks as they led further into the dark grotto. The group agreed that the tracks had been made by a four-wheeled vehicle, and that the overall wheelbase was slightly smaller than Rhea's. A portion of the tracks had been swept away by winds, but the team managed to find where they picked up again.

Suddenly, Rhea's wheels sank into the loose soil, causing her to stop abruptly.

Glenn shook his head and looked over at Viktor. "What have you done now?"

"She's stuck in the sand," Viktor answered. "But I can initiate the traction spikes and allow her to auto-recover, right?"

Glenn looked around. "Everyone okay with that?"

The rest of the team nodded in agreement.

Viktor selected a few command prompts and sent them off into space. "Come on," he said, as if addressing Rhea, "dance for me, baby." He looked over at Jason, who apparently found that amusing. "What?"

"Nothing," Jason answered. "It just sounds kind of funny with your Russian accent."

"To me, you're the one with an accent."

After everyone laughed at that they sat in quiet anticipation as they awaited Rhea's response. Minutes later, the image on the screen began to move as Rhea's wheel spikes engaged and rolled, first into reverse, and then forward. In auto-recover, Rhea would normally proceed on to the destination point and retract her spikes. In this case, however, the pointed wheels stumbled over some rocks and gravel, causing her to lunge forward and spin unexpectedly to the right.

The camera slowly rose back up to its normal angle as the dust settled.

Keri looked up at the big monitor. "Oh my Goodness…"

"Sorry," Viktor said. "I don't know what happened there. She must have—"

"No," Keri said, pointing to the screen. "Look!"

The team was stunned. One by one, they stood from their chairs and walked up to the monitor. The camera now revealed to them what they had hoped for didn't fully expect.

The other rover.

While the team wondered at the strange, almost alien-looking machine, Derrick Haut stepped back to his console and hit a key on the secure line. After a few rings, Richter answered.

"We found it," Derrick said.

"Good. Is it another rover, or...?"

"I guess so, but—"

"I'll be right down," Richter said. "Whose is it, anyway?"

"Like, who built it?"

"Yeah. Is it from the Chinese or...?"

"It doesn't look like anything I've ever seen," Haut said. "Maybe it's not even from here."

"Of course, Derrick. We already know it's not from Cronus."

"I mean...maybe it's not from *Earth*."

Chapter 11

Lucas Richter ended the call, then quickly composed a brief public message explaining that Rhea had experienced a critical malfunction. The message also explained that the control room team was attempting to restore communication with the rover.

Rather than heading straight to the control room, he walked over to the wide sliding-glass door at the rear of his office where he took a moment to contemplate what had just unfolded. He tried to imagine how another planetary rover had found its way to Venus without anyone at Cronus knowing about it.

Thanks to Derrick Haut's calculations, the parachute delay allowed Rhea to touch down exactly where he wanted, which was the precise location that Wright Aerospace had planned to send their own rover. That mission, of course, had been terminated.

Wright was on to something, he thought.

Through the glass, he watched as his dog, Phobos, lay sleeping just outside the door. The dog, a twelve-year-old Doberman, awoke as though he'd sensed his master watching him. Phobos looked at Richter with his dark, once-keen eyes and slowly sat up. He then stood on all fours and went to the glass door as it slid open.

Richter crouched down and petted his long-time companion. He glanced over at the pet's doghouse. *Wright had chosen that spot,* he thought. *They already knew about the cavern and what was inside it.* He wondered if this machine could be of the same origin as the one discovered long ago, the one found buried in the remote hills of central Mexico.

Like many others in his profession, Richter had heard rumors of the discovery in Mexico. He'd heard how a planetary rover had been dug out of the dirt after being buried for centuries. He'd also heard stories of its advanced technology and how it was being studied under the strictest secrecy. Richter was a true believer. Since his youth, he'd read every book and article he could find on the topic. At age twenty, he traveled to the small village of La Chona, Mexico where he spent days exploring the surrounding hills with metal detectors and soil samplers, searching for clues but finding none. Until now, perhaps.

Wright wasn't going to Venus to explore, he thought. *They were going there to find this machine and to bring it to Earth.*

He began to devise a plan. Secrecy, he knew, would have to be the top priority. For that reason, the control room team, with the exception of Derrick Haut, would need to be silenced.

Inside his coat closet was a small two-drawer dresser. From it he emptied underwear and socks from the bottom drawer and then lifted out a false bottom, revealing a small, hidden compartment. From there he removed a square electronic device equipped with a short plastic antenna and a cord. This device, an Electromagnetic Interference Transmitters, or EIT for short, is used for jamming radio signals and to create electronic interference over short distances.

Next, he slid on a pair of beige Spandex gloves before picking a weapon. From the compartment, he selected a custom Smith & Wesson M&P-22. The barrel had been modified and rifled for specially-made carbon bullets while the end of the barrel had been threaded. Richter checked the magazine and loaded the chamber. Each carbon bullet was implanted with a tiny capsule containing a toxic blend of arsenic oxide and cyanide gel. He screwed a black titanium suppressor onto the end of the barrel.

He placed the items into his briefcase and put the dresser back in order before heading to the door. He paused for a moment to consider the details of his plan, then took a deep breath and exited the office.

Glenn Hosato heard the buzzer and turned to check the security monitor, forgetting that the cameras were off due to the lockdown. He pressed the button for the intercom. "Who is it?"

"It's Lucas. Open up."

Immediately, the control room door unlocked and Richter entered, placing his briefcase atop an empty console. He joined Glenn in front of the large monitor where they viewed the newly discovered machine.

Glenn shook his head. "Fascinating, isn't it?"

Richter was mesmerized by what he saw and studied the machine for a long moment before making a reply. He could see the machine had four bright alloy wheels, each connected to the main body by a short arm. The machine's one-piece body appeared egg-shaped with a flattened underside. Protruding up and forward from the top was a long smooth limb-like appendage. At the end of that was a sphere-shaped component the size of a golf ball. Richter figured this was the camera eye. "'Fascinating' is an understatement," he finally replied.

Viktor leaned close to Keri's ear and asked, "Where's all the food he'd promised?"

She whispered back, "You didn't believe that, did you?" She then asked, "Do you think they'll give us a bonus for finding this thing?"

Viktor laughed under his breath. "Not in a meellion years, but I bet your friend Lucas will be driving a Lamborghini very soon."

Richter continued studying the image of the rover. After a minute or so, Glenn mentioned, "Whoever built this knows more about planetary rovers than we do."

"Who do you suppose built it?"

"That, I don't know," Glenn replied. "The Russians landed several probes on the planet as far back as 1970, but certainly nothing with wheels. Nothing like this."

"What's your initial evaluation?"

"My evaluation? We haven't had time to study it, Lucas. All we have are a few guesses and—"

"That I understand. What have you found so far?"

"Well…there are a couple of things we've noticed." Using a remote control, Glenn positioned four different images of the rover onto the big screen before he continued, "From our preliminary observations we've noticed the machine is missing a few things. It's what it *doesn't* have that makes it interesting."

"Such as...?"

Glenn directed Richter's attention to each of the images and explained, "The first and most obvious thing is that there are no symbols, flags, or insignias anywhere. We don't see any antennas or communication devices on its exterior, either."

Richter nodded.

"Also, there are no visible cooling devices, no solar panels or collectors, and no hydraulic components. Other than the wheels, there are no external drivetrain mechanisms. All of the usual sensors and electrical apparatus are nowhere to be seen."

"What do you suppose powers it?"

"That, I'd love to know." He pointed to one of the images and explained, "In some ways, this machine makes Rhea look like a Ford Model T. If you look carefully, you'll see no visible fasteners or assembly seams anywhere. Whoever designed it didn't like sharp corners or right angles, either. Aside from the wheels, there are no machined parts visible. Viktor and Jason believe the body and appendages could be bio-mechanical."

Richter appeared surprised. "Is that possible?"

Glenn shrugged.

"How long do you suppose it's been sitting there?"

Glenn thought about that. "From the amount of dust accumulated and the general condition of the tracks, I'd say it's been there for at least a year. Maybe longer. *Why* it's just sitting there is the question."

Richter stared again at the four images. After a long moment, he leaned close to Glenn and mentioned, "Decades ago, a planetary rover was found buried in the hills of central Mexico. In scientific circles it is known as Rita. Have you heard of it?"

"Rita?" Glenn began to chuckle before noticing Richter's serious expression. He then cleared his throat and replied, "I've heard the stories, Lucas. I also know there are many books written on the subject."

"Do you think this could be another one? Another Rita?"

"Frankly, Lucas, I've always considered the story of Rita to be a hoax. Most scientists I know dismiss it. If it actually does exist, then—"

"It exists." Richter snapped. "Don't allow yourself to be fooled, Glenn. Look around this room." He waved his hand in the direction of the consoles, computers, and monitors. "Where do you suppose all this technology came from?"

"Look, Lucas, I don't know anything about Rita," Glenn said in reply. "You're asking the wrong guy. All I've heard are rumors and tall tales."

"It's no rumor," Richter insisted. "I've been to the village where it was found, and I've explored the hills where it was dug out."

"Have you ever actually seen it?"

"I wish I could say I have, but only a select few have ever laid eyes on that incredible machine. According to reliable sources, Kennedy was one of the first to inspect it after it was smuggled into the United States."

"*President* Kennedy?"

Richter nodded and then gestured to the images on the screen. "In your opinion, Glenn, is this machine from Earth or somewhere else?"

Glenn went to his console and sat down. He could feel the eyes of the team upon him. "Right now I have no way to know," he answered, "and it would be useless to start speculating. Perhaps if we assembled a team of researchers and gave it enough time, we could come up with a reasonable scientific answer."

Lucas remained standing and folded his arms.

Glenn glanced over at Viktor and Jason who both shrugged. He then turned back to Richter. "To my knowledge, there is no corporation or any nation on Earth that could have designed and built such a unique machine and sent it to Venus without us knowing at least *something* about it."

The rest of the team seemed in agreement.

Glenn asked Richter, "Was it by sheer chance that Rhea happened to land so close to this machine, or…?"

"It was dumb luck," Richter replied, "and that's all. As you know, the parachute delay caused Rhea to miss the planned landing site by hundreds of miles." He turned and stepped back to the monitor, effectively ending the conversation.

After a minute or so, Richter stepped over to Derrick Haut's console. He bent down close to Haut and whispered, "I think you know what we have to do here."

Haut shrugged. "Um…what would that be?"

"You and I are going to have that machine brought here, to Earth."

"What are you talking about? How can we do that?"

"Just stay calm," Richter told him. "What I'm about to do will seem crazy at first, but I know what I'm doing. Okay?"

Derrick saw that Richter had a strange look in his eyes and was trembling as well. Nonetheless, he nodded in agreement.

Richter walked over to his briefcase where he removed the spandex gloves and slid them on. He then glanced over his shoulder at the team members who were busy at work except for Derrick, who was watching his every move.

From the briefcase, Richter removed the cord from the EIT and plugged it in. As he flipped it on, the lights flickered and every monitor went black.

Now he was ready.

Chapter 12

A small commotion began as the video monitors went black. All at once, the control room operators stood from their chairs and began troubleshooting. Glenn Hosato tapped at his touch-screen a few times while attempting to diagnose the problem.

Aside from Derrick Haut, no one in the room was aware that Lucas Richter was now holding a gun. Richter knew there would be no room for error. The weapon would need to be fired at close range for the carbon bullets to penetrate and for their poison contents to enter the victim's bloodstream.

In shock, Haut watched as Richter approached Glenn from behind. He held the end of the barrel less than two inches from Glenn's right ear. Without hesitation, he pulled the trigger. Though muffled by the suppressor, the sound of the gunshot startled everyone in the small room.

Richter stepped aside as Glenn's body fell forward onto his console before dropping to the floor. Quickly, Richter turned and stepped toward Keri Jenkins. She let out a piercing scream. As he prepared to fire, Keri desperately reached and grabbed the end of the silencer, pointing it away.

Richter yanked the gun from Keri and fired one shot at her chest. Almost at once, she dropped to her knees, then fell at the feet of Jason MacQuaid.

Jason gazed down in shock at Keri's limp body. He then glared at Richter and yelled, "You monster! What have you done?"

Richter ignored that. He kicked Keri's chair out of his way and went straight for Jason, who tried to scramble backward. As Jason stumbled, Richter swung the gun close to his throat and fired one shot.

Just then, Richter noticed something from the corner of his eye. He turned to see that Viktor Ivanov had picked up a chair and hurled it at him. Richter ducked just in time as the chair sailed over his head, crashing loudly into another console before tumbling across the small room. He turned to Viktor and their eyes locked.

"You murderer!" Viktor cried. "Why are you doing this? Tell me!"

Richter offered no reply. Instead, he aimed and fired one shot at Viktor's chest. That was enough to land him on the floor, though Richter knew he'd have to move in for a second, closer shot. Before proceeding, he glanced over at Jason MacQuaid, who was lying on the floor and no longer breathing. Richter saw the blank stare on Jason's face and could tell the poison had already taken affect.

He stepped toward Viktor, who was on the floor, clutching his chest in pain.

Viktor caught his breath and looked up at the killer. "You sick son of a—"

Before Viktor could finish his statement, Richter stepped toward him with the barrel of the weapon held out. Right then, Viktor swung his leg up, striking Richter's right forearm. The gun flew from Richter's hand and tumbled through the air. As Richter stopped and turned, Viktor swung his leg again. This time, the heel of his shoe slammed into Richter's right knee, bringing him to the floor in pain.

The gun landed at the feet of Derrick Haut.

Viktor called to him, "Grab it, Derrick! Shoot him!"

As Haut reached for the gun, Richter warned him, "Wait Derrick—don't touch the gun. We can't have your fingerprints on it."

"Shoot him!" Viktor yelled. "He's going to kill us!"

Derrick looked into Viktor's desperate eyes for a brief moment. He then turned to Richter, who signaled him to kick the gun across the floor to him.

"What are you waiting for?" Viktor cried.

Derrick placed his foot beside the weapon. He paused for a moment, then, with a flip of his foot, he slid the gun across the floor to Richter.

Richter reached down and grabbed the weapon. While Viktor stared at Derrick in disbelief, Richter stepped toward him and fired one shot into the side of his head.

Carefully, Richter stepped away from the four bodies. He then looked over and saw Derrick was pressed against the far wall. His face had turned white and he was breathing rapidly. "Sit down," Richter told him. "It's okay."

Haut remained frozen against the wall, trembling. "*Okay?* How is it okay?"

"Just sit down, Derrick," Richter repeated, this time more calmly.

Haut hesitated and then staggered over to his chair.

"Relax and try to breathe," Richter said. "I need to fire one more shot, but don't worry, I'm going to miss. Okay?"

Derrick nodded while covering his ears.

Richter aimed to the left of him and fired. Derrick flinched as the carbon bullet shattered into the wall. Carbon fragments ricocheted across the control room.

After that, Richter stepped back to where Glenn Hosato lay dead on the floor. He lifted Glenn's right arm and carefully placed the gun into his lifeless hand and closed his fingers around the grip. He moved Glenn's index finger onto the trigger, then lowered his hand back to the floor

Richter looked up at Haut and instructed him, "Listen carefully to everything I say. When asked, you'll explain that Glenn had been acting strangely all week. Right?"

Haut nodded nervously.

"After the communications went out, Glenn became convinced that Rhea had burned up on the planet's surface. The thought of failure was too much for him."

Haut acknowledged that.

Richter continued, "Glenn went mad. He produced a gun and shot the team members one-by-one. He also fired at you without realizing he'd missed. After seeing you hit the floor, he killed himself." He looked into Haut's eyes. "Do you understand all this?"

Haut was nearly in shock and could make no reply.

Growing impatient, Richter stepped in front of him and slapped him across the side of his head. He asked again, "Do you understand?"

Haut was stunned by that. "Yeah—it was Glenn—he shot himself. Got it."

"Good. And remember that I wasn't here when it happened."

Haut agreed.

"I'm heading back to my office while you wait here. After I leave, adjust Rhea's camera to face away from the other rover, then place Rhea into sleep mode and remove the control room copy of the video. No one is to lay eyes on anything except what went to the website. After you've done that, contact security and report what Glenn did." He added, "Stick to one story—the one I told you. You got it?"

"Yeah. But why…why did you—?"

"I know all this seems crazy," Richter said, gesturing to the four bodies, "but it was necessary. We're on to something huge, Derrick."

"Like what?"

"I'll explain everything later. It will all make sense." Richter unplugged the EIT, placed it into his briefcase, and quickly headed to the door. Before leaving, he turned to Haut and added, "Don't say anything to anyone about the other rover."

"Of course."

At that, Richter exited the control room.

Soon after returning to his office, Richter's phone rang. This was the facility Security Chief who called to inform Richter that a shooting had occurred. The Chief also explained that, although it was too early to make any conclusions, it appeared that the shooter was Glenn Hosato, and that Glenn had taken his own life.

Richter feigned astonishment and instructed the Chief to contact 9-1-1 at once. Hoping to disturb the crime scene as much as possible, he authorized entry to the room for all guards and emergency medical personnel. He also advised that a full in-house response team be sent to the control room immediately to perform emergency first aid and attempt resuscitation. He also explained that he would inform Corporate Management of the tragedy before coming to the control room himself.

After ending the call, Richter quickly removed his clothing and placed everything into a trash bag along with the EIT device and the gloves. After showering, he changed into a clean set of clothes. Carrying the trash bag, he exited the office, limping slightly from the kick he'd received to the knee. He rode the elevator to the basement, then walked past the trash compactor and recycling bins and headed straight to the incinerator. There, he opened the heavy steel door of the machine and tossed the bag inside. After activating the incineration process twice, he went to the elevator and headed to the scene of the crime.

Chapter 13

The video transmission from Venus had stopped abruptly, and I figured that either my spy transmitter or Rhea had failed. Just as I was about to give up, the video suddenly resumed. On my screen, I could once again see the mysterious new rover. I suspected the six-minute picture loss had something to do with electromagnetic interference, which has a different appearance than a reception problem or a total loss of signal. Anyway, whatever was jamming the signal decided to stop.

On a whim, I checked the mission website and found what I'd expected: the website video had been shut down since earlier this morning. There was also a message from Lucas Richter claiming that Rhea had malfunctioned. This, of course, was not true because I happened to have the live video in front of me. Since one lie usually leads to another, I read on. Sure enough, Richter's message went on to say that the control room team was working to reestablish communication with the rover, though I knew better.

Just as I went back to watching the control room video feed, Rhea's headlight turned off. Her camera turned away from the newly found rover and slowly aimed to the ground. Soon, the live video ceased and I realized that Rhea had been placed into sleep mode. I assumed the team had decided to put the mission on hold until they came up with a plan of action concerning their little discovery. I wasn't going to hold my breath for a press release.

My first cup of coffee had reached the end of its long and winding journey, so I set my tablet on the arm of my recliner and headed for the bathroom. While there, I took a few minutes to shave, shower, and put on some fresh clothes. Once finished, I headed back to the living room. To my unpleasant surprise, I found my neighbor Kaui sitting in my recliner with his twin brother Kekoa crouched beside him—and they were studying my tablet.

Kekoa looked up to see me entering the room. "The door was wide open," he explained. "We just came in."

I held my hand out for the tablet. "I'll take that, please."

"Not so fast," Kaui said, holding the device out of my reach. "First, I think you need to explain how it is that you have the entire video from Rhea on your personal tablet."

Usually, I can lie my way out of anything, but I wasn't prepared for this. I told him, "I'm the Director of Security, remember?"

"Yeah. So?"

"So, I have access to what's going on at the facility, including the video from Rhea."

"From your living room?" Kaui looked at me doubtfully. "C'mon, Mike, give us a little credit. *Nobody* has access to this except the control room team."

"Well, I guess there are a few things you guys don't know."

Kaui shook his head and reminded me, "Kekoa and me personally designed the mainframe that handles this data. Its primary purpose was to keep all the data received from Venus in one place—"

"Never mind that," Kekoa interrupted. "What really matters is that they've found something amazing."

I was hoping they hadn't noticed that. "Look," I said, "that video is top secret. The people we work for are keeping this quiet for a reason and it might be dangerous for you guys to stick your noses where they don't belong."

"I think it's too late," Kaui said.

I gave them a look. "You don't realize what you're messing with. Just hand me the tablet and we'll pretend none of this ever happened. There are things going on that you don't need to know about, and—"

"Are you a spy or something?" Kekoa asked. "Tell us the truth."

"He must be," Kaui said, "and he must have placed some kind of transmitter into the mainframe."

I keep forgetting how smart these two are. "I'm the Director of Security for the Venus mission," I said. "I'm certainly not a *spy*."

"Whatever," Kekoa said. "Let's check out what Rhea found. It looks like another rover, doesn't it?"

I went to my front door and closed it before anyone else decided to stroll in. I then thought things over for a minute while the twins looked at the video, studying the newly discovered machine from different angles.

"Where do you think it's from?" Kekoa asked me.

"I have no idea. I was going to ask you guys that same question."

Kekoa looked up and asked, "Did you see the message Richter posted on the mission website?"

I nodded. "Obviously, they don't want anyone to know what they found, which is one reason why you two would be better off if you forgot all about this."

Kaui told me, "After Richter's message posted we tried calling the facility, but they weren't allowing incoming calls."

"That can only mean one thing," I said. "The facility must be in lockdown."

The twins looked at each other in disbelief. "Why would they do that?" Kekoa asked.

"Apparently, the bigwigs at Cronus plan to keep this a secret. Or maybe they found my transmitter in the mainframe."

"I *knew* it," Kekoa said.

Kaui appeared concerned. "If they *did* find such a thing, they'll probably think Kekoa and I put it there."

"I wouldn't let you take the rap for that," I said, "but you might still be legally responsible for what you now know."

They both nodded.

I went to the couch and sat. After thinking, I turned to the twins and asked, "Where's Raquel Richards right now? Is she at the facility?"

"I think so," Kekoa answered. "But if there *is* a lockdown she'd be evacuated."

"Call her cell phone and find out—"

"I tried already," Kekoa said. "I left a message for her to call us."

It occurred to me that the twins could be in danger simply by knowing too much. They know about the discovery of the other rover. They also know that the message Richter posted is a lie. In addition, they know about my transmitter and that I seem to have access to everything. On top of that, they've probably figured out that I'm a spy, too.

I told them, "If they find the transmitter, the first thing they'll do is bring both of you in for questioning. They'll separate you, and if your answers don't jibe they'll have you arrested."

Kaui seemed shocked. "Arrested? For what?"

"For espionage," I replied. "And if they find out you know about their little discovery, you'd have an even bigger problem."

"What do we do?" Kekoa asked.

"You'd have to tell them the truth about everything," I said, "though they could still accuse you of being accomplices."

"C'mon," Kekoa said, "They know we're not *spies*,"

I nodded. "Still, Cronus won't want you running around with all these secrets in your head. They'd rather have you locked up or silenced."

Kekoa assured me, "We wouldn't tell anybody anything."

"I believe you, but keep in mind that we're talking about a multibillion dollar mission, plus all the years of research, planning, and preparation. And don't forget about all the stockholders and financiers involved. Is Cronus going to look the other way with all that at stake?"

"Then what do we do?" he asked.

I thought for a few seconds and explained, "Right now, there are a number of wheels in motion. I'm not at liberty to discuss much, but I can tell you this: things are not going to end well for Cronus *or* for this mission." I stood from the couch. "To play it safe, I think the three of us should disappear for a while."

They both seemed surprised.

I went on, "If the security team has found the transmitter, they could be on their way here right now. I suggest we pack a few things and head out within the next five minutes."

"To where?" Kekoa asked.

"We'll decide that later," I answered. "Right now, this apartment complex is the last place we want to be. Go to your place and grab all of your ID's as well as anything that has a digital record. That includes your phones, tablets, flash drives, memory cards—all that. Throw everything into a carry-on bag or a pillowcase and we'll head out. Now hurry."

While the twins left to gather their things, I went to my room where I picked out a carry-on bag and tossed it on my bed. Wasting no time, I grabbed a few items from my closet and dresser. I also packed my two handguns, a Colt .380 Mustang and a Sig .22 Mosquito. From a hidden compartment under my mattress, I grabbed a plastic bag containing my stash of cash, wallets, and passports. I put that in the case along with all of my phones, cameras, and memory cards. Once I'd finished, I zipped the overnight bag and left the apartment, locking the door behind me.

When I got to the twin's place I found they had little to say. I could tell by their faces they were frightened. Cronus had been their first job out of college, and this was their first real apartment. Unfortunately, their simple lives were about to change.

Quickly, we loaded everything of importance into pillowcases and headed to the door. Before stepping out, they both turned and took one last glance at their little apartment. After that, we headed straight to my car.

And never went back.

Chapter 14

As the twins and I reached the parking lot of our apartment building, I surprised them by unlocking the doors to my shiny new Acura Motarái, a solar-charged MPV. As it turns out, this would be last time I'd ever drive it.

"Nice ride," Kaui commented. "Whose is it?"

"Just get in," I said, "and try not to ask too many questions."

We placed our things in the rear compartment and climbed in, with Kaui commandeering the front seat. Without delay, I exited the parking lot and turned onto South Atlantic Avenue.

Naturally, Kaui had more questions. "Why are we heading north? Are we going to the Cape?"

"We need to stop at Wright Aerospace," I replied. "I want to meet with Craig Van Essen, if he's in."

Kekoa asked, "Is that who you *really* work for? Craig Van Essen?"

"Not anymore," I told him. "I was with Wright Aerospace for nine years before I quit and went to work for Cronus. Nonetheless, Craig and I have remained close friends." I think. "Now please shut-up for a minute and let me concentrate, okay?"

They both nodded.

I looked over at Kaui and asked, "Why hasn't Raquel called?"

He made no reply.

"Hello? Anybody home?"

"You said to shut-up, remember?"

So I did. I reached forward and slid the in-dash tablet in front of Kaui and told him, "I need you to send an email to the HR Department. Explain that after what happened with Rhea, the three of us have decided to take a day or two off." I thought for a second and added, "Tell them we're going to visit my family in Ocala, a town about three hours northwest of here."

Kaui started typing. "That's not really where we're going, is it?"

"Nope. But I hope it sends anyone who comes looking for us in the wrong direction."

He glanced over at me. "I'm beginning to realize you have the ability to be an amazing liar."

I smiled at that. "You, my friend, are in the presence of a master."

Using the phone app, I spoke some numbers. A few seconds later, a ringtone came up over the speakers. I said to the twins, "Don't make a peep."

After one ring, the phone picked up. "Wright Aerospace. Paige speaking. May I help you?"

It was Paige O'Neill, Craig's long time personal assistant.

"Good morning, Paige. This is Mike Brennan."

"Hello, Mike. Have you missed me?"

"Actually, I need to speak with Craig right away. It's kind of an emergency."

"Okay. I'll try to put you through. I hope everything's okay."

"I hope so, too." I continued driving while I waited.

After a minute or so, Van Essen came on the line, "Good morning, Mike. Are you okay?"

"I'm fine, thanks. But I have an urgent situation on my hands."

"What can I do to help?"

"Well, I know that you're a busy person, Craig, but we need to meet with you ASAP."

"We? Who are you with?"

"I'm with Kaui and Kekoa Hamilton, two engineers from Cronus. Right now the three of us are heading north on Highway 1A, close to 401. We should be arriving at your facility in about ten minutes."

There was a moment of silence, so I asked, "Mind if we stop by?"

"You can vouch for the two engineers, right?"

Meaning: *You're sure they aren't spies, right?* I glanced at the twins, who looked like two kids on a school trip. "Yeah, I think I can vouch for them."

"Use the East Entrance," he said. "I'll have Paige meet you downstairs."

"Thanks, Craig." I ended the call.

Kaui looked over at me. "He probably knows that something's going on at Cronus."

That may be true. I suspected that Craig had a spy or two of his own planted there and could know more about the situation than we did. I told Kaui, "You should try calling Raquel Richards again."

Kaui turned to the back seat and told his brother, "You call her, Kekoa. You know her number."

I looked in the mirror and reminded him, "Don't tell her *anything*—not even where we're heading. Just let her do the talking."

He nodded. Using the rear seat tablet, Kekoa entered her number.

After only one ring, Raquel answered, "Hello?"

"Raquel? It's Kekoa. Are you okay?"

"I'm fine. Where are you guys?"

"We're with Mike. Are you at the facility?"

"I'm outside in the parking lot. The whole place went into lockdown for some reason. They evacuated the building, but they won't let anyone go home."

"Why not?"

"The police don't want anyone leaving the premises until we've all been questioned."

"The police? What are they doing there?"

"*That* I don't know," Raquel replied, "but emergency vehicles are arriving right now. Something serious must have happened." She advised him, "If I were you, I'd stay away from here."

"We plan to."

"You guys heard what happened to Rhea, right?"

Kekoa hesitated, then asked her, "What did *you* hear?"

"Well, the website only explains that the control room lost communication and there was some kind of malfunction."

"That's what we heard, too."

While Kekoa continued the conversation, I turned into the main entrance of Wright Aerospace. After being waved through the security checkpoint I headed straight to the East Entrance and parked at the front doors. I spotted Paige O'Neill, who was making sure her hair was in place before coming out to greet us. I also noticed she was with an armed security guard. As I got out, I handed the keys to the guard. "I have an important carry-on bag in the back," I told him. "I'll need it for later."

He nodded.

"You'll also find a pillowcase full of items. That needs to be locked up and kept out of sight."

"Yes, sir."

I gestured to the car. "You'll need to find a place to hide this thing, too."

The guard looked at me to see if I was serious. He then began speaking into his radio microphone.

After that, I turned to Miss O'Neil. "It's good to see you again, Paige." I gave her a quick hug.

I let Kaui and Kekoa know, "Paige is Craig Van Essen's executive assistant. She and Craig go back a lot of years."

She nudged my elbow and reminded me, "So do you and I." At that, she turned to the twins and winked.

"We should get moving," I said abruptly. "I don't want to keep the great and powerful Mr. Van Essen waiting."

Paige laughed under her breath. "Right this way, gentleman." We were escorted through the lobby and to the executive elevator. On the way up, Paige whispered to me, "Please tell me you've decided to come back."

I smiled. "Maybe someday."

Seconds later, the elevator stopped at the top-floor suite. As the doors opened, I was surprised to see Craig standing there waiting for us. While I greeted him and introduced the twins I could tell something was troubling him.

"Let's step into my office," he suggested as he directed us in the direction of his sprawling corner suite. Once there, he and I sat opposite each other on two white leather couches positioned in the center of the room.

I glanced over at Kaui and Kekoa. The two were studying some framed photos which Craig had arranged atop an ornate antique cabinet. One of the photos was a young girl, a gymnast, performing on a balance beam. This, I knew, was Craig's daughter, Chandis, who'd died tragically along with her mother while in Tokyo. Next to that was a nice portrait of the lovely and famous Michelle Fontaine, Craig's current wife.

I know you're not supposed to covet your neighbor's wife. Luckily, Craig wasn't my neighbor.

Kaui bent to look closer at a small framed photo nestled behind the others. The portrait appeared to be a younger, leaner Craig, though I knew it was actually his older brother, Martin, who'd also died in a tragic way. Kaui then picked up a framed photo of Craig with someone who looked much like one of the recent Presidents. In the picture, the two men were posing alongside a huge marlin they'd apparently caught together.

Kaui looked over at Craig. "Is this...?"

Craig nodded. "Yep. That's a marlin."

"No, I mean the guy with you."

"Oh, the President? Yeah, that's him." He looked at me and grinned.

On the coffee table were four glasses of orange juice in a tray of ice. Craig grabbed one and took a sip before he got down to business. "So, Mike, when were you last at the Cronus facility?"

"I left last night about ninety minutes after Rhea landed. Around 11:00 p.m."

He looked over at the twins.

Kaui answered, "We got home just after midnight. Why?"

"Are you aware that Cronus evacuated the entire facility this morning?"

Kaui turned his eyes to me.

I replied, "We confirmed that just before we arrived here."

"Do you know *why* they went into a lockdown?"

I shrugged. "I have no idea."

Craig leaned back. "I received some information from an anonymous source a few minutes before you called." Meaning: *One of my spies made a report.*

He continued, "In this business, as you know, bad news travels faster than our own rockets. All of this is developing as we speak, but the initial report is that there has been a shooting at the Cronus facility."

"Who was shot?" Kekoa asked.

Craig paused for a moment, then told us, "The preliminary report I received was disturbing—to say the least." He turned to the twins. "What I'm about to tell you is strictly confidential."

They nodded.

"I'm sure you are both familiar with Glenn Hosato."

"He's the control room chief." Kaui replied.

"And I'm sure you know all of the senior control room operators handling the Venus mission."

The three of us nodded.

He drew a deep breath. "This won't be easy for you to hear."

"What happened?" I asked.

"It appears Glenn Hosato may have been the shooter."

We were stunned.

Kaui looked at Craig with disbelief. "That can't be right."

Before Craig could reply, Kekoa asked, "Who was shot?"

Craig looked down at his juice as he replied, "The initial report suggests that Glenn shot and killed three of the team members while inside the control room. After that, he took his own life."

I felt like I was hit by a truck.

Craig added, "There was only one survivor: Derrick Haut."

"This can't be true," Kaui said.

"Kaui is right," I said. "Glenn would be incapable of such a thing."

"Keri is dead?" Kekoa asked. "Viktor and Jason, too?"

"That's what I've been told," Craig answered. "According to a reliable source, all communication with Rhea was suddenly lost. Apparently, the failure was too much for Glenn to handle and he—"

Kaui shook his head and told Craig, "Rhea isn't lost." He glanced over at me.

I signaled him to be quiet about that.

Craig noticed that. "Is there more to this?"

"Much more," I replied. I looked over at the twins and saw grief written on their faces. I told Craig, "This morning, we discovered several major concerns involving Rhea and what was happening inside the control room."

"Tell me everything."

I sat forward and found myself speaking in a low voice. "What we found," I said, "could place us in great danger. Unfortunately, we can't share what we know with anyone right now—not even you."

Craig held out his hands. "You know you can trust me, Mike."

"We do trust you, Craig. It's just that we've uncovered something huge. Knowing what we know could place *you* at great risk as well."

He shook his head at that. "What kind of danger are you talking about?"

"The worst kind. Whoever murdered those people is still alive."

He couldn't argue with that.

I went on, "Kaui and Kekoa are caught in the middle of all this. I aim to keep them out of danger until this is over."

"What's your plan?"

I leaned back. "That's where we need your help, Craig. Do you happen to have a jet available?"

He made a smirk. "I thought you might ask. Where are you planning to go?"

"That's undecided right now," I answered, "but it would be a good idea to be nice and far from here."

"I have a beach house in California," he offered. "You could hide there until—"

"They could trace us to there."

"Who's 'they?'"

"I wish I knew, Craig, but until I find out, I plan to keep the three of us off the grid." On that subject I asked, "Can you arrange to have new citizen cards made for the twins?"

"No. But I might know someone who can." Meaning: *Yes*. "I'll be right back. Don't go anywhere."

After Craig left, I gestured to the twins indicating there could be a listening device planted in the room.

In a whispered voice, Kaui asked me, "Why can't we just tell him the truth about Rhea?"

"Right now, it wouldn't benefit Craig to know," I said, "and it wouldn't do us any good to tell him. The less people that know the better."

A moment later, Craig returned accompanied by Paige. She gestured to the twins to come with her.

After they had left, Craig closed the door and returned to his seat opposite me. He finished what was left of his orange juice, then asked me, "Since we have a few minutes, is there anything you'd like to discuss?"

"Not really. I just hope you're not offended that I won't tell you everything I know."

Craig shook his head. "I understand. Besides, I have plenty of my own information sources." He stood and walked over to the side cabinet, then returned to his seat with the framed picture of the President and himself posing with the marlin. "That was a hell of a day."

"Hell of a fish, too."

I noticed a faraway look in his eyes. "The President had just finished his term in office," he told me. "He and I were exhausted from it all and I guess we felt we deserved a vacation. We booked this charter and told the captain we'd be going out every day until one of us hooked a big one. On the third day, I landed this." He pointed to the marlin.

"What were you doing that you were so exhausted?"

"I was working for the President."

This caught me by surprise. "You never mentioned that before."

"It wasn't something I could discuss with you. Not until now."

"What was your job?"

He looked me in the eye. "The same thing you do, Mike."

This surprised me even further. "So, you were once…"

"A President's Agent."

I exhaled slowly while that eight-ball landed in the pocket, and then asked, "So, when you and I met in Rome, you were working for the President?"

He smiled. "That was my first mission."

"Does your wife know about it?"

"No. And neither does Paige. In fact, you're the only person I've ever mentioned this to."

He and I leaned back and took a moment to laugh at ourselves. After that, I looked at his right hand and noticed the ring on his third finger was identical to mine, with gold inlay on one side and platinum on the other.

"So, what have I gotten myself into?" I asked.

"A world of trouble," he said, "but it's worth it, especially considering what you can do for this country."

I nodded.

"Let me show you something." He unbuttoned his shirt to show me what looked like an oval-shaped scar over his heart.

"What's that from?"

"I took a nice-sized bullet in the chest," he said. "It broke a rib going in and landed in my pericardial sack less than half an inch from my heart."

"I guess I have that to look forward to."

He smiled at my wry comment, then asked, "If you leave Cronus, will your mission be negatively affected?"

I shook my head. "I'm essentially finished here…though I'm half-tempted to look into this murder case—"

"Leave that to the police."

"Should I try to report what I know to the President?"

"I wouldn't. Does he ever allow you to contact him?"

"Actually, no. His instructions were for me to gather information and wait for him to contact me for a report, and not to—"

"Then there's your answer. Just focus on your assigned mission. That, and protect your two friends. If I were you, I'd go to the last place anyone would think of and hide there until the man contacts you."

I took a moment to consider Craig's advice. I'd finally managed to collect plenty of evidence to use against Cronus. I just needed to keep Kaui and Kekoa safe until this whole thing blew over. I grabbed an orange juice from the tray and drank half of it down. After that, I looked at Craig and let him know, "You might want to begin making preparations for the acquisition of Cronus Space and Communications."

Craig simply nodded, and I realized he already knew about that.

Just then, a knock came to the door, followed by Paige, who entered along with the twins. She set a small package on the coffee table and gave me a smile.

"Thank you, Paige," Craig said.

After she'd left, Craig commented, "What would I do without her?" He then turned to me and suggested, "Actually, you could probably use an assistant."

I shook my head. "No thanks. I've got enough trouble."

Craig smiled at that. He then stood and handed me the package from the coffee table, which I assumed contained Kaui and Kekoa's new citizen cards. As we got up to leave, Craig told the twins, "When this is all over, I want you both to come work for me. Understand?"

I could have knocked them over with a feather.

"Thanks for everything," I said, "including the use of the jet."

He waved that off like it was nothing. As we shook hands, Craig leaned close and asked in a low voice, "You *do* have a weapon, right?"

"Of course."

"Good. Before all else, be armed." He gave me a pat on the back and added, "Find a place to hide and stay out of trouble. Okay?"

"I will," I promised, though I knew trouble had a way of finding me no matter where I hid.

Chapter 15

The twins and I followed Paige to the elevator and headed downstairs. After retrieving my bag from the security guard we traveled by golf cart to a nearby hangar where Craig Van Essen's sleek new Gulfstream G850 sat waiting. If you are familiar with Craig, you know he always had to have the latest greatest thing, and the G850 was apparently it. Across the tail gleamed the blue and gold Wright Aerospace insignia, an elegant ellipse orbiting the letter W.

Paige pulled the cart beside the aircraft and we all hopped out. Right away, we were greeted by our young co-pilot, Scott McGuire. Scott let us know our pilot, Captain Tom Bennett, was inside making final preparations.

I noticed Scott was wearing his Wright pilot uniform which consisted of a navy ball cap, a gold polo shirt, and a navy wind breaker—all with embroidered Wright logos on them—and navy cargo pants to match.

This reminded me of a domestic spy mission that Craig sent me on a few years ago. I'd dressed in a similar outfit, disguising myself as a pilot. The simple costume worked surprisingly well and I was given access to almost everything I wanted. It was working so well, in fact, that I wondered why I hadn't tried this trick before. That is, until I ran into a few of the *real* pilots. About then, everything went down the tubes.

Anyway, I looked in the distance and saw my new Acura being driven at a high speed across the runway to another hangar where I knew it would be tucked away out of sight. Maybe buried. I also noticed the sky was clear over this part of Florida and I hoped it would be like this at our destination, wherever that was. I knew Scott would be asking me about that within the next thirty seconds.

"You boys have a good flight and be careful," Paige told us as she began to drive away. "The pillow case with its contents will be locked away safely until your return."

I gave her a nod. "The twins and I appreciate your help."

Paige turned and blew me a kiss, which Kekoa happened to notice.

Just as Scott looked like he was about to inquire about our destination, Kekoa asked me, "Did you and Paige ever have, like, a thing?"

I laughed, perhaps too loud. "Of course not," I told him. Unless you count that thing in Rome. At that moment, I was suddenly distracted by our flight attendant as she emerged from the doorway of the jet. Gracefully, she descended the stairs and walked over to greet us.

"Good morning," she said with a bright smile. "I'm Crystal. I'll be your flight attendant today. How is everyone?"

Crystal was young, perhaps in her late twenties, with brilliant blue eyes and long blonde hair, which was pulled back and braided nicely.

"I understand that there will be three passengers flying today," she said.

"Just us three," I replied.

She smiled. "Fine. I'll go check that everything's ready while you find your seats." As she headed back up the stairs she turned to me. "Oh, by the way, what's our destination?"

Well, Paris crossed my mind, or maybe Greece. I then considered the twins and replied without further thought.

"Honolulu."

Chapter 16

The twins and I followed Crystal aboard the jet and took a quick look around. The floor plan made the interior appear roomy and I thought the décor might have come out of a starship. The seats were extra wide and could be leaned way back for sleeping. In the aft section was a divan, which could berth into a double bed that faced a large TV. The galley was located in the tail section where I could hear Crystal tinkering and from where I smelled coffee brewing.

I could live here.

A few minutes later our pilot stepped out of the cockpit. After speaking with the co-pilot for a moment, he came over and introduced himself to me. "Welcome aboard," he said. "I'm Tom Bennett. I'll be your pilot today."

We shook hands and I introduced the twins and myself by our first names. I noticed that, like most pilots, Tom was over six feet tall and had no shortage of grey hair. At a glance, I saw his ID badge included a winged symbol fashioned with a star in the center. Fastened to his lapel he wore a gold pin, a small star-shaped image emitting a beam. Apparently Tom had been an Air Force Astronaut.

"Our flight attendant tells me our destination is Honolulu International."

"That's correct," I said. I lowered my voice and added, "For the record, Tom, this trip never took place and your crew has never seen us."

He nodded. "No problem."

After thanking Tom I headed to the aft section where I placed my bag into a storage closet. Scott shut and sealed the door while the twins and I went to our seats and buckled up. After the plane was towed out of the hangar the pilots started both engines and taxied out to the runway. We were airborne within minutes.

Before long, Crystal appeared from the galley and let me know, "The pilots estimate our arrival to be approximately 12:40 p.m. Hawaii time." She handed me a small card with a lunch menu. "Coffee?"

"Yes, thank you."

She walked to the back and spoke with the twins, though I knew they'd be holding off on food until we arrived in Hawaii. Once there, the two could feast on some of the local dishes they constantly talk about. I decided to hold off too.

As comfy as all this was, I couldn't enjoy it much. I was sure Kaui and Kekoa felt the same way. Four of our coworkers had gone to be with the angels this morning, and that was heavy on our hearts. I also was troubled with the possibility of the twins being in danger, which was partly my fault. At least we were heading somewhere where I knew we'd be safe, a faraway place where no one would find us.

I'd been to Hawaii once before, and that was with my ex-wife, Julia. I remember it as the most enjoyable time she and I ever spent together. This trip, however, would be no vacation. I didn't have much of a plan yet but my main objectives were simple: protect the twins, lay low, and wait for the President to contact me. I also wanted to monitor Cronus and try to figure out what they were up to. Hopefully, my transmitter was still operating and no one had discovered that yet.

After my coffee, I took a moment to set my wristwatch for Hawaii Time. I wore a thin titanium watch with an alarm feature which Julia had given me as a gift. I looked to the rear of the plane and saw that the twins were both asleep, which was probably a good idea. I thanked Crystal for the coffee and requested a blanket. She brought me a thick ivory-colored down comforter that matched the seating. I adjusted my seat into the feet up and fully reclined bed position.

"Is there anything else you need?" she asked in a low voice.

"If it's no trouble," I said, "let me know when we're about one hour from Hawaii."

"No trouble at all."

Just before nodding off, I remember promising myself that I would hunt down and kill whoever murdered Glenn Hosato and the others.

When I awoke, I glanced at my watch and saw that it was 11:10 a.m. Hawaii time. The twins were still asleep, so I quietly repositioned my chair and got up to stretch. I decided to change my clothes, so I went to my bag and removed a black polo shirt along with a pair of leather sandals and khaki shorts, then stepped into the small lavatory. After changing, I splashed some water on my face and combed my hair. From there I headed to the galley where Crystal was sitting and reading an eBook. I spoke to her using my best French: "Bonjour mademoiselle," I said. "Un café, s'il vous plaît."

"Oui monsieur."

As she prepared my coffee, she let me know, "I think we're about one hour from Hawaii now."

"Good. I'll need to talk with Scott as soon as he's available."

From the bulkhead, she picked up a phone and called the cockpit. Moments later, Scott emerged from the cockpit carrying his tablet and joined Crystal and me in the galley.

"Can I help you?"

"Yes, Scott. I have a question and I think you can help me." I explained, "Years ago, while visiting the island of Maui, I drove out to the small town of Hana. It's way out on the east end of the island."

He nodded. "I've been there."

"I remember a small airport there," I said, "and I was wondering if it would be possible for us to land there rather than Honolulu."

He shrugged. "Let's find out." He tapped at his tablet screen for a moment, then told me, "Apparently, the runway was recently expanded to seven-thousand feet, which is definitely long enough. Would you like us to radio a request to land there?"

I nodded. "If it's okay with Tom, then Hana will be our new destination."

Scott excused himself and headed to the cockpit.

I'd feel safer staying on the island of Maui, which is more rural than Oahu and easier to disappear in. Also, all of the twin's relatives and buddies live in Oahu and I wanted to avoid them being spotted by someone they know.

After a few minutes, Scott phoned and explained that we were cleared to land in Hana. After chatting with Crystal for a minute, I looked and saw that the twins were finally awake. I stepped over to their section and explained, "I decided to change our destination from Oahu to Maui. Sound okay?"

They shrugged.

"Good. We'll be landing in Hana."

Kaui seemed surprised. "They have an airport there? In *Hana?*"

"They do now," I said. "I called ahead and had one built."

For some reason, they both looked at me like I was making that up.

Just then, Crystal stopped by and told us we were nearing our destination and that we would need to prepare for landing.

I went back to my seat and buckled up. After a minute or so, I heard the two jet engines slow as the nose of the aircraft dropped slightly and we began our descent. Once the aircraft dropped below the clouds I looked down and could see the island of Hawaii, The Big Island, and it really was big. I remembered how Julia and I were surprised when we discovered how enormous the islands actually were. After the Big Island, Maui is the next largest, though over ninety percent of the state's population reside on the island of Oahu, which was another good reason not to go there.

The engines slowed further as we continued our descent. Before long, I could see Maui in the distance. It was magnificent. The north side of the island seemed to rise up out of the turquoise sea like a green jewel, jagged and carpeted in rainforest. The sunlight was shimmering over the clouds which were scattered along the summit of the island's towering volcanic mountain. The easternmost tip of the island, I knew, was where we'd soon be landing.

I recalled that Hana was a remote, quaint, and unspoiled old Hawaiian town. It was a place visited by few tourists except those who, like Julia and I, had braved the famous 'Road to Hana,' a rugged but picturesque drive along the island's north shore. I remembered how the narrow road twisted along steep sea cliffs, over countless single lane bridges, and past endless waterfalls through one of the wettest tropical rainforests on Earth.

For a brief moment, I allowed myself to think back to the last time I was here. It was the year 2021 and I'd rented a convertible for the drive to Hana. Julia had worn a white bikini top that day, along with skimpy jean shorts and white Wayfarer sunglasses. She'd also worn the nice diamond and platinum earrings I'd bought for her, and I remember noticing how her matching wedding ring sparkled in the sunlight. She was young and thin and her skin was smooth and tanned. It was a wonderful time for the two of us. She and I were together in paradise and it seemed as though nothing else on Earth mattered.

We were in love.

More memories began flashing through my mind and my heart began to feel heavy. I opened my eyes and watched out the porthole as we banked gently to the south. Captain Bennett lowered the landing gear and extended the flaps. Through my small window, I looked out and saw the rocky shoreline and towering coconut palms blur along as we fell from the sky. After the pilot leveled the plane and made some final adjustments, we dropped further until our wheels skidded on the asphalt runway. Once on the ground, we coasted to the end of the runway and turned around, then proceeded onward to the taxiway before coming to a stop in front of the tiny terminal.

Feelings of sadness and regret suddenly loomed over me. My thoughts had gone back to a time that I shouldn't be thinking about and I already regretted that I'd selected this destination. For me, it was a place with too many memories. For so long, I'd closed my mind to that page from my past, but here it was again.

Right now, I didn't need any distractions. I stood up from my seat and walked to the bathroom where I quickly washed my face with cold water. I looked in the mirror and studied the reflection for a few seconds, then turned away. After thanking the crew, I grabbed my bag from the storage closet and stepped out of the aircraft. I stood on the pavement and breathed in the fresh tropical air as I watched the tall palms waving in the wind as if to greet me.

The memories of my earlier life seemed to trouble me, though I no longer resembled the man I was when I last visited this place. This time, I was here to complete a mission and to protect my only friends from danger. My life with Julia was behind me now and things would be different from here out. I was no longer just a common corporate spy. That was behind me, too. I was now involved in something far more important, something beyond what most men dare to dream.

I was now the President's Agent.

At that, a strange feeling of despair came over me. I suddenly felt cold and broken inside, not unlike a man who'd just realized he'd allowed his soul to slip into the hands of the devil.

And it was too late to buy it back.

-PART IV-

Maui, Hawaii

"Heroes may not be braver than anyone else. They're just braver five minutes longer."
~Ronald Reagan

Chapter 17

Kekoa could tell something was troubling me, as I wasn't my usual wonderful self. "Are you all right?" he asked.

"I'll be fine," I said. "It's just that my ex-wife and I had come here once. The place brings back a lot of memories."

"I didn't know you were ever married. What was her name?"

"Julia," I replied, "though by the end she went by 'Plaintiff.'"

Kekoa grinned.

"Let's find a car and a place to eat. After that we'll hit the road."

He didn't argue with that.

Kaui soon joined us and the three of us headed to the one-and-only car rental booth. There, a woman wearing a white flower lei greeted us warmly and directed our attention to a dark grey all-electric Ford SUV parked behind the booth. It looked roomy enough for the three of us and had plenty of space for cargo. Plus, it was the only vehicle she had available, which sealed the deal.

Once the paperwork was done we piled into the Ford and left for a local eatery called Bruddah Kim's, which the woman had told us about. As soon as we arrived, I could tell it wasn't one of those fancy places, like the ones that are licensed and inspected. Apparently, Kim was a guy with some grills in his front yard, plus a garden hose and a picnic table. Nonetheless, the twins seemed delighted.

Kaui ordered a plate of barbecued chicken while his brother decided on grilled Ahi with a pile of jumbo shrimp on the side. The meals, known here as *grinds*, came with heaps of white rice and a big scoop of macaroni salad.

After their meals arrived I took the opportunity to explain a few things to the twins. "Until things clear up back in Florida," I said, "we need to be careful to stay disconnected. No matter what, we can't leave any kind of digital fingerprint that can be traced to us."

Kaui asked, "What about the credit card you used for the rental?"

"For that, I used a card with an untraceable debit feature and an alias name."

He seemed impressed. "What about the phone and the tablet that came with the car?"

"Those are okay," I said, "as long as we don't log-in to anything. Whatever happens, don't check any accounts, don't post anything, and don't email or text anyone."

They agreed with that.

Using my own tablet, I looked over a map of the island to familiarize myself with the roads and towns. Once Kaui and Kekoa had finished grinding their meals, I paid Kim in cash and headed to the car. We pulled away and started down the road on what I knew would be our address for the next few hours: Hana Highway.

"We're heading for a place called Paia," I announced. "It's a small town with only a few roads. We'll see if we can find some rooms for rent there."

"We should try to find someplace that takes cash," Kekoa suggested.

I glanced at him in my mirror. "You're going to make an excellent fugitive."

He smiled.

Using the in-dash tablet, Kaui began checking for short-term rentals in Paia. Within minutes he found a place. "How does this sound?" he asked. "*Rooms for rent. Ocean front luxury home in Paia. White sandy beach, indoor steam room, hot tub, pool, and gourmet kitchen.*" He turned the in-dash tablet in my direction. "Check out the pictures."

I pulled over and looked at the photos of the place, which was called the Ocean Breeze. To me, it seemed perfect. The twins agreed.

Once that was decided, I began driving again, continuing along the winding road while crossing over countless narrow bridges, alongside steep cliffs, and past numerous flower stands on the side of the road. Most of the flower stands had colorful bouquets for sale along with a variety of tropical fruits to choose from. They also had a small box for people to insert money into after making a selection. *The last bastion of the honor system,* I thought.

Kaui downloaded some Hawaiian music and began reading to us from the internet about the Hana Highway. "We'll be crossing over fifty-nine bridges," he informed us, "and almost every one is a single lane."

I joked, "Since we're not coming back, one lane is all we need. Right?"

No answer.

Anyway, I was enjoying the drive. To the sound of ukulele music from the radio we headed through the thick green rainforest, dense with tropical plants and flowers of all types and colors. We spotted a variety of fruit trees including guava, papaya, coconut, and mango trees all along the highway. There were plenty of waterfalls, too. Some flowed from small crevices in the rocky ledges while larger ones poured down from the mountains in huge cascades.

Kaui and Kekoa were like tour guides and made sure I didn't miss anything. I had to be careful not to drive off any of the cliffs as they pointed out bamboo forests, distant mountains, and plush green valleys. It was easy to see how the two of them were proud of Hawaii, their paradise home, where natural beauty seemed to meet us at every turn.

Somehow, being together made it easier for the three of us to forget what terrible things had caused us to come here in the first place.

After an hour or so, cell service picked up. I asked Kaui to call the Ocean Breeze to check on available rooms, so he found the number and placed the call using the car's phone. A woman named Malia answered, and she agreed to set aside three rooms for us, including what she called 'The Ocean Room,' which was somehow special.

"I can give you a special rate," she said, "and I guarantee you'll love them."

We booked the place.

My co-pilot, Kaui, programmed our new destination into the vehicle's GPS. After another thirty minutes or so, we spotted signs for Mom's Fish House and I slowed down. Following the commands, we found ourselves in a residential neighborhood and soon arrived at the home. I parked in the tiled driveway next to a Jaguar convertible. From this viewpoint, the place looked okay. The three of us were aching and exhausted from the long trip and we stretched and yawned as we stepped out of the car. A warm breeze blew through my clothes, which felt refreshing.

Malia had instructed us to come right in when we arrived, and so we did. We entered through the ornately carved wooden double doors and found ourselves standing inside a lavish courtyard filled with tropical gardens.

From the courtyard we walked to a set of white French doors that opened to the main home. To the side of the doors was a small plaque which read, "Please remove your shoes."

"It's a local custom," Kekoa explained. "In Hawaii you always remove your shoes before going in someone's home." We left our sandals at the door and entered.

The twins and I walked quietly down the hallway toward the living room and adjacent dining area. The place was spotless and nicely decorated. Nonetheless, what caught my eye was the breathtaking view. Floor-to-ceiling glass spanned the rear of the home which overlooked a plush green lawn with towering coconut palms swaying in the wind. Just beyond that was the ocean.

The three of us gazed out at the postcard-perfect white sand beach at the water's edge. About a hundred yards from the shoreline was a rock-lined coral reef. For a moment, I watched the waves turn to white spray as they collided upon the rocks. Inside the reef was a turquoise tide pool where children were playing and splashing.

I looked over at the twins, "Not too shabby, huh?"

A voice from behind surprised us, "I knew you'd like it."

We turned to see a woman standing in the kitchen.

"I never tire of that view," she said. "We spoke on the phone, right?"

"That's correct," I said. After we shook hands and introduced ourselves, I told her, "This is an amazing home, Malia."

She nodded. "It is beautiful."

Though I certainly wasn't in the market, I couldn't help but notice that Malia was rather beautiful herself. She had pretty eyes and island features with light brown skin and dark shining hair. She seemed a couple years younger than me, maybe late-thirties or early forties, though it was hard to tell. From the way she was looking at me I could tell she had some thoughts racing around in her head too.

"My room is the one above the garage," she said. "Besides me, there's only one guest and she's usually gone most of the day. If you decide to stay you'll have the place mostly to yourselves."

"That's perfect," I told her. "I'd like to see the Ocean Room, if you don't mind."

She smiled. "Right this way."

I followed Malia upstairs. The large bedroom there featured dark cherry flooring and a high vaulted ceiling. On one side were wide French doors opening to an outdoor lanai. At the far end, an oversized window overlooked the ocean and the tide pool. The thundering sound of crashing waves and ocean spray could be heard through the louvered vents below the window, which allowed cool air to move through the room. Above, two ceiling fans spun lazily over an inviting king sized bed.

Malia stepped over to the window. As the reflected light shone upon her pretty face, I thought I heard her say, "I'll try to slip in here tonight."

Well that didn't sound right. I asked, "What did you say?"

She turned to me and smiled. "I'm sure you'll sleep well here tonight."

Oh.

Chapter 18

After checking out the upstairs, Malia and I returned to the kitchen where we found Kaui and Kekoa checking out the refrigerator.

I told Malia, "Apparently the twins like the place, and so do I."

"Great. So you'll take the rooms?"

"Yes, but before that, I should probably explain a few things."

I saw her pleasant expression fade slightly. In this situation, I knew I had to air some of our laundry out in the open. I knew it was possible that someone back in Florida might try to find us, especially if they discovered my hidden transmitter. In fact, there was a chance they would implicate the twins or me in the murders in an attempt to force us out. Therefore, I had to have Malia's confidence in case that happened. I told her, "To be truthful, we need a place where the three of us can lay low for a while."

One of her eyebrows raised.

"Don't worry," I added, "we're not criminals or anything. I can promise you that."

"I certainly hope not," she said. "I don't want to be harboring fugitives."

I faked a laugh, and the twins followed suit. I then explained, "Back home, Kaui, Kekoa, and I worked for the same corporation. By chance, we happened to stumble across some sensitive information that we…"

"Something you weren't supposed to find?"

"Right. You could say it was above our pay scale. When our employer realizes what we've discovered they'll probably become worried that we'll go public with it. To keep things simple, we decided to come to Maui and wait until the storm blows over."

"I hope the storm doesn't come knocking at my door."

"I don't think they'll be able find us," I said. "We've done a good job of covering our tracks."

Malia let that roll around in her head. "I guess I'm okay as long as no one here is in danger. You're not going to be on the TV news or anything, are you?"

I shrugged. "If that happens, just remember not to believe *anything* they say. It's possible they'll become desperate and start offering rewards or make up lies about us until someone turns us in."

She gave me a look. "You don't think *I'd* turn you in, do you?"

"Of course not," I answered. "I feel I can trust you, Malia, and I want you to trust us, too. That's why I'm telling you all this up front, so you know I'm not hiding anything from you." Of course, there was a lot more laundry in our basket than what I was willing to air.

"Who did you guys work for, anyway?"

I wrinkled my nose and told her, "The less you know about that, the better."

She smiled politely. "I guess that's your way of telling me not to ask too many questions."

I returned the smile.

"All right. Show me some money before I change my mind."

I opened my wallet and counted out some big bills, which added up to much more than she was asking. "This is for one week," I told her, "plus a little extra for your discretion."

She thumbed through the bills.

"So, we're good?"

"Oh, yeah." She grabbed her purse. "Now that I have all this cash, I feel like I need to spend it. I think I'll head over to the grocery store and pick up a few things. Anything you guys need? Maybe some snacks or drinks?"

I shook my head.

Kekoa spoke up, "Some Mountain Mist soda, if you don't mind."

"Gotcha covered." She grabbed her sunglasses and headed to the door. As she slid into her slippers and stepped out, she turned to us and made a suggestion, "It's a beautiful day. You should go check out the beach." She then left for the store, closing the door behind her.

Taking her advice, Kaui, Kekoa, and I grabbed our sunglasses and went outside. On the back porch, I stopped to breathe in the fresh air and watched the birds as they flew from tree to tree and sang to each other.

We headed down a walkway and passed a large and ornate gazebo which housed a hot tub. From there, we continued down the stairs and through a heavy teak gate to the white sand beach.

We walked barefoot through the sand to the turquoise tide pool. Once there, I walked out until the water was about knee deep while the twins followed me.

"I'm glad we found this place," I told them.

Kaui nodded in agreement. "Malia seems nice, too," he said. "Did you notice how she acted around you?"

"I'm sure she liked the way I just paid her more than she was asking for the rooms. Women always act funny when you do that."

"Well, I think she—"

"Let's forget about Malia," I said. "We've got more important things to think about right now." I looked at the two of them. "I know the control room operators—Glenn, Keri, Jason, and Viktor—were your friends."

They both nodded.

"I want you to know I'm sorry about what you're going through right now. Also, I'm sorry I let you become involved in all this—"

"It wasn't your fault, Mike," Kekoa interrupted. "Kaui and I shouldn't have been looking at your tablet without asking. *We* got us involved in all this—not you."

I felt something and looked down to see two or three tiny fish nibbling at the hairs on my legs.

Kekoa asked, "So, what's our plan, anyway?"

"Most importantly, we need to be sure we stay under the radar," I replied. "In the meantime we can try to find out more about what actually happened back at the Cape and why. If we're lucky, we might be able to figure out what Cronus and the murderer plan to do next."

"Do you think someone will actually try to find us?"

"Maybe," I replied. "We left no digital fingerprints pointing to here, but—"

"But they might try to flush us out," Kaui said.

"Exactly. If Cronus wanted to, they could accuse us of something. Possibly even the murders. They could use the media to start a nationwide manhunt."

Kekoa asked, "If something like that happened, would you trust Malia not to turn us in?"

I shook my head. "Not enough to bet our lives on it. To be safe we should trust no one but ourselves."

They didn't argue with that.

"Let's review what we know," I suggested. "First, the control room operators discover they aren't the only ones with a planetary rover on Venus." I looked at the twins. "The rover they found doesn't look like anything anyone has ever seen before, right?"

Kekoa shrugged. "*We've* never seen anything like it, that's for sure."

"Okay. So the next thing that happens is the website is shut down. Then the outside team is cut off and the facility is evacuated. Soon after that, the control room itself becomes a crime scene."

I looked at both of them for a moment and then said, "Maybe you guys have a better theory, but I think someone at Cronus believes they've discovered an alien rover."

Kekoa made a face. "Alien? From where?"

"From wherever alien rovers come from," I said. "Have either of you ever heard the story of a planetary rover named Rita?"

"That's an old urban legend," Kaui said.

"I'm sure you're right, but a lot of people believe that stuff. According to what I've heard, it was discovered in a remote area of Mexico in the early 1960s—"

"After it had been buried for centuries," Kekoa interjected. "Conspiracy theorists believe it's the source of all modern technology."

"Right. And someone at Cronus believes it too. If I'm correct, that person wants it brought here to Earth for themselves."

Kaui pointed out, "That would be a violation of international law without the authority of the U.N. council."

"Correct. And that might explain why your innocent friends were murdered."

After that, none of us had much more to say. From the restaurant next door I detected the aroma of seasoned meat sizzling on the grill and I started to think about food. I knew the twins needed some time, so I stepped out of the water and headed back up to the house by myself.

As I entered through the sliding door, I saw Malia carrying groceries and I helped by bringing in the rest of the bags from her car.

After we'd put everything away, Malia told me, "While I was at the store, I ran into an old friend of mine, Chuck Kruger. He and his son have a boat and he told me they're planning a fishing trip this coming Sunday. I mentioned you and told Chuck you might be interested in joining them. You seem like the kind of guy that would enjoy that type of thing."

"What did you tell him about me?"

"Nothing, other than that you're a guest here."

I thought about that. "I'll give Chuck a call later."

"Great."

"And thanks for thinking about me."

She gave me a warm smile. "Well, *someone* has to think about you."

While Malia began preparing dinner I gazed out the window and watched as the wind moved the tall palm trees from side to side.

I'd thought about my ex-wife earlier today and I couldn't help but wonder if she still thought about me. I wouldn't blame her if she didn't.

I also thought about my boss, the President, and I wondered if he'd forgotten about his agent. *Him* I could blame.

My thoughts then went back to Florida and all that had happened. Someone there had killed four innocent people today. I had a feeling that the murderer, whoever it was, was thinking about me right now.

Chapter 19

I helped Malia with the grill while Kaui and Kekoa showered. I had a few marinated teriyaki steaks cooking and the aroma was making my mouth water. In the meantime, Malia put together an interesting salad made with spinach, diced apples, walnuts, and chunks of cheese.

Before long, the twins returned and I noticed they still had on the same clothes they'd been wearing all day. I made a mental note to take them shopping in the morning. I saw Kaui point to the TV and mouth the words 'The news' to Kekoa without Malia hearing him. His brother got the message and went to the living room while Kaui assigned himself to kitchen detail.

Once dinner was ready, we all sat down at the table. I noticed no one wasted much time digging in. Over dinner, Malia explained she was a *hapa*, which I learned was an island way of saying you have a mixed ethnic background. "I'm part Hawaiian," she told us, "plus some Filipino, Chinese, and Irish."

"It's a nice combination," I told her.

She smiled at the compliment.

Kaui asked, "What kind of work do you do, Malia?"

"I work for a lending company as a mortgage broker," she replied. "My late husband was a real estate broker. We met through our jobs."

Which explains the house, I thought.

After a while, she got tired of talking about herself. "All right," she said. "You guys have heard enough about me. Now it's your turn." She turned and looked at me.

"What would you like to know?" I asked

"Anything. Where are you from?"

"I'm originally from New Jersey," I replied. "After high school I attended college for a while, then quit and joined the Navy. After that, I lived all over."

"That's it?"

"What else would you like to know?"

"I don't know. Have you ever been married?"

I figured that was coming. "I'm recently divorced," I said.

Malia nodded at that and looked at the twins. "What about you guys?"

Kekoa shrugged. "We've never been married."

After a while, Malia gave up trying to extract information from us. Once we'd finished our meals, Kaui and Kekoa helped by clearing the table. They also loaded the dishwasher and wiped down the counters before heading to the living room to watch TV.

"Your friends are so helpful," Malia told me.

"I'm shocked," I said. "This is the first time I've seen either of them do anything."

She smiled.

"We appreciate you making dinner for us," I said. "How about I make something tomorrow night? Does Mexican sound good?"

She thought about that. "Can you make it Wednesday night instead? Tomorrow I'm bringing home pizza from Fat Bread's for their annual fundraiser."

I agreed with that and asked, "Do you mind if I use your phone to give your friend Chuck a call?"

"Not at all." She reached for her phone and selected Chuck's number from her contact list before handing it to me. She then excused herself to use the bathroom.

After a couple of rings, Chuck answered and the two of us spoke for a few minutes. I explained I was a guest at the Ocean breeze and I was interested in joining him and his son on their next fishing trip.

"We'd be glad to have you," Chuck said. "The boat is a twenty-eight footer with twin outboards. We'll be launching out of Kahului Harbor early Sunday, around half-past four."

"I'll be there."

"We look forward to meeting you. If it's not too cloudy we should be able to catch a total lunar eclipse just after five a.m."

"I hope that's a good omen."

"I hope so, too."

After he and I finished our conversation, I set Malia's phone next to her purse and went to the living room. There, the twins were streaming a popular spy movie on the big TV. To me, movie spies are the worst spies in the world. Instead of maintaining a low profile and quietly going about their business, they do everything they can to draw attention to themselves—guns, car chases, explosions, and whatever makes a lot of noise. And they're usually more concerned with the girl than the actual mission.

I asked Kekoa, "Anything on the news?"

Without taking his eyes from the TV he told me, "There was a lady reporting from outside the Cronus facility. She said the police are calling it a murder/suicide."

"They're right about the murder part," Kaui said. "But there was no suicide."

We all seemed in agreement on that.

After watching the movie for a minute I told the twins, "I'm going outside for some fresh air. Okay?"

They made no reply.

"Always let me know if you go anywhere. Understand?"

"How about for breakfast?" Kekoa asked. "Kaui and I were thinking about going to Da Kitchin in the morning."

"I thought that was in Oahu."

"They have one here, too. Right in Kahului."

Well, talk about luck. I'd been hearing about Da Kitchin for the past five months. I pulled a few bills from my wallet and handed them to Kekoa. "The keys are on the counter. Just don't go anywhere other than the restaurant and don't talk to anyone anywhere about anything."

He agreed.

I remembered that my things were still in the car, so I went out and grabbed my carry-on bag and tablet and brought them up to my bedroom. Once upstairs, I slid my Sig .22 under the bed mattress along with the tablet. I then placed my Colt .380 under my pillow, just to be safe.

After that, I went back downstairs and placed the car keys on the kitchen counter before stepping outside into the cool of the evening. The moon was low in the eastern sky as I walked with no particular destination in mind. From the restaurant next door, Mom's Fish House, I could hear the sounds of voices and laughter. I decided I wanted a look at the place so I headed that way.

Minutes later I arrived at the restaurant. I saw it was decorated in an eclectic but inviting way with a blend of rustic décor and island-style furnishings. Next to the entrance was a reservations booth where a woman wearing a bright cotton dress and a flower lei was focused on a computer screen. Out of curiosity I walked up and asked her, "Any tables available?"

She looked up at me. "Do you have a reservation?"

"Actually, no."

"I'm sorry sir, but we have nothing available for tonight. In fact, we're booked solid until lunchtime Friday. Would that work for you?"

I thought it would be smart to treat Malia to a special meal, especially since I wanted to stay on her good side. I decided to book a table for two overlooking the beach.

"What name would you like to reserve that under?" the woman asked.

I wanted to avoid using my real identity, so I gave her the first name that popped into my head. "Lucas Richter," I said. I spelled it for her.

She entered the name on the register. "Richter. That sounds like a German name."

"It is," I said. "My great-grandfather lived in Germany before moving to Argentina."

"Oh."

I left Mom's and decided to walk down through the towering palms to the beach, which was the same stretch of white sand that fronted our rental.

I removed my sandals and stood at the water's edge. Tonight was almost cloudless and the reflection of the moon was shimmering over the quiet, tranquil pool. Above, an abundance of stars sparkled in the heavens. To the southeast, I could easily pick out Venus.

The water appeared calm and inviting. I moved further down the beach and removed my shirt. I took a quick look around, then removed the rest of my clothes, and waded in.

It was surprisingly cold. I continued in until the water was almost up to my crotch, which I knew was going to be the challenging part. At that point, I remembered there were small fish here that liked to nibble on things. I decided to turn around. Suddenly, I heard voices and laughter coming from behind me, so I dove in and swam out to the far end. From there, I looked and saw two couples walking along the beach. I floated quietly for a while.

After the couples had passed, I got out of the water, pulled on my shorts, and ran up to the house. The twins had apparently headed to bed, so I went upstairs to my room.

After a quick shower, I toweled off and slid into my king-size bed. From outside, the rhythmic sounds of waves and familiar scent of the sea came to me while the cool evening air swept through the open vents and flowed gently through the room. I rested my head on the soft pillow and let out a deep breath.

Two seconds later I was out.

Chapter 20

Once asleep, my body quickly surrendered itself to the night while the weight of the world dissolved into the great void of nothingness. Soon, my subconscious mind crept forth, taking control of my most idle thoughts as though it had been waiting for the moment.

I began to dream. I imagined myself aboard a boat, the same one Malia's friend Chuck had told me about. It was the hours before dawn and I was sailing slowly toward the mouth of a harbor. The light of the full moon sliced through the blackened sky, casting my shadow against the white deck.

The temperature was cool and the sea was remarkably calm. I dreamed of the wind in my face, light and fresh. The boat itself appeared seaworthy and well rigged, though it was puzzling to find no one else aboard.

I checked the gear and found only one rod and reel, which was secured in a sturdy mount. Attached at the end of the rig was a ragged-looking lure, scarred from battle and strung together with huge steel hooks scarcely hidden under a tattered black skirt. I looked at the transom and noticed a small door for hauling in large catch. Tucked away in a storage bin at the stern I discovered an old wooden club.

After the craft had entered the open ocean, I tossed the lure into the water and let the line out, attaching it to the starboard outrigger.

At the same time, I dreamed the edge of the moon had begun to dim. I watched as the eerie darkness crept slowly along until its entire surface was eclipsed. At that moment, the stars disappeared from the heavens while ominous black clouds arrived from the north. It seemed as though a page had been turned and a new chapter, a dark chapter, had begun. At that, a cold wind arrived, chilling my skin.

On the distant horizon, the sun began to rise and the whole of the eastern sky soon turned blood red. After that, a heavy fog swept over the sea and I felt the air grow damp and still.

Off the starboard bow I spotted a shadowy silhouette of a lonely figure moving over the murky water. I saw it was a young girl. As her eyes fell upon me she smiled. In an instant, however, the smile was swept from her face as she was pulled into the darkness below, her cry for help silenced.

After that, a feeling of desolation came over me and I began to feel as though I'd fallen into the grasp of darkness itself. Just then, I saw a fin slice through the water on the port side. In that same moment, the rain began.

I dreamed of heavy rain pouring down while strong winds stirred the waters. Then, all at once, it happened.

The line flew from the outrigger and I watched as the pole snapped forward violently. I could tell that whatever had taken the bait was swift and powerful. Quickly, I grabbed hold of the drag knob and gave it a slight turn.

From the depths, the fish fought with great strength while I turned at the crank. One-half turn. Again. Another half turn. Spasms raked through my spine and forearms until my knuckles became numb. Pain shot through my neck and arms.

For a brief moment I considered severing the line.

I was startled by the sound of the ship's radio as it crackled loudly with a distorted and indiscernible message. As I tried to listen, a rogue wave collided violently into the starboard bow of the boat, sending me sprawling across the deck.

I pulled myself up from the deck and wiped blood from my knees. My right shoulder was throbbing and I realized I'd suffered a deep wound.

I stepped to the rig and started to turn the crank again. I winced in pain from my injuries but continued to work the reel. Soon, I felt the great fish weakening and I fought even harder. Finally, I spotted its shadow just below me and I knew at once what sort of creature it was.

A shark.

I reeled in the line until the fish rose to the surface, then brought it along the side of the boat. The shark's body was tattered and its head and snout were scraped and torn.

I retrieved the club from the rear bin and leaned over the side to finish him. As I swung down with the club, the shark spun itself unexpectedly. I was struck across the face by its powerful fin and I stumbled backward.

After that, I leaned back over the side again and began to beat the shark ferociously. Once done, I grabbed hold of the heavy leader and pulled him through the transom door and onto the deck.

Looking it over, I gasped as I saw the fish's right eye had been beaten out of its head. The eyeball itself was hanging from its socket by only a few strands of tissue.

Without warning, the shark suddenly flung itself upward and knocked me to the deck. To my horror, I found myself pinned under its weight. Desperately, I scrambled to escape as it snapped at my face with rows of razor sharp teeth, missing my face by mere inches while its hideous eyeball flung about. I cried out in terror and kicked wildly as adrenaline poured into my veins. All at once, it spun one last time, flipping itself out of the boat and back into the darkness of the deep, taking the rod and reel with it.

I sat up in bed and found myself panting and trembling. My face and chest were wet with sweat. In the faint moonlight I could see Malia standing at the top of the stairs with a frightened look on her face.

"Are you all right?" I asked.

"Me? I heard you screaming and came to see if you were okay."

My heart was still pounding. "I'm sorry," I said, wiping the sweat from my forehead. "I had a bad dream, that's all."

"My goodness. I thought someone had come in and attacked you."

"I'm fine. Thanks Malia."

"All right then. Good night."

After she'd gone, I reached under my pillow to make sure my gun was still there, which it was. I thought about what Malia had said, though I knew the chances of someone coming for me were a million-to-one.

Nonetheless, I'd be keeping an eye out.

Chapter 21

Thursday, April 22, 2032

Ellis Lacorde entered the office.

Lucas Richter glanced up at him and mentioned, "As I'd predicted, Cronus stocks are steadily dropping."

Lacorde looked at Richter's tablet screen for a moment and nodded in agreement. "I guess you were right."

"That means now is the time to buy," Richter said. "After that, we'll stun the world with the news that Rhea is back in operation." He grinned.

Lacorde shook his head. "Let's hope the world doesn't catch on that they've been duped."

"You can always bank on people being greedy and stupid, Ellis. We can also bank on what we've discovered on Venus." Richter leaned forward and began entering a number on his phone.

"Yeah. I have a few questions about that—"

"Hold on a minute." While the phone began to ring, Richter brought up a message from the HR Department on his tablet.

After a few rings, Raquel Richards answered. "Hello?"

Richter cleared his throat. "I'm glad you answered, Raquel. This is Lucas Richter."

Raquel was surprised to be hearing from the mission director. "Oh. Hello Mr. Richter. Are you…okay?"

"Well, I suppose we're all still in shock after what happened," he replied. "Aside from that, I guess I'm okay."

"Is it true what everyone is saying?" she asked. "I mean, on the TV they said the police think Glenn Hosato was responsible for…"

"Honestly, I don't know any more than you, Raquel. And even if I did, I can't comment on anything until the investigation is over."

"I understand. So why did you call?"

"Two reasons, really. First, I wanted to offer my condolences on the loss of your friends and co-workers, Jason, Keri, and Viktor."

"And Glenn."

"Yes, of course." He continued, "Secondly, because I wanted to ask for your help—if you feel you're up to it."

"*My* help? With what?"

"I think it would be better to discuss that here in my office. Where are you right now?"

"I'm in my car heading east across the causeway, and I'm—"

"Then you're only about ten minutes away. Is it possible you could stop by?"

"Aren't we still in a lockdown?"

"Technically, no," Richter replied. "The facility is still closed while the investigation continues, but I can have the guards escort you in." He added, "It's important."

She thought for a moment, then told him, "I'll be there in ten minutes."

At that, Richter ended the call.

"Why did you invite her here?" Lacorde asked.

"I've got a special job for her, Ellis. It seems that Mike Brennan, our Security Director, has disappeared."

Lacorde seemed surprised by that.

"Yesterday, a message was sent to the HR department from Kaui Hamilton, one of the secondary team members. The message explained that he and his twin brother, along with Mike Brennan, decided that now would be a good time to take a few days off."

"Sounds fishy."

"I agree." Richter looked at the email message from Kaui on his screen and continued, "According to this, the three of them have headed to Ocala, a city about two hours north of here. Supposedly, they went to visit Brennan's parents."

Lacorde shrugged. "Why should we be worried about Brennan right now?"

Richter leaned back in his chair. "I think he knows something. He's traveling with the Hamilton twins and suddenly they're not answering their phones, texts, or—"

"So…?"

"It strikes me as odd that the Director of Security would disappear like this in the middle of a crisis. I'm sending Raquel Richards to Ocala to try to find him and the twins."

"Why her?"

"Like Brennan, she's close to the twins. They might get spooked if someone like you or I came knocking on their door, but they'll trust her. In the meantime, I'll need you and your partner, Safire, to check their apartments for anything unusual or suspicious."

Lacorde let out a breath. "You should really think about ditching Safire already. That lady is a complete—"

"She stays, understand?"

Lacorde rolled his eyes. "The Hamilton twins are just kids."

"They're *smart* kids," Richter said, "especially with computer stuff. And now they're involved with Brennan. As you know, Brennan had access to an awful lot of information here. Together, they could be trouble."

"Has it occurred to you they might be spies?"

Richter nodded at that. "We need to make finding the three of them a top priority. As soon as Raquel locates them she'll report to me. When that happens I'll need you to take care of them."

Lacorde gave Richter a look. "We're leaving quite a body count, don't you think?"

"It's worth it, believe me."

Lacorde leaned over the desk. "Tell me how it's worth it."

Richter looked up at Lacorde. "The rover we discovered on Venus is no ordinary machine, Ellis. In fact, I'm almost certain it's not from Earth."

Lacorde shrugged. "So, where's it from?"

"It's from the same advanced race that sent a similar rover to Earth long ago. That machine became the foundation of all our modern technology."

Lacorde chuckled. "And you honestly believe that?"

Richter shook his head. "I can't expect you to believe something you don't understand, Ellis. However, I can assure you that what I'm saying is true. I've spent years researching and investigating the machine that was found on Earth. That was only the beginning. What we've found on Venus will be the key to all future technology."

"So…we'll be rich, right?"

Richter let out a laugh. "Beyond your wildest dreams, my friend."

Lacorde thought about that, then asked, "How do you plan to bring the thing here from Venus? Have you thought about that?"

"I have, and I think I know a way. There are a lot of details to work out, but I can tell you this: when the Zeus lander returns from Venus, it won't be carrying soil samples and rocks."

Lacorde grinned.

"I'll be assembling a new team to work on the details, and this time the team will be made up of *my* people."

"Including Derrick Haut?"

"Of course. Why do you ask?"

"I don't know. He doesn't seem to have a lot of confidence in how we do things."

Richter considered that. "We'll keep an eye on Derrick, but in the meantime we have a lot of work to do. In fact, the launch date for Zeus isn't far off."

Just then, Richter's desk phone rang. He answered and spoke for a moment, then ended the call and turned his attention back to Lacorde. "I'm glad you're with me on this, my friend. Right now, however, I'll need you to step out for a bit. She's on her way up."

"Who?"

"Raquel Richards. Remember?"

Chapter 22

Lucas Richter checked his hair and adjusted his shirt at his closet mirror before heading back to his desk. As he waited for Raquel to arrive, he pulled up Mike Brennan's employee file on his computer and began to read through it. He saw that Brennan had named his parents as his emergency contacts and listed their address and phone number in Ocala. Richter wrote down the information on the back of his business card.

Raquel appeared at the door. "Good morning, Mr. Richter."

He stood from his desk. "Ah, Miss Richards. Please come in and have a seat."

She sat at a chair in front of Richter's desk while he closed the door.

He could see her usual cheerful expression was gone. "I appreciate you coming over here, Raquel, especially on such short notice."

"You made it sound important."

"It is," he said. "I'm sorry I can't discuss any details about what happened, but I hope you accept my sincere sympathy. My heart goes out to the families and loved ones of those we lost."

She nodded.

"I want to do everything I can to help the mission team deal with this tragedy. To do this, I'll need your help, which is why I've asked you to come here this morning."

"How can *I* help?"

"I believe that staying in contact with the staff and keeping connected is important during this difficult time. In addition, the police have asked that Cronus keep track of everyone's location for the purpose of the investigation—especially those in management and anyone directly involved with the control room team."

Raquel shrugged. "I guess that makes sense."

"So far we've been able to contact just about everyone. Kaui and Kekoa Hamilton, however, have still not responded to our calls or emails. Our Security Director, Mike Brennan, is also missing."

Raquel now understood why she was here. "I haven't seen or heard from them either."

He leaned back in his chair. "Actually, we did receive a brief email from Kaui Hamilton."

"What did it say?"

"It was addressed to the Human Resources department," Richter replied. "Basically, the message explained that the three of them had left the Cape area to visit Mike Brennan's parents in Ocala."

Raquel was surprised by that. "Why would they leave at a time like this?"

"That's a good question, Raquel. I suppose people react to tragedy in different ways." He leaned forward and looked at her closely. "Are you sure you haven't heard from them?"

"I already told you I haven't."

"Right. I'm sorry. I just need to know where they are in case the police have questions. Plus, I want to be sure they're safe."

Raquel nodded. "So…how can I help?"

"You're their close friend, right? So, wouldn't it be better if *you* tried to locate them instead of me or some stranger—or the police?"

"Are the police looking for them?"

"Not yet, but I know they plan to speak with everyone employed here. And I'd expect the investigators will want to talk to our Director of Security, right?"

She nodded again.

"Sending you to find them is my way of handling this in a more personal and sensitive way, without involving a manhunt."

"You want me to go to Ocala?"

"Yes, I do," Richter replied. He handed her his business card along with a corporate credit card "As you can see, I wrote the address for Brennan's parents on the back of my card. Use the credit card for your expenses and contact me the moment you find them."

She thought for a moment, then placed the cards into her purse and prepared to leave.

Richter walked her to the door. "You're doing all of us an important service," he said. "Thank you for this—and good luck."

After leaving the Cronus facility, Raquel drove to the apartment building where Mike and the twins lived. On the way she tried calling their phones, all of which went straight to voicemail.

Upon arriving at the apartment building, she went first to Mike's unit and rang the doorbell. After a few tries she gave up. She then tried the same at the twin's apartment, but again with no luck.

On the way home, Raquel decided to call her friend, Emma. The two spoke for a minute before Raquel asked, "How do you feel about going on a quick road trip?"

"Where to?" Emma asked.

"Ocala. It's about two hours from here. Kaui and Kekoa are there along with Mike Brennan. My boss wants me to try to find them."

"Mike Brennan? Is that the guy you told me about?"

"He's my co-worker Em. This is business."

"But you said he's cute, right?"

"I don't know. Yeah, I guess so."

"Okay. So why would your boss—?"

"I'll explain on the way there," Raquel said. "Can you be ready to go in, like, fifteen minutes?"

"I'll be ready to go before you get here."

That, Raquel thought, *would be a first.*

Chapter 23

I got up the next morning just in time to share coffee with Malia before she headed off to work. I also had a chance to speak with the twins who were up early for once, anxious to get to their favorite restaurant, Da Kitchin.

"As soon as you guys get back," I told them, "the three of us need to sit down and review what's happening at Cronus."

They agreed.

I reminded them to drive safely, then poured myself the last few drops of coffee and went back to my room.

Once upstairs, I linked my tablet with the large TV mounted on the wall. After that, I logged onto a special site where I could check to see if any new videos had been recorded by the hidden security camera I'd installed outside my apartment back in Florida. The camera was activated by a proximity sensor which would cause it to begin recording if someone stood near the door for more than ten seconds.

Beginning the video at yesterday morning, I watched a quick clip of the twins and me coming and going. After that, it showed a young woman at the door who I recognized as Raquel Richards. She rang twice, then knocked a few times before she gave up.

Up to that point there was nothing out of the ordinary. The next segment, however, was classic. A man and a woman appeared at my door and they didn't look like they'd come to invite me to church. The man was about my height, but *big*. Even with his jacket, I could tell the guy was a serious weightlifter. The woman, who might have been a couple of years younger, was light-skinned and slim. Like her boyfriend, she was wearing dark glasses and dressed entirely in black.

They rang the door a few times and tried knocking. Once they were certain no one was home, the woman pulled a device out of her purse. I recognized this to be a card-key pick. Crooks, as well as people like me, use these to break into places with bar code or magnetic card entryways. I've seen these things go cheap on eBay auctions. Because of that, I had my lock set up with a micro switch connected to the door's thumb lever which needs to be lifted for the reader to be energized. That prevents card-key picks like hers from working.

Good luck, schmucks.

I watched in delight while the woman gave it several tries, then became frustrated and shoved the device back in her purse. They both walked away and returned a few minutes later with plan B. This time, the woman pulled out a J-bar. This is a special metal bar that inserts into the jamb next to the door bolt. They sell these on eBay, too. When inserted correctly and pushed hard enough, the bar will usually break the door open. Of course, my two guests didn't know I'd driven a pair of three-inch hardened steel screws through the bolt plate deep into the door frame itself. Therefore, when the big guy pushed on the bar, all that happened was the outer door trim popped off. They tried this again with even less success, and I could tell they were becoming exasperated.

This was much better than last night's spy movie.

With the exception of my recliner, I'd already removed everything of value or interest from the apartment. I had no plan of ever going back there, so at this point I actually found myself rooting for them.

After more failed attempts with the J-bar, one of them had a mental epiphany and tried placing the bar near the bottom of the door. It was comical how they both tried to appear nonchalant while doing this. This time around, the bottom of the door leaned in and the leverage broke the framing. With a few more pushes, they finally were in.

I found myself applauding.

The next segment of the recording was of their exit. It was a good one, too. After they stepped out of the apartment and closed what was left of my door, they looked around. They'd both removed their sunglasses, which made it a photo op moment. By chance, they also glanced in the direction of the camera before walking away.

I watched the remaining videos, which weren't quite as interesting. A neighbor noticed my door and guessed correctly that something was wrong. The police and my property manager soon showed up and snooped around. After that, the final videos showed a maintenance man trying to make everything nice again.

I went back to the part of the recording where the woman faced the camera. I froze it there and took a print-screen snapshot of her mug. I did the same for the guy and then took a few minutes to crop and enhance both shots. After that, I logged-in to the FBI records website, which is loaded with more classified information than any one person should ever have access to. Naturally, its entry requires the highest security clearance. In fact, most of it can only be accessed by two types of agents: top-level federal agents with special authority and a need to know, and me.

Once I figured out the website, I submitted the big guy's photo and waited while the facial recognition software matched details from my photo with those in their current file. After a few seconds three possible matches popped up, but I quickly narrowed it down to one guy: Ellis Lacorde.

I glanced over his file and soon realized it was a good thing I wasn't home when he came knocking. A career criminal, Lacorde had spent almost two years in a Texas prison for industrial espionage. To me, this seemed forgivable. As I read further, I found he'd also had arrests for assault, money laundering, tampering with evidence, resisting arrest, and a few probation violations involving firearms possession. Not so forgivable.

Lacorde was described as six foot one, two-hundred eighty-five pounds, and possibly armed and dangerous. Apparently, Ellis was often in cahoots with his two brothers, Luis and Maxwell, who I assumed were career criminals as well. At one point the three had been arrested together as suspects in a homicide. The charges, however, were later dropped due to missing evidence and a lack of witnesses.

The Feds believed Lacorde was loosely connected with the criminal underworld, though there was no active investigation being pursued on that. From the FBI's data I saw no connection between Lacorde and Cronus Aerospace. That is, until I noticed one of his possible addresses was located very close to the Cape.

Next, I submitted the woman's photo into the facial recognition software. I was hoping she'd turn out to be a librarian or maybe a kindergarten teacher. But no. Within seconds, the software matched her with an international crime figure known professionally as Safire.

Interestingly, Safire's file showed she had no arrest record at all. From what I could tell, most of her file had been compiled from the testimony of informants— jailhouse squealers providing information as a deal to reduce their time in the slammer. Her file was comprised mostly of guesswork, but suggested she was born in Eastern Asia. Reportedly, she could speak fluent English, Korean, and Russian. She was thought to be between thirty-six and forty-one years old, around five feet two, and about one-hundred five pounds. Said to be an expert with weaponry— including sniper rifles—and practiced in martial arts. To be considered armed and dangerous.

According to her Match.com profile, she's a chocolate lover who adores puppies. Just kidding.

The FBI had no known addresses, but linked Safire to crimes in cities such as Las Vegas, Los Angeles, and Los of other places.

It was no surprise that Safire was thought to be associated with a known crime syndicate and possibly hired from time to time as a contract killer and sniper. Her criminal profile also suggested she might suffer from numerous psychiatric illnesses commonly associated with criminal behaviors including antisocial personality disorder.

Come to think of it, I may have dated this woman.

Anyway, all this raised a few questions. Like why are two career criminals interested in my apartment? And what about the twins? Did Lacorde and Safire break into their apartment, too?

After a while, Kaui and Kekoa returned and came up to my room.

After they told me all about their wonderful breakfast, I told them all about the wonderful couple who visited my apartment.

"I'm glad we left Florida when we did," I said, "and it's a good thing we covered our tracks, too." I went to my server site and logged in.

"What are we watching now?" Kaui asked.

I pointed to the screen and explained, "I still have a live transmission coming from the control room mainframe. As you can see, Rhea is completely functional and fully charged, but currently in sleep mode."

They both stared at the screen in awe.

"I have everything recorded," I said, "including the discovery of the other rover."

Kekoa looked at me. "You must know a lot about gathering confidential information."

"Gathering information is easy," I told him. "Knowing what to do with it is the hard part."

Chapter 24

Raquel and Emma reached the town of Ocala by two p.m. Soon after that, they arrived at the address Lucas Richter had provided. Emma waited in the car while Raquel went to the front door and knocked.

Emma watched as an elderly woman opened the door a few inches and peer out. While Raquel and the woman spoke, she noticed she appeared puzzled.

A minute later Raquel returned to the car.

"Let me guess," Emma said. "They're not here. Right?"

Raquel began backing out of the driveway. "This is so weird, Em. The lady told me her son had once worked at Cronus."

"In Cape Canaveral?"

"Right. She said her son's name was Nathan, and he died almost two years ago. She's never heard of Mike Brennan or the twins."

Emma thought about that. "Does your friend Mike Brennan happen to have access to the employee files at Cronus?"

"He's the Director of Security, Em. He has access to practically everything."

"Well, it sounds like he may have used the contact information from the file of a dead person."

"Why would he do such a thing?"

Emma shrugged. "Maybe he has something to hide. Do you trust him?"

"I guess. But I wouldn't put anything past him either."

"From what you say, he's nice looking and has a good job. Right?"

"Right."

"So why is he single and unattached?"

"I don't know."

Emma smiled. "Maybe you could fix that."

Raquel rolled her eyes. "Please, Em. He's like *forty*-something, okay?"

"Well, I like guys that are forty-something."

"Admit it, Em, you like guys that are *any*-something."

Emma giggled at that. "So, anyway, where do the twins like to go? Any favorite restaurants or—?"

"Da Kitchin," Raquel replied. "That's their favorite place to eat. They talk about it every day."

"Okay, great. Where is it?"

"In Hawaii."

"Okay, not great." Emma turned on her tablet and Googled *Da Kitchin*. "There are two of them," she announced, "and they're both in Hawaii. One's in Kahului and the other is in Honolulu." She asked, "Which one do they usually go to?"

"I have no idea, Em. Why do you ask?"

"I'm gonna call there and ask if they've seen them, that's why."

"You're calling *Hawaii?* You actually think they went all the way out there?"

"That's where I'd go if I could," Emma replied. "What's the time difference between here and Honolulu?"

"Six hours, I think."

"Good. They're probably open." Emma entered the number on her phone.

After a few rings a man answered, "Da Kitchin."

"Hello," Emma said. "I'm sorry to bother you, but I'm trying to find two friends of mine, Kaui and Kekoa Hamilton."

"The twins?"

"Yeah!"

"I remember those guys," the man said. "They haven't been here for a while though. At least a year."

"Oh."

"Do you want to leave a message in case they come in?"

"Yes. Tell them to contact Raquel. They know the number."

"Contact Raquel. Got it."

"Thanks!"

Emma ended the call and began to enter another number.

"Who are you calling now?"

"The one in Kahului."

After a few rings a woman answered, "Da Kitchin. Can I help you?"

"Hello," Emma said. "I'm sorry to trouble you, but I'm trying to find two friends of mine. Kaui and Kekoa Hamilton."

"Can you describe them?"

"Well, they're twins, and have—"

"They jus' left, honey. Was it important?"

Emma looked at Raquel in shock and quickly put the call on speakerphone. "Yes, it's important—but let's make sure we have the right guys, okay? Can you describe them?"

"All right. Um…black hair, about six-foot, both kind of quiet. They said they've been working on the mainland for a while, in Florida—"

"That's them! Do you know where they're staying?"

"I have no idea."

"If you see them again, can you ask them to contact Raquel as soon as possible? They know the number."

"I'll pass on the message. Aloha." At that, the call ended.

The two looked at each other in astonishment before Raquel said, "Em—you're a genius."

"It was luck," Emma explained. "I didn't think we'd actually find them."

"*I* can't believe they're in Hawaii."

Emma nodded. "Should you call your boss now?"

"Richter? Uh…"

Emma noticed Raquel's reluctance. "You don't trust him, do you?"

"Actually, no."

"Okay. So what next?"

Raquel drew a deep breath. "We need to get to Orlando."

"Why?"

"That's the nearest major airport. I'm going to Hawaii."

Two hours later, Raquel arrived at Orlando International with only a purse for luggage. She hugged Emma before heading to the security checkpoint for her nine p.m. flight to Honolulu.

"Thanks for everything, Em, including loaning me money for this."

"No problem," Emma said. "Just remember not to use your phone for any reason. And don't use that credit card your boss gave you, either."

"I'll remember."

"Good. I'll park your car in its spot at the apartment and slide the key under your door, all right?"

"All right, Em. And don't worry, I'll be fine."

"Yeah. You'll probably come back with this Mike guy wrapped around you."

"Shut up!"

"Promise me you'll at least *try*. All right?"

They both giggled at that, then waved goodbye to each other before Raquel turned and disappeared into the crowd.

Hawaii. With three guys, Emma thought. *Lucky girl.*

Chapter 25

The twins and I finished watching the video of my apartment being broken into. After that, I felt it would be a good idea for us to get out of the house where we could take our minds off our current situation for a while. Plus I hate sitting around.

I managed to convince Kaui and Kekoa to join me on a road trip to the summit of Haleakala, Maui's big volcano mountain that takes up half the island. I grabbed my gun while the twins each grabbed a Mountain Mist, and off we went.

I remembered the twins had packed no clothes aside from what they were wearing, so I decided to make a quick stop at the local mall. I figured we'd also need jackets for when we get to the summit.

We soon reached the mall where I parked in front of Macy's. Before we got out of the car I told the twins, "Look, this is going to be a hit and run mission. Okay?"

Kaui looked at me. "What do you mean?"

"I mean I hate mall shopping. I want us in and out of there as fast as possible, all right?"

"And what if we take too long?"

"Then I start going crazy," I said. "Last time that happened the mall cops had to wrestle me down and give me a tranquilizer. I woke up in a coroner's office."

That brought the message home.

Anyway, we all went into to the store and I headed straight to the men's department. There, I picked out a few things including some casual shirts, a pair of pants, and a light windbreaker jacket. While I was at it, I grabbed a pair of sandals and some walking shoes. All this took me less than fifteen minutes.

I found the twins in the young men's section where they'd each picked out a pile of beachwear and a couple of hoodies. Wasting no time, we hit the register where I paid with cash. We then headed straight to the car. Within minutes, the three of us were on the road to Haleakala. Mission accomplished.

We left the central valley and began the long uphill climb. Soon, I turned onto Haleakala Crater Road where a sign indicated that we'd already reached an elevation of thirty-two hundred feet.

After that, we found ourselves winding along a narrow, picturesque road. Along the way we saw beautiful trees filled with purple flowers as well as sprawling horse pastures and rolling hills. The twins and I also spotted wild hens and roosters, and even a few peacocks walking along the roadside. The highway zigzagged back and forth through sharp hairpin turns as we climbed higher.

My copilot, Kekoa, was managing our in-dash computer. He informed us we'd be navigating thirty-two of these switchbacks on the way up and that the current temperature at the summit was a mere forty-five degrees.

Good thing someone thought of jackets.

Driving further, I noticed numerous cattle crossing signs posted. I also saw that we were heading into a dense cloud layer. Soon, we found ourselves surrounded in a thick fog. Fine mist began settling on the windshield and the automatic wipers came on.

Visibility was near nil, so I let off the accelerator—and just in time. Straight ahead, I spotted a huge cow standing in the road. Quickly, I slammed on the brakes. At the same time I swerved to the side, missing the thing by inches.

After that close call, I slowed even further until we'd reached the six-thousand foot elevation. There, the fog began to thin and I could tell we were above the tree line. Plant life at that level was almost nonexistent, but the rugged and deeply sculpted terrain had turned to a brilliant volcanic red which shimmered in the bright sunlight.

At about ten-thousand feet we arrived at the Visitor's Center where we were greeted by strong winds and frigid air. I put on my new jacket while the twins slid into their hoodies. From the car, we headed to the Information Center, a small stone structure situated precariously on the edge of a steep vertical cliff. The cliff itself dropped hundreds of feet into the massive crater below.

A stream of air blasted up the side of the cliff carrying occasional tufts of cloud with it. The base of the crater, which was over seven miles wide, was strewn with richly colored cinder cones and volcanic debris. Its dark rocky surface was beautifully streaked with bright reds and brilliant yellows.

"This is awesome," Kaui observed.

His brother and I nodded in agreement.

After a minute or two, the twins noticed a trail heading into the crater and decided to go exploring. I wasn't in the mood for a hike, especially at this altitude, so I suggested we meet back at the car in forty minutes.

After they'd left, I looked further up where I could see a number of observatories at the very peak. Most people probably think these are used for space exploration, but I knew they were actually operated by the Department of Defense and used primarily for orbital surveillance and good old American spy stuff. I had a few minutes to kill, so I went to the car and drove up to check it out.

Once there, I parked and found a long, steep stairway leading to a lookout post. I was winded by the time I reached the top, though the view was even more breathtaking. To the east I could make out the Big Island with its distinguished twin peaks high above the clouds. To the west, I could see most of central Maui including some of the beaches and small towns which dotted the landscape below. Beyond the central valley were the beautifully jagged West Maui Mountains.

On the way back to the visitor's center I spotted Kaui and Kekoa walking along the side of the road, so I pulled over. As they climbed into the back seat I could see they were pale and out of breath.

"You guys look terrible," I said. "Are you okay?"

They both went straight for their Mountain Mists. After a long swig Kekoa managed a reply, "The air's so thin…we ran out of breath."

"Your brain cells might have taken a hit," I said. "Quick: what's twelve times twelve times twelve?"

Without hesitation they responded in unison, "One thousand seven hundred twenty-eight."

Okay. So I guess I should've asked something I knew the answer to. Nonetheless, I saw the color returning to their faces which told me their Mountain Mist levels were returning to normal.

A few miles down the road, a huge rainbow came into view. I pointed it out to my passengers only to find they'd fallen asleep already. I put the radio on low and set it to the front speakers. I still hadn't heard from the President and I was starting to wonder if he was okay. I selected an all-news station to find out.

I continued driving, keeping an eye out for cows while enjoying the magnificent panorama before me. As I maneuvered through the sharp bends, I began to think about things. In some ways it seemed my life was like this winding road, and I wondered if I'd been traveling in the right direction. I also wondered where I was heading in life and where I'd be when I got there. Until recently, I felt I was in an enviable position and at the top of my game. I was now starting to realize I may have been deceiving myself all along.

As I thought this through, it occurred to me I was forty-four years old, yet had no wife, no children, and no actual home. Besides my expense account, I had no money and no tangible assets. I had no one I could share things with, no past I could talk about, and no predictable future. I had a job that I couldn't discuss and I was always at risk of being captured, jailed, or killed. Aside from Kaui and Kekoa, I had no friends. In fact, there was no one in the world I could confide in without placing them in danger.

Just then, I heard the radio announcer say something about Cronus Aerospace, so I turned up the volume. The reporter explained that the newly staffed Venus mission team had successfully rebooted their troubled planetary rover and that it was once again fully operational.

That, of course, was a lie, though the twins and I were among the few people alive who knew Rhea had never failed to begin with. I had to wonder who else was in on that little secret.

Oddly, the announcer had nothing to say about the murder investigation, but went on to report that Cronus stocks were 'skyrocketing.' I turned the radio off.

Kaui awoke when we were about halfway home while his brother continued sleeping until we reached the driveway. We unloaded our things from the car, and I remembered to bring my gun upstairs with me. I checked the magazine and then slid it under my bed pillow. I doubted I'd ever need to use the thing, though it felt reassuring having it close.

As a President's Agent, you can never be too safe.

Chapter 26

That night, Malia arrived home with pizzas in hand, as promised. After changing into a black sleeveless top and a pair of snug-fitting jeans, she joined us on the patio where the four of us enjoyed dinner and conversation together.

After the meal, Malia and I stayed out on the patio while Kaui and Kekoa headed to the living room to watch TV. As the sun drew low in the sky, Malia removed her sunglasses. I noticed she'd touched up her makeup after arriving home, which told me something, though that something wasn't going to happen. It can be tricky trying to keep things friendly and platonic without it becoming romantic and sexual. I'm all for sexual, but when it's with the one person who happens to know your exact location while you're trying to stay under the radar, things can get complicated.

I hope the President appreciates all the sacrifices I make.

Before long, the sky began to darken. Malia smiled at me. "It's such a nice night," she said. "Let's walk down to the beach." Without waiting for my reply, she led me barefoot through the backyard and to the gate. From there, we headed down the stairs to the beach and began walking along the sandy shoreline.

Right away, she slid her hand into mine. "I have a confession to make," she said. "I thought about you today while I was at work."

I thought for a second, then stopped and told her, "I have a confession to make, too."

I felt her hand pull away. "Don't tell me—you're married, right?"

I shook my head. "I already told you I'm divorced." This was true. "If I was married I wouldn't be here with you." This was semi-true. I looked her in the eye. "I would never lie to you." That, of course, was a lie.

"I'm sorry. What is it then?"

"Let's keep walking while I explain." As we continued along the shoreline I let her know, "I want to be honest with you about the twins and myself, but I need to do so without telling you *too* much."

"Why is that?"

"In truth, I'm worried that too much information could place you in danger."

"What do you mean?"

"Yesterday morning, four of our coworkers were brutally murdered right in our workplace."

Malia was startled. "That was on the news! At the space center, right?"

I nodded. "The twins and I thought we might be in danger, too, which is why we decided to leave Florida and go into hiding."

"*That's* why you're here?"

I nodded again.

We came to the end of the beach where we turned back. After a quiet moment, she looked over at me and said, "You must feel terrible about your coworkers."

"I do," I replied, "but Kaui and Kekoa were closer to the victims than me. In their own way, they're in mourning." I added, "I suppose I am too."

We soon found ourselves at the stairs again. I sat on the landing and looked up at the stars which were beginning to appear one-by-one. Malia sat herself between my legs with her back leaned against me. I rested my chin on her head and closed my eyes for a moment, listening as the wind flowed through the palm branches high above us.

I could smell her perfume, which I liked, and some ideas started rattling around in my mind. I recognized I was at a crossroad, so to speak, a place where a lot of guys lose circulation to their brain and do things they wind up regretting. This has happened to me more than once. One way would land the two of us in bed, while the other way would keep things between us simple, which was what I needed right now.

I noticed her arms were cold and her hands were shivering. "You're freezing," I said.

"I felt hot a minute ago," she told me, "but I guess the moment passed."

I made no reply.

She turned and looked at me. "Sorry about that, Mike. You're probably going through a lot right now with everything—"

"No apologies needed."

She looked at me and let out a breath. "I wish we'd met under better circumstances."

I nodded at that and gave her a light kiss on the forehead. After that, we headed back to the house where we said goodnight and went to our separate rooms.

After a quick shower I climbed under my sheets and thought about what had happened tonight. Part of me wanted Malia in my bed while the other part, the smart part, knew that would only lead to trouble. After thinking about it, I was convinced I'd done the right thing.

Though that may have been a lie, too.

Chapter 27

Friday, April 23, 2032

The landing gear lowered with a soft bump as the plane approached Honolulu International Airport. Earlier, the pilot announced the flight would be arriving at 9:45 a.m. Hawaii Time, which was a few minutes early. Raquel had been awake during most of the flight, feeling more than a little apprehension about what she was doing. She was also worried that Mike and the twins may have already returned to Florida and that they'd crossed paths in the air. For the moment, however, she was able to forget all that as she gazed down at the tropical landscape and natural beauty of Oahu.

Minutes later, the plane made a smooth landing and taxied to the terminal. Once inside the airport, Raquel went directly to the nearest activities counter. There, she studied a map of the island looking for the town of Kahului where the restaurant was located.

"Can I help you find something, ma'am?"

Raquel looked up from the map to see a young man standing behind the counter. "Yes," she said. "I'm trying to find Kahului on this map, but I don't see it..."

"I think you're looking at the wrong island," he told her. From an information rack, he removed a map of Maui and pointed out the town of Kahului. "It's on Maui. See?"

Raquel looked at the map for a moment. "Yikes. I'm on the wrong island." She turned to the young man and asked, "How do I get to Maui from here?"

He pointed to a long corridor behind the counter. "Go that way," he said. "There's a tram at the end that takes you to the inter-island terminal."

She thanked him and hurried off.

At the inter-island counter, the teller looked over Raquel's ID. "You want the next available flight to Maui, right?"

"Yes," Raquel replied, "I have no luggage, just a pocketbook."

The teller was an older, world-weary woman. She gave Raquel a blank stare, then focused back at her monitor. "Good news," she said. "I have you booked on the next flight. They start boarding in thirty minutes, sweetie, so you'll need to head straight there."

"Okay. How much—?"

"Two hundred thirty-two dollars." She held out her hand. "You have a card?"

Raquel shook her head. "I'm using cash." From her purse she pulled out all her money, two hundreds and a ten. "Oh."

"Not enough," the teller observed. "No credit card?"

"I have one," Raquel replied, "but I don't want to use it." She turned to a young couple standing in line behind her. "Excuse me, but could you spare twenty-two dollars, please? It's important."

The couple looked at each other, then shook their heads.

Raquel turned back to the teller. "Schmucks."

The teller smiled at that as she checked her screen. "It says here you're a Travel Partner member. Why not use that account for the remaining twenty-two dollars?"

"Wouldn't that be the same as a credit card?"

"Not if you pay it before the end of the current billing-cycle, which isn't 'til May. Up to then it's the same as cash."

"It can't be traced? I'm trying to do this trip without my—"

"Let me guess. You don't want your husband to know you're going to Maui, right?"

Raquel leaned forward and confided, "Actually, I don't want my *boss* to know."

The teller grinned. "Honey, I thoroughly understand. My boss is a pervert and a porn addict. I wouldn't want him to know if I was going to the ladies room, much less Maui." She tapped at her screen. Seconds later, a ticket printed out. "Your boss won't be able to trace *this*." She handed the ticket to Raquel and pointed in the direction of the terminal. "Gate seventeen, sweetie."

"Thanks!"

After passing through the security checkpoint, Raquel headed directly to the gate. Once there, she sat facing away from the windows and rested her eyes.

While waiting for boarding to begin, an idea came to her. She had a feeling the twin's phones and email accounts were under surveillance, but was sure a message from her wouldn't reveal their location. She pulled out her phone and composed a cryptic message. Once done, she read it through and smiled. Rachel was certain only the twins would understand the hidden meaning of the message and no one else would think anything of it.

Passengers started boarding. Raquel read the message one more time and began to wonder if it was a good idea. She looked again at the line of passengers and saw it was moving quickly.

She thought for a few more seconds, then hit 'send.'

Chapter 28

I awoke to the sound of birds chirping and the aroma of fresh coffee. I sat up and checked the other side of my bed to be sure Malia hadn't slipped in during the night, then climbed out from under my sheets and got dressed.

I went downstairs where I found Malia preparing to leave for work. She was dressed kind of sexy, wearing a black blouse that looked kind of low-cut, a beige skirt that looked kind of short, plus a pair of black heels that looked kind of high. If I understand women, which I don't, I'd conclude this was her way of showing me what I'd missed out on. Lucky for me, I'm impervious to silly tactics like this. As long as I'm looking the other way, that is. Still, there was enough sexual tension in the room to trip a breaker.

"You look nice this morning," I told her. "You make me want to apply for a mortgage."

She smiled politely.

I headed to the coffee pot and poured a cup.

"Are you still planning to make dinner tonight?" she asked.

Whoa. I'd totally forgotten about that. "You didn't think I forgot, did you?"

"Just asking." She grabbed her things and went to the door. "I have a big day planned," she said, "but I should be home by around five." She threw me a kiss and left.

I stood there for a moment in quiet thought. Malia appeared to be happy. Prickly, yes, but still happy, which was the main thing. I was glad I'd been truthful and forthcoming with her about things. Of course, if she knew I was a secret agent with two loaded handguns hidden in her house, or that I was using her television for spy stuff, or that two known killers were interested in finding me, she might not be so happy.

I took my cup outside and sat at the patio table. The sun was rising over distant clouds, casting brilliant colors across the eastern sky. The sea was calm as glass and birds were singing as they flew playfully from tree to tree. All signs of trouble.

Before long, Kaui and Kekoa came outside and joined me. Both were wearing their new beachwear and baseball caps, which looked exactly like their old beachwear and baseball caps.

Kekoa asked me, "Wanna come with us to Da Kitchin?"

I held up my cup. "I drink my breakfast, but thanks anyway."

"Where's Malia?"

"She left for work already. Why?"

"Just wondering," he said. "I saw you and her walk down to the beach last night."

Sidestepping that topic, I told him, "When you and your brother return from breakfast we'll check the news and finish going over the videos from Rhea."

They agreed.

After they'd left, I went upstairs and I sat in front of the TV. I placed my ICD charger under my ear and turned on a news channel. The President, who appeared to be alive and well, was discussing his upcoming campaign. He seemed like a shoe-in for re-election, which meant I'd be a shoe-in for another four years as his agent. Assuming I live that long.

In other news, the scientific community was busy applauding the new Cronus control room staff for resurrecting Rhea back in the midst of the horror of recent events. Photos of the original team, including Jason, Keri, and Viktor, as well as Glenn, were flashed across the screen. Nothing about the investigation was mentioned, other than that it was being ruled a murder/suicide on the part of poor Glenn.

After that, I spent some time researching the La Chona Rover, or 'Rita' as it was sometimes called. I was surprised at how much information there was on the subject including eBooks, websites, and blogs. Obviously, it was a hot topic for all the conspiracy theorists out there. These, of course, are the same loonies who believe there's a flying saucer hidden at Area 51, that there was a second gunman in Dallas, and that Humpty was actually pushed.

To my surprise, they had their facts remarkably straight concerning the so-called 'President's Agent,' so maybe they weren't completely off their rockers. In fact, some of their theories about all the king's horses were starting to make sense. Or maybe I needed more coffee.

Concerning Rita, the theorists agreed on only two things: one, that the supposed discovery occurred in the year 1963, and two, that it was found and reported by a local rancher by the name of Ignacio Soto. Before disappearing, that is.

From downstairs, I heard the sound of the twins returning from the restaurant. They both came straight to my room and made themselves comfortable in front of the TV.

"So what's our plan for today?" Kaui asked.

"After we go over the videos from Rhea," I said, "we'll make a quick run to the grocery store."

"For what?"

"I told Malia we'd prepare dinner tonight."

"Seriously?"

"Yeah. I promised we'd make Mexican food."

He looked at me funny.

In the meantime, Kekoa used my tablet to make some picture adjustments before pulling up the video of the mysterious rover. After he'd finished, the three of us studied the images closely, pausing at times to check details of the rover's design and construction. Our late coworkers had done a good job of photographing the machine from almost every possible angle.

"Where do you suppose it came from?" Kekoa asked.

"It has to be from Earth," I replied. "And I don't think it's been on Venus for more than a couple of years."

He seemed surprised. "Why do you say that?"

"The tracks on the planet's surface can't be too old or they'd have been eroded away by the wind, dust storms, and quakes. Also, the amount of dust on the rover seems minimal, which tells me it hasn't been sitting there for long."

Kaui asked, "What makes you so sure it's from Earth?"

I pointed to the image on the screen. "If you look at it long enough, you'll see it vaguely resembles most of the rovers we've sent to other planets. Basically, it has wheels and a main body, plus what looks like a camera mount projecting out of the top."

He nodded.

"Besides, it would be too far away to be controlled from some distant planet—"

"Maybe it's self-guided," Kekoa suggested.

"If it was smart enough to be self-guided, it wouldn't have wandered into a cavern and become stuck, would it?"

While he contemplated that, I added, "If extraterrestrial beings wanted to study what's interesting in our solar system, they'd study *Earth.*"

Kaui paused the video. "Look at that right there," he said. He got up from his chair and directed our attention to a blurred oval spot on the front of the main body. Only then did Kekoa and I notice it.

The spot was faint and dust covered while the lighting and camera angle were less than ideal. I asked Kaui to zoom in and take a screen shot, which he did. He then transferred the photo to a digital image editor and began tweaking. After that, he transferred the file onto a 3D converter, amplified it to the highest projection setting, and pressed *enter.* Instantly, the details stood out. In fact, we could tell right away what it was. The image was an insignia with an ellipse orbiting a wide letter W. The symbol for Wright Aerospace.

I told Kekoa, "I think this answers your question about where it came from."

After that sunk in, he looked at me and asked, "How could Wright have put a rover on Venus without anyone knowing?"

"And why?" Kaui asked.

I shrugged. "And where did Wright come up with such an advanced design?" As I thought about it a possible answer came to me, but I kept that to myself.

Chapter 29

Once we were done reviewing the video, Kaui asked me, "Do you think it's safe for me to check my email?"

"I guess you can look at it," I told him. "Just don't open or change anything."

His brother seemed in agreement.

Kaui opened his email portal while Kekoa and I watched on the big TV screen. At the top of his inbox we could see a message had recently arrived from Raquel Richards.

Kaui pointed out, "Look at that. It's already been opened."

"That means someone out there is monitoring your email," I said.

He and his brother appeared concerned.

I told Kaui, "Since it's already been opened, let's see what she had to say."

He clicked on the message and the three of us read it on the big screen:

HI. I just wanted you guys to know I'm okay.

In my heart, though, I'm sad after what happened in the control room.

You're probably devastated. Let's hope that those we lost are never forgotten and that their dedication to the success of the mission was not in vain.

Know, please, that you two are my best friends and I hope you are being extra-safe. I miss hanging out together and all the good times that we shared. I remember how we'd spend entire nights just sitting in my kitchin talking and laughing about things. You guys would tell me about your favorite place to eat, and we'd play 50 different video games. We'd stay up after twelve pm, even when we all had to work in the morning.

I hope you find your way here soon. I'm sitting in the kitchin right now and looking forward to seeing you. Keep being safe. God bless. Raq

Something about the message seemed peculiar. I asked the twins, "Do you guys notice anything strange about this?"

"I do," Kekoa answered. "For one thing, nowhere in the message does Raquel ask us to contact her. Also, her place is a studio and has no kitchen. We always hung out in her living room in front of the TV."

Kaui spoke up, "And look how she spelled it: k-i-t-c-h-i-n. That's how Da Kitchin, spells it." He added, "It also says 'We'd stay up after twelve p.m.' That would be noontime. Twelve *a.m.* would be more like it."

Kekoa pointed to the screen. "She mentions how we talked about our 'favorite place to eat,' and then, 'I hope you find your way here soon.' She also wrote, 'I'm sitting in the kitchin right now and looking forward to seeing you.'"

"Raquel is here in Hawaii," I told them. "That's why she used the number '50.'"

Kekoa nodded. "The fiftieth state."

"And look at the first word of each paragraph, starting from the bottom."

Kekoa read it, "I—Know—You're—In—HI."

Kaui looked at me. "How did you notice that?"

"I saw that both letters of 'HI' were capitalized like the abbreviation for Hawaii. I took it from there."

"It's like she's worried about us," Kekoa said. "The message tells us to be safe—and mentions it *twice*."

I nodded. "She must have figured someone would be monitoring your emails, so she wrote the message in a cryptic way that only the two of you would understand. I think she's telling us she's here in Maui and wants us to meet her at the restaurant at twelve p.m."

Kekoa thought about that. "How did she find us? If Raquel managed to track us down, what's stopping anyone else from doing the same?"

We all looked at each other.

"It's almost 11:30," I said. "Let's head to the restaurant—and let's just hope she didn't leave a trail."

I turned off the TV and hid my tablet where it was out of sight. After the twins had gone downstairs, I grabbed my gun and wrapped it in a t-shirt before following them out to the car.

Kaui claimed the front seat this time, and he saw me hiding the t-shirt under my seat. "What's that?" he asked.

"My insurance policy."

"It looked like a gun. Where'd you get that?"

"It's from a gun store in Miami," I told him, which was true—though it was the kind of gun store that operated out of a suitcase in a dark alley. As I backed out of the driveway, I let him know, "It's a compact automatic handgun, a Colt .380 Mustang with laser sighting."

"Cool."

"When we get back, I'll show it to you and Kekoa. In the meantime, don't say anything to Malia."

He agreed with that and asked, "What do you think about the whole gun control thing?"

"Me? Oh, I'm a big believer in gun control."

"Really?"

"Sure. If there's a gun around, I want to be the one who's in control of it."

I thought about a few things on the way to the restaurant. At this point, it was reasonable to assume Raquel had been followed and that her trip, phone calls, and charges had already been traced. Also, I couldn't eliminate the possibility that someone had read Raquel's email and deciphered the same thing we did. Maybe I was over-thinking all this, but the email could have originated from someone other than Raquel and we were walking into a clever trap.

I told the twins, "If we *do* find Raquel, the less she knows the better. In fact, don't even mention the other rover. All right?"

They agreed.

"And don't say anything about Craig Van Essen, either. Or his jet."

Again, they agreed.

I thought for a second, then added, "And don't tell her I have a gun."

"Is that it?" Kekoa asked.

"Uh...don't tell her I have access to the control room mainframe either. I think that's it."

"Maybe we shouldn't say anything."

"Good idea."

Within minutes, we arrived at the small shopping center where the restaurant was located. I stopped in front of a surf shop.

"It's down that way further," Kekoa said, pointing.

"I'm taking a precaution in case Raquel was followed." I scribbled a phone number on a piece of scrap paper, then handed it to Kaui and asked him, "Can I borrow your baseball cap?"

He looked at me funny, but handed it over.

I adjusted it to my size and explained, "Just to be safe, I want you guys to duck into this surf shop and wait there until I'm sure everything's clear. If I don't come back within ten minutes, then something bad has happened."

Kekoa asked, "What do we do then?"

"If ten minutes pass, I want you to call the police. When the cops arrive, tell them you're in danger and need to be placed into protective custody immediately."

"What's this phone number for?"

"When the police allow you to make a phone call, call that. It's Craig Van Essen's cell phone. You'll also need to contact Malia at Maui Pacific Mortgage. Tell her to join the two of you in protective custody. Tell her I said it's important."

"Why Malia?"

"Just a precaution. If our location has been compromised she could be in danger."

"What do we tell the police?"

"Don't say too much until you've contacted Craig. After that, tell the cops everything you know and don't lie about anything." I looked at my watch and saw it was 11:49 a.m. "Now go—and start counting down ten minutes."

Without a word, they stepped out of the vehicle and went straight into the surf shop.

I drove past Da Kitchin and parked under a shade tree at the far end of the lot, reversing into the space so I faced the restaurant entrance. I had my sunglasses on as well as Kaui's ball cap with the bill pulled low. I scanned the area for anything suspicious but saw nothing.

Just as I got out of the car a blue minivan entered the lot. I waited behind the open driver's door. The van slowed and came to a stop in front of the restaurant. I watched while a young woman hopped out and waved goodbye as the vehicle drove off.

Raquel Richards.

Before she entered the restaurant, I tooted the horn. As she turned around I removed the ball cap and waved. We began to walk toward each other. Once we got closer, she began running and leaped into my arms. Almost immediately, she began to weep and I held her tightly while tears of every emotion fell from her eyes.

"Oh, Mike! I was so worried about you!" she cried. Suddenly she pulled herself away and looked at me.

"The twins are fine," I said before she could ask. "They're here with me."

She fell back into my arms.

I knew I had to get back to Kaui and Kekoa before they called the police, so I opened her door for her, then hurried to my side and hopped in. As I began to drive I explained, "I wanted to be extra cautious in case you were followed, so I asked the twins to wait inside one of these shops." I pointed up ahead.

"There's no way I could have been followed," she said, "but I'm glad you guys are being safe."

I stopped in front of the surf shop and gave Kaui and Kekoa a thumbs-up signal as they came out. Raquel jumped out and gave both of them a hug. After they all climbed in I looked around one last time, then drove off.

Raquel let out a breath. "You don't know how good it is to see the three of you. I was so worried."

I looked over at her and smiled before checking my mirrors. I took a few evasive maneuvers to be sure we weren't being followed before turning onto Hana Highway.

Though it was great to see Raquel, her unexpected and uninvited arrival in Maui meant I now had one more person to worry about. That, plus all the drama and complexities that go along with having an attractive young woman around.

I thought about Malia and wondered how she'd react to having Raquel with us, though I didn't see how it would be a problem.

Then again, I don't understand women too well.

Chapter 30

Kaui and Kekoa seemed happy to have Raquel on board and the three of them sounded like chatterboxes. While they were busy catching up, I was busy driving and thinking of what our next step should be. I had a few questions for our new team member. Like how she managed to find us. More importantly, I needed to be sure she hadn't left a money trail or any evidence that could be traced here.

If she did, our next stop would be the airport.

I decided it would be better to take Raquel to a secluded place to talk rather than go straight to the house. Ahead on the left I noticed a beach access sign, so I turned there.

"Where does this go?" Kaui asked.

"There's a beach up here I want to check out." I turned to Raquel and said, "We have a few things to discuss once we're there."

She made a face. "So you can *debrief* me, right?"

I smiled in reply.

Soon, the road ended at a remote beach where I pulled over and parked. The four of us got out and removed our footwear before heading down to the water's edge.

We walked together for a while, until we rounded a small peninsula and came upon a pristine cove of brilliant turquoise water. There was no one around, making it an ideal spot for Raquel and me to discuss recent events. While the twins ventured ahead, Raquel and I found a shaded area under a tree.

After we'd made ourselves comfortable, I took a moment to offer my condolences concerning the loss of her friends, namely Jason, Keri, Viktor, and Glenn. After that, I got down to business. "I'm glad you found us, Raquel, but I need to know exactly how you managed to do that."

"It was mostly luck," she said. "I was looking for a way to find you guys when my friend had the idea to call Da Kitchin. Sure enough, Kaui and Kekoa had just been there for breakfast. That's when I went to the airport and got on the next plane to Hawaii."

"And how did you pay for the trip?"

"Aside from my friend, I didn't want anyone to know where I was going, so I borrowed cash from her and used that to pay for the tickets."

"Good move."

"Other than the one email message I sent the twins, which you guys obviously figured out, I haven't called or contacted anyone."

I was glad to hear that. "So, you didn't use a credit card for *anything*?"

"Nope. I have Lucas Richter's corporate card with me. But I never used it."

"Richter? Why would you have *his* credit card?"

"For my expenses," she said. "Yesterday, he told me the police wanted to interview everyone employed at the facility. He was worried about you and the twins and explained that the three of you had gone to visit your parents in Ocala. He asked me to go there and try to convince you to come back to the Cape."

"Did you actually go to Ocala?"

"Yeah. And I found out you'd used a dead guy's contact information."

I held back a laugh. "Does Richter know you're here?"

"I was supposed to call him when I found you, but I didn't."

"Why not?"

She thought about that. "I guess because I don't trust him."

I nodded.

After that, I briefed Raquel on the basics of our current situation, including the story of Ellis Lacorde and his partner, Safire, and their haphazard visit to my Cocoa Beach apartment.

She gave me a look. "I think there's a lot you're not telling me."

And she was right. I assured her, "If I've left anything out, Raquel, it's for your own good."

She didn't seem to appreciate that.

It got quiet for a while. To break the silence, I told Raquel about our temporary residence, the Ocean Breeze. I described the proprietor, Malia, as a friendly person whom the twins and I felt we could trust. I neglected to mention that Malia was also an attractive and sexually mature woman who seemed interested in Mike Brennan. Raquel could find that out on her own.

She stared out at the ocean for a moment. "I hope you don't mind that I came out here."

"I'm glad you're here, Raquel."

She turned to me. "I couldn't rest until I saw you guys again, face to face."

I gave her a smile.

"Do you think what they're saying is right? That Glenn did it?"

I shook my head. "He wouldn't have been capable of such a thing."

"How about Derrick Haut? He was the only survivor."

"If he's not the killer, he knows who is."

She scooted herself closer to me, then lay her head on my shoulder. I glanced over at the twins who appeared to be either comfortable or asleep. As we rested, I took the opportunity to think about Glenn Hosato. I also thought about Haut and the murders and the horror and the senselessness of it all.

Somehow, I knew the murderer and I would one day meet.

And it would be face to face.

Chapter 31

As we headed back to the car I told Raquel, "We need to stop at a grocery store on the way home. I volunteered to make dinner tonight."

"*You're* cooking?"

"Yeah. I was thinking Mexican food, like tacos."

She let out a laugh. "This I've got to see."

Another doubter.

In Paia, we stopped at a natural-food store. Once inside I started filling the cart with boxed taco shells, canned beans, and jars of salsa.

"Why are you buying that garbage?" Raquel asked. "You either use fresh ingredients or I'm not eating it."

And so it begins. Having been married, I've learned it's not worth arguing with women about trivial things. Along the way, I've also learned that practically everything is trivial—which just kills me.

Anyway, the twins and I followed Raquel through the store while she loaded the cart with organic meats, onions, tomatoes, avocados, flour, spices, and more. As we headed for the checkout, I saw the twins had picked their lunch rations for the day: two frozen pizzas and a six-pack of Mountain Mist.

After our organic shopping adventure, the four of us headed to the house. Once there, the twins took care of unloading groceries while I showed Raquel the shaded courtyard and the view from the kitchen.

"Wow. This place is beautiful," she said, looking out at the ocean and the lagoon. "How are we paying for all this?"

"Don't worry," I said. "I brought enough cash to cover us for a few days."

"And when that runs out?"

"I don't know. How do you feel about camping?"

She smiled. "So, what made you volunteer to make dinner tonight?"

I shrugged. "Malia made dinner for us the first night and brought home pizza the second. I thought it would be nice to reciprocate the gesture. Besides, we want to do whatever it takes to stay on her good side."

"Why do you say that?"

"Because right now she's the only person on Earth who knows our location. And we want to keep it that way."

She nodded.

"She also knows the twins and I worked together at Cronus, and that we came here to lay low for a while."

"Are you sure you can trust her?"

"I think so."

"You're not sleeping with her, are you?"

Well, I knew that was coming. "I can assure you that Malia and I have not slept together."

She looked at me in full lie-detector mode for a second, then grinned. "Just asking."

For once, I was glad I hadn't had sex.

After that, Raquel and I began preparing dinner. Kaui and Kekoa joined us and were assigned to the tortilla production department while I was placed in charge of grill detail. Our leader, Commander Richards, gave out orders while expertly preparing fresh salsa, guacamole, and refried beans.

We finished the meal preparations just as Malia arrived home from work. Kaui greeted her at the door. "You're just in time for dinner," he said.

She drew in a whiff. "It smells great."

Malia came to the kitchen and gave me a warm smile. She then noticed Raquel, who was busily setting the table. In an instant, the smile vanished from her face. At the same time, I thought I felt the temperature drop a few degrees.

I told Malia, "This is Raquel Richards, our coworker from Florida. She surprised us by showing up in Maui this morning."

She looked at me and forced a smile. "I hope she'll be joining us for dinner."

"That's the plan," I said. "In fact, we were hoping she could stay here with us. If you have a room, that is."

"That shouldn't be a problem." She glanced over at the table, which was set with plates of guacamole, tortillas, and all the trimmings.

"Dinner is ready," Raquel said. "Why don't we sit down before it gets cold?"

After we'd begun eating, Malia looked over at Raquel. "So, Mike said that your arrival was a 'surprise'…?"

Raquel nodded. "That's right."

"I was under the impression no one knew where they were. How did you find them?"

Raquel looked at me and smiled. "It was mostly a lucky guess."

Malia picked at her meal while continuing the inquisition. Raquel seemed to handle it well, though I'm sure she was wondering why Malia was so green-eyed. After a while, Malia's internal self-awareness alarm must have gone off and she gave it a rest.

After dinner, the twins began operation cleanup while Malia, perhaps to compensate for being so frosty, showed Raquel to her room. Coincidently, this was on the second floor of the opposite end of the house, as far as possible from me. Malia also offered to loan Raquel some clothes since the two were about the same size: extra-puny.

I advised Raquel to get some sleep, reminding her that it was past midnight in Florida. After that, I headed up to my room where I showered and hid for the rest of the night.

I could only hope that things between Raquel and Malia worked out. In the meantime, I'd have to be careful while dealing with two strong-minded women under the same roof.

God help me.

Chapter 32

Saturday, April 24, 2032

I found myself tossing and turning before I finally gave up and climbed out of bed. I glanced at the clock on the wall and saw it was only 4:42 a.m. Though it was early, I decided to go ahead and shave. After that, I dressed in a t-shirt and surf shorts and headed downstairs.

I noticed a lamp was on in the living room. On the couch, cross-legged and covered with a large feather-filled comforter, sat Raquel Richards. She had a cup of coffee in one hand and a magazine in the other.

She looked at me and smiled. "I thought you'd never wake up."

I was sure everyone else in the house was still asleep, so I kept my voice down. "Is there more coffee?"

"Of course."

I went to the kitchen and filled a cup, then went back to the living room and sat next to Raquel.

"I want to show you something." She handed me a copy of *Maui Discovery Guide Magazine*, which was opened to an article.

I took a sip of coffee and glanced over the page. The article described a place known as Mile Marker Fourteen, and a photo showed a young couple snorkeling among tropical fish and colorful coral.

"I want you to take me there," she told me.

I nodded at that while I read further.

"I love the names of all the towns and places here," she said. "The place you're reading about is actually where the highway mile marker fourteen sign is posted. Isn't that cool?"

I looked up from the article. "So, when were you planning on going?"

"They say early morning is the best time, when the water is calm and the visibility is clear."

"So, like, *now?*"

"C'mon—it'll be fun!"

"Can I finish my coffee first?"

"You can finish it on the way." She threw her comforter aside and hopped up from the couch. "According to Malia there's tons of snorkeling stuff in the garage for guests. Let's check it out."

Malia's room was located right above the garage, so we kept the noise down as best we could. Once there, Raquel and I found containers filled with masks, fins, snorkels, and vests of all sizes and styles. I sifted through the collection and came up with an assortment that I felt would work for us.

I saw there were a few standup paddleboards stored neatly on racks, also for the use of the guests. I picked out a smaller board for Raquel along with a short, narrow paddle. For myself, I selected the biggest board there was along with the longest paddle I could find. I also helped myself to a tube of sunscreen, a few beach towels, and a collapsible cooler.

We filled the cooler with the masks and fins and carried that and the rest of the gear out to the SUV. After folding down the rear seats I loaded everything into the back with the boards sticking out of the rear hatch. I made sure to pack my Colt too, and I hid that under the seat. Before leaving, I went inside for one more coffee.

From the kitchen, I looked out and saw the predawn light was already beginning to glow in the east. I pointed this out to Raquel and the two of us stepped out to the deck for a better look.

We watched while the distant horizon became further illuminated. Over the next minute or so we watched as brilliant rays of red, yellow, and orange streaked skyward from behind glimmering clouds.

Raquel seemed in awe of this and watched silently as the surface of the sea began to sparkle like a mirror before her. Above, the night sky slowly vanished as its stars disappeared from sight one-by-one.

Raquel seemed moved by the beauty of it all, and I noticed she had a small tear in her eye. Without a thought, I dabbed it with the back of my finger. As I did so, she took my hand and softly kissed the drop from my finger with her lips.

For a second there, I felt my heart skip.

After that, she and I returned to the kitchen where I left a brief note for the twins and Malia explaining where we were headed. I then refilled my coffee and we were off.

As we turned onto Hana Highway I told Raquel, "You probably need a swim suit. Should I stop somewhere?"

"I borrowed one already," she said. "I'm wearing it under these clothes."

She had on a pair of white jeans with a grey sweater under a black and white jacket. "Nice clothes. Where did you—?"

"Malia gave them to me, along with a ton of other stuff."

"I'm glad you two are getting along so well."

According to the magazine article, Mile Marker Fourteen was located just before the small town of Olowalu, so Raquel entered that into the GPS. We headed through quaint Paia, then into Kahului and the central valley where the road widened and car dealerships, shopping centers, and fast-food restaurants dominated the scenery for a while before transforming again into rural countryside and farmland. To our left were vast fields of some kind of tall green plants.

"What's all that?" Raquel asked, pointing to the crops.

It could have been asparagus for all I knew, but I felt like I needed to give some kind of answer. "Pineapples."

"Really? They look so huge."

I looked more closely and noticed the plants were at least nine feet high. "Hawaiian pineapples are taller than most."

"Right." Using the in-dash tablet, Raquel did a quick search and found a photo of the crops in question. In fact, the picture looked like it had been taken from our exact location. She positioned the tablet where I could see the caption under the photo: *Sugar Cane.*

Being a man of experience, I knew to stick to my story. "You can't trust anything on the internet," I told her. "Half of that stuff is written by fourth graders. What website are you looking at anyway?"

"The State of Hawaii Department of Agriculture."

"See what I mean?"

We both smiled.

Behind us, the sun had begun to cast a rich amber glow across the landscape. To the left and right of us endless fields of tall pineapple plants were spread out as far as the eye could see. Ahead in the distance stood the jagged West Maui Mountains whose seven-thousand foot volcanic slopes were carved with countless ravines and crevices from centuries of erosion.

As we continued west, the highway began to curve through the rugged mountainside. Before long, the road fed through a tunnel, then descended gradually until we were close to sea level. On the left, white sand beaches seemed to stretch for miles alongside glassy smooth water. Countless palm trees shimmered in the golden glow of the morning light while flocks of small birds dotted the sky.

Raquel was noticing this too. "I should move here," she said. "It's so beautiful and tropical."

"Wouldn't that interrupt your career as a…?"

"As an astronautical engineer? Yes, but at this point I'm probably unemployed anyway."

That was probably true. It occurred to me that between her, the twins, and myself, I was probably the only one who still had a job. At least I think I did.

The GPS let us know we were close, so I slowed down until I spotted highway mile marker sign number fourteen. I turned and parked under a large tree only ten yards from the shoreline. I went around to Raquel's side to find she'd already hopped out and walked over to the water's edge.

I removed our boards and paddles from the back, fastening the collapsible cooler with our snorkel gear on the front of my board. Just as I finished with that I heard Raquel call to me.

"Did you see this?" she asked, pointing to a signboard posted high on a tree.

I looked up at the sign, which read:

WARNING
SHARKS MAY BE PRESENT
SHARK BITES HAVE OCCURRED IN THIS AREA

No wonder we were the only ones here. "We can go somewhere else," I said, "unless you want to stay."

"It's all the same ocean, isn't it? I mean, what are the odds?"

I shrugged. "Maybe a thousand-to-one."

"There's two of us, so that means it's more like two thousand-to-one." She looked at me and smiled. "Besides, they'd probably go for you anyway. You have more meat on you."

"Thanks."

I went back to the car and removed my t-shirt, then grabbed the sunscreen and took a moment to apply a small amount to my nose and shoulders. While I did this, Raquel went to the other side of the vehicle and began preparing for the water.

Once I'd finished, I went over to Raquel's side to offer her some sunscreen. As soon as I saw her I stopped in my tracks. She was standing with her back to me and adjusting her bikini. I'd never seen her in anything but loose jeans and frumpy-looking sweaters before. Now I could see she had long thin legs, toned muscles, and flawless brown skin. Holy smokes.

She noticed me and turned around. "Does this look okay?"

"You look great, Raquel."

She smiled. "Can you rub some of that sunscreen on my shoulders and back?"

See what I go through?

Anyway, after we'd finished with that she and I went to our boards and strapped on our leashes, then entered the water in a kneeling position as we paddled out over the glassy water.

Once the water was deep enough, I stood and paddled beside Raquel. After seeing me she decided to try it. She was shaky for only a few seconds until she got the hang of it.

We followed an underwater path of white sand which led us through the turquoise reef. As the water became deeper, the coral below us grew richer and more colorful. The water was remarkably calm, which allowed for exceptional visibility.

So far, it was a perfect day. The water was warm, the sky was clear, and it seemed as if all our troubles were behind us. Nonetheless, I knew if I didn't stop staring at Raquel I was going to find myself in a whole new kind of trouble.

Chapter 33

Raquel and I continued paddling while gazing down at endless acres of coral.

All at once, she stopped and waved me over. "Come look at this."

I paddled closer and saw a huge black Manta ray, no less than five feet wide, gliding effortlessly below us. After a few seconds it changed direction and turned upward, heading straight toward Raquel. It was just under her board when it suddenly turned upside-down, revealing its bright white underside along with rows of gills and a long thin tail. After turning right side up again, it swam off into deeper water.

"That was so cool!" Raquel said. "Aren't you glad we came?"

I nodded at that, then looked around and suggested, "Let's head closer to shore where we can snorkel for a while."

She agreed, so we turned and paddled in that direction. When we'd reached shallower water we grabbed our masks and fins from the cooler, then strapped everything on and dove in. Using our snorkels, the two of us swam slowly through the crystalline water while the boards, still strapped to our ankles, followed behind us.

We had entered another world, a beautiful place where golden sunrays streaked down from above, reflecting and dancing over everything in sight, including Raquel's skin. Colorful tropical fish of all kinds darted about while we moved through mounds of coral divided by paths of glistening white sand.

Raquel swam beside me with graceful strokes of her fins. To my surprise, she reached out and took my hand and held it as we continued. She and I were just friends, of course. As far as I was concerned it was going to stay that way. Nonetheless, holding her hand felt good.

We explored the reef while heading in the general direction of shore. Before long, we found ourselves in only four feet of water. We stood and removed our gear and I placed everything onto my board.

"This place is amazing," Raquel said. "I've never seen anything like it."

I was about to reply to that when I caught a glimpse of movement in the water. Behind Raquel was a big grey creature—and it was swimming straight for her.

Raquel noticed my eyes had locked onto something and turned in time to see it. "Sh…shark!" she screamed.

In terror, Raquel jumped into my arms. Wasting no time, I darted to shore with our boards trailing behind us. Once I'd reached knee-deep water, I looked back and saw that it wasn't a shark at all, but a huge seal.

I assured Raquel we were safe and set her on her feet. I then strapped on my mask and went back to take a look. Keeping my distance, I dove underwater to watch the animal as it swam gracefully along the sandy bottom with short strokes of its tail. The seal was probably seven feet long and around five hundred pounds with a small head, a short snout, and thick, funny-looking whiskers.

Soon, it became curious and began to approach me, coming closer until we were less than ten feet apart. I glanced to my right and noticed Raquel had waded out and was watching us. For a long moment, the seal stared at me with huge black eyes before it finally swam off.

I went to Raquel and removed my mask.

"I feel so dumb," she said. "I really thought it was a shark coming at me."

I rubbed her shoulder. "And so did I."

We smiled at each other's silliness.

After that, she stepped closer and used her fingers to comb my hair away from my face. "There. That looks better." She then combed her own hair back and asked, "Do I look okay?"

I looked at her for a moment and confessed, "I've never seen anyone so lovely."

She seemed surprised by that. Perhaps even more surprised when I held her waist and pulled her close.

We gazed into each other's eyes for a long moment before our lips met.

As we kissed, my heart quickened. At the same time, everything around us seemed to come to a stop. In that extraordinary moment, nothing else seemed to exist.

Her kisses soon moved from my lips and down my neck until her face rested against my chest. We were both breathing heavily.

I looked up and glanced around at our surroundings. Near the shore, towering palms were swaying gently in the warm breeze. The golden sunlight was glimmering across the surface of the water. I could feel the warmth of Raquel's body as I held her close. At the same time, I could sense that neither of us wanted this moment to end.

We looked into each other's eyes once again, and we knew.

We were no longer just friends.

Chapter 34

I felt half-intoxicated as I steered through the twisting roads leading back home. I glanced over at Raquel, who smiled at me and placed her hand on mine. I hadn't planned on adding a new dimension to our friendship, and I knew this was going to take getting used to. At the same time, I was in heaven.

I had no doubt the twins would be fine concerning Raquel and me, though I wasn't so sure about Malia. I made a mental note to hide all the kitchen knives as soon as we get home.

I noticed it was eleven a.m. already and I remembered I'd made reservations for Mom's Fish House. My original idea was to take Malia out for a nice lunch, but plans change, right? In fact, I had a feeling a lot of things were about to change.

I asked Raquel, "Are you hungry?"

She looked at me like that was a dumb question. "I'm starving already. Feed me."

"How's Mom's Fish House sound?"

She smiled. "Is that a date?"

I took her hand and kissed it, which answered the question.

Before we knew it, we were back home. I backed up to the garage so it was easy to unload the boards and gear. After that, I followed Raquel to the living room where we found Kaui and Kekoa playing video games.

Raquel described to them our encounters with the manta ray and the seal. After she was done I mentioned, "The two of us are heading next door to grab lunch."

At that, Raquel turned to me. "I'll go upstairs and change." Before she headed off she gave me a quick peck.

Kaui noticed that and gave me a funny look. I took that as my queue to head up to my room.

After I'd showered and dressed, I went downstairs and watched Kaui and Kekoa play their game while I waited for Raquel. Waiting for women, I've found, is a refined art requiring a special degree of patience and tolerance that is learned over time. Once perfected, a guy can stand like a statue for hours without a complaint. I was still in the beginner phase.

I'd been watching Kaui and Kekoa blasting and killing things for a few minutes when I heard footsteps behind me. I turned to see a lovely young woman wearing a short black dress with black heels and a pearl necklace. It took me a second or two to realize this was Raquel.

The twins looked astonished.

Raquel smiled and took a moment to model her outfit for us. I noticed she was wearing makeup, which was something I'd ever seen on her before. Her brown hair was still damp from showering, but it looked pretty as it flowed over her tanned shoulders.

I told her, "You look just stunning, Raquel."

Kaui joked, "That's *Raquel*?"

She turned and wrinkled her nose at him.

We left the twins behind and headed to the restaurant.

Once there, I led Raquel to the reservations booth where a young woman wearing a flower lei greeted us.

"I have a lunch reservation," I told her. "Last name: Richter."

Raquel looked at me. "Richter? What's with that?"

"It's just a joke." I lowered my voice and explained, "I didn't want to use my real name for obvious reasons. Somehow, his was the first name that popped into my head."

"When did you make a reservation?"

Without the slightest hesitation I replied, "I called the restaurant while you were in the shower." Personally, I think it's a good idea to begin new relationships with a nice lie or two. That way, when things move along and you *really* start lying, it doesn't feel so weird.

Anyway, Raquel and I were taken to a table next to an open window with a spectacular view of the beach and ocean. The island-style décor gave the place a relaxed tropical atmosphere. All the tables appeared to be taken so I figured Mom must be doing well.

The waiter took our orders, after which Raquel and I began to converse. I'm sure she was curious to know more about me and my secretive past, though she seemed to know better than to probe too deep. I suspected the twins had advised her not to ask me too many questions and I was glad for that. I'd hate to use up all my lies on our first date.

Our meal soon arrived and we continued chatting while savoring our grilled seafood and steamed vegetables, all of which was delicious.

After dinner, Raquel excused herself to the ladies room. When she returned to the table, she told me, "I'm not used to high heels. Was I walking funny?"

"You seemed fine to me," I replied. "You have a pretty walk, Raquel. Very feminine."

She smiled for a moment, then lowered her eyes and confided, "I've never felt pretty or feminine before." She glanced up at me. "But you make me feel like I'm beautiful."

After our lunch, she and I went outside and took a few minutes to look over the grounds. We strolled the property hand in hand under the shade of dozens of tall palm trees. I asked Raquel, "What do you think of the place where we're staying?"

"I think it's great," she said, "except for one thing."

Well, I think I knew what that was. "Malia?"

She nodded. "I think she has you in her sights, Mike. In fact, I have a feeling she won't take too warmly to seeing us together."

I thought about that. "If that's true we might need to relocate. In fact, we should probably go to the house and pack our stuff."

"Right now?"

I looked at her. "As you know, some dangerous people are looking for the twins and me. By now, they could be looking for you, too. In the meantime, Malia is the only person who can blow our cover. To play it safe, I think it's best to leave on good terms and find a new hideout."

She nodded at that and then gave me a look. "Are you sure you and her never had anything going?"

"I'm quite sure."

Raquel continued studying me for a few seconds, but didn't pursue that question any further. That's what's nice about the early stages of a relationship, when people are reluctant to argue or point fingers and there's not much animosity or bitterness going around.

All that comes later.

Chapter 35

Raquel and I headed back to the house. As we walked up from the beach, I noticed the sliding door at the living room was open. Inside was Malia, and I realized she'd come home early.

It was time to face the music.

As we entered, I saw that Kaui and Kekoa were there too, and the three of them were staring at the TV in the corner.

Malia glanced over at me for a second, then looked Raquel up and down, no doubt recognizing her dress. "Kaui and Kekoa were just on the news," she told us, "and so were *you*."

Uh oh.

Kekoa turned to us and explained, "According to the news, the police in Cape Canaveral want the three of us to come in for questioning."

"About what?" Raquel asked.

He shrugged. "About the murders, I guess. They showed photos of Kaui and me and advised anyone who knows where we are to call the police."

Malia noticed the four of us had turned intuitively to her. "What?"

"The reporter says we aren't official suspects, but because we disappeared right after the murders, they—"

"We made the decision to leave Florida before we even *heard* about the murders," I said.

Kekoa nodded at that and continued, "They also said the police won't close the case until they've interviewed everyone at Cronus. I guess we're the only ones they haven't been able to locate."

And they won't. "What photos did they show of us?"

Kaui answered that: "Our employee photos, the same as the ones on our name tags."

Malia let me know, "Yours was blurry and didn't look like you at all."

Then my photo editing software has paid off. I asked her, "Did they say anything about Raquel?"

"Not yet."

Kekoa looked worried. "If we don't contact the police they'll think we had something to do with it."

Raquel nudged me. "He's right. You should probably call."

I saw Kaui and Malia nod in agreement.

Well, I knew better than that. I told them, "Let's keep in mind that we've committed no crime. We have more than enough evidence to prove we weren't involved with the murders. In fact, we were nowhere near the facility when the crimes took place. The police know that, so we have nothing to worry about."

No one argued with that, so I continued, "I believe there are dangerous people out there looking for us and they hope to flush us out by going to the media with this lie. This means they don't know where we are and—"

"And they're becoming desperate," Raquel said.

"*Who's* becoming desperate?" Malia asked. "Who are these people?"

I explained, "I believe two criminals, a man by the name of Ellis Lacorde and a woman known as Safire, are trying to find us. Calling the police or turning ourselves in would lead them straight to us."

Malia let out a sigh.

I told the twins, "Malia has been our friend and ally all along, and we don't want to place her in any further danger. For her safety we'll need to find a new hide out. In fact, I think we should relocate immediately."

"We're moving?" Kekoa asked.

"That's right. I need you and your brother to load your things into the car."

Malia spoke up, "I know another place where you can stay. It would be perfect."

"Where is it?"

"Way out in Haiku," she said, "in the middle of nowhere. It has three oceanfront cottages on ten acres, plus a garage and a barn."

"How many people live there?"

"That's just it. I'm having the place renovated right now so there's no one there. It's so remote; no one would ever be able to find you." She managed a smile. "Even *I* have a hard time finding the place."

I glanced over at my troupe, who seemed sold on the idea. "We'll take it."

Malia advised us, "Just so you know, there are no standard utilities out there, but the property does have its own solar power, plus a wind turbine and a diesel generator. It also has a cistern with reverse osmosis for drinking water."

"Is there internet?" Kaui asked.

She shook her head. "Sorry. But there are a couple of Honda ATVs in the garage. You and your brother can help yourselves to those if you like."

He and Kekoa both grinned.

She went on, "The entire estate is fenced, and the entry gate is pass code protected."

"Why all the security?" I asked.

"The usual tenants are a celebrity couple who like their privacy. They're happy as long as there are no paparazzi sneaking around with cameras, which is why I had the gates and fences put in."

"Anyone we know?" Raquel asked.

Malia smiled. "I'm sure you'd recognize them if you saw them."

"It sounds perfect," I said. "We'd like to head out there right away if that's possible."

"It's ready, as far as I know. I just need to call my construction guys and tell them to stay off the property. While I'm at it, I'll write down the pass code for the gate and find the keys for you." She began to step away, then stopped and turned to us. "Just so you know, I'm not going to say anything to anyone, including the police."

Raquel stepped forward and took Malia's hand. "Thank you, Malia. We appreciate that and everything you've done to help us."

Malia smiled at that and headed off.

Once Malia was out of earshot Raquel asked me, "Do you think it's safe to stay here in Maui?"

"We don't have much of a choice," I replied. "After that news broadcast, every cop and every airport in America will be on the lookout for us. The best thing we can do is to continue hiding, and the property Malia described sounds like our safest bet."

Everyone agreed with that, so we gathered our things and began loading it into the car.

Malia met us in the driveway with the keys, which she gave to me along with the pass code and directions to the place. She insisted, "You need to load a cooler or two with some food before you leave. There aren't any grocery stores after you leave Paia and there's probably not a speck of food in any of the cottages."

I looked over at the twins, who got the message and headed to the kitchen.

I pulled out my wallet and handed some large bills to Malia. "This should cover it for a while, plus a little extra for all the trouble."

She looked at the money. "This is way too much, Mike."

"I want you to have it."

She shrugged and slid the bills into her pocket.

Minutes later, the twins returned with coolers of food. After everything was loaded we thanked Malia one last time and left. As we started down the road I looked over at Raquel. "This new place sounds interesting."

She squeezed my hand. "As long as we're safe I'll be okay."

"We will be," I assured her. "Everything will be just fine."

And she believed me.

Chapter 36

Ellis Lacorde crouched down and stared through the sliding glass door at Lucas Richter's dog, Phobos. "I think your dog likes me," Lacorde told Richter.

"That's only because you'd make a full meal," Richter replied. Just then, he felt his cell phone buzz and saw it was Derrick Haut calling. He answered, "I hope you have good news, Derrick."

"Hello to you too," Haut replied. "Where are you?"

"I'm sitting at my desk. Why?"

"Is this a secure line?"

"This is an unregistered cell phone, Derrick, and the SIM card doesn't record call histories. But I'm glad you called to ask."

"Actually, I have some good news," Haut said. "As you know, I've been monitoring Raquel Richard's accounts."

"And…?"

"And something's turned up."

"I'm listening."

"Well, I noticed a hold showed up on her checking account for the amount of twenty-two dollars. It was just a hold and not a charge, but I researched it and made some inquiries. It looks like she used a travel account to cover part of a flight."

"A flight to where?"

"That was the hard part, actually. But I was able to use my—"

"Just tell me where she is, Derrick."

"Okay. She's somewhere in Maui."

It was quiet for a moment, so Haut added, "That's an island in Hawaii, and—"

"I know that."

Half-joking, Haut offered, "Maybe I should take the Gulfstream out there and look around."

Richter ignored that and asked, "How about Brennan and the twins? Anything on them yet?"

"Nothing on the twins," Haut replied, "but Brennan is another story."

"What have you got on him?"

"Not a thing—and I mean *zero*."

"What are you talking about?"

"Well, for one thing, it looks like his keystroke log and our spyware was either deleted or disabled. Also, I can't find any financial accounts other than payroll deposits which, by the way, have never been touched. I also checked all the social media sites, his corporate email, and his phone history. Those were all dead ends—"

"So…?"

"So, that tells me he's either a spy or some kind of secret agent."

After a moment of silence Haut asked, "Do you want me to keep monitoring them, or what?"

"Yeah. And call me on this line if anything comes up."

"All right. And by the way, you're welcome."

At that, Richter ended the call.

"What was that all about?" Lacorde asked.

Richter smiled. "Haut managed to track down the girl. She's in Hawaii of all places."

Lacorde thought about that. "The Hamilton twins are from Hawaii. The four of them are probably there together."

"If not, one will lead us to the other. Right?"

Lacorde nodded. "So what's the plan?"

Richter stood from his desk. "I intend to release another media statement offering a reward for information on any one of them."

"Good idea."

Richter continued, "Haut believes Mike Brennan is a spy. If that's true, he probably knows about what happened in the control room. We can also assume he knows about the other rover by now—"

"That explains why he went into hiding," Lacorde said, "which was probably smart."

"Well, he's dragged the twins and little Raquel Richards into all this, which was not so smart."

Richter stepped over to Lacorde and looked him over. "You look like you could use a vacation, my friend. Ever been to Maui?"

Lacorde smiled.

"I need you to head straight there. Do everything you can to hunt down these four as quickly as possible."

"No problem."

"And bring Safire with you."

Right then, the smile disappeared from Lacorde's face.

Chapter 37

Rather than drive straight to the Haiku house, we decided to stop and stock up on extra food and supplies while in Paia. This way we'd avoid having to make a run into town any time soon.

The twins were now TV celebrities. Because of that, I advised them to stay in the car while Raquel and I went into the store, quickly filling two shopping carts with everything we could think of.

Ironically, we wound up with lots of boxed, canned, and long shelf-life items that Raquel had previously referred to as 'garbage.' While we were there, I also grabbed some deli sandwiches, a few pounds of jumbo shrimp, a tub of marinated olives, and some thick steaks. I also remembered to pick up a supply of Mountain Mist for the twins.

At the checkout I paid in cash and gave Raquel some pocket money for herself. After we'd loaded the items into the back of the SUV, we took off for the Haiku house.

It was another warm sunny day and the clouds were few as we traveled west on Hana Highway. Raquel checked the directions Malia had provided, which were mostly landmarks. Before long, we drove past the banana bread stand she'd described, followed by a produce stand and then a cemetery. After another mile or two we spotted a small surfboard rental place that marked the entrance of the Haiku property.

Immediately after the surf shop, I turned left onto a gravel road which led us under a canopy of high shade trees. Before long, we arrived at the entrance gate where I entered the six-digit code into a small security box. The gate slowly opened. After driving through, I continued along the narrow drive for a few minutes until we spotted the cottages in the distance.

Once there, I parked at the end of the circle driveway. The cottages were older wood-framed structures. Two were built on stilts, which was probably a good idea being only a few hundred feet from the shoreline. To my left was a three-car garage. About two hundred feet beyond that I saw a rustic barn in the midst of an empty pasture.

Raquel and I got out and looked around while the twins went straight to the garage. I directed Raquel's attention to the largest cottage. "You and I could share that one," I said, "assuming you're okay with that." We were still on day one of our relationship and I wasn't sure how she'd react to that.

"Let's go check it out first."

Well, that answered that.

We went up the stairs to the door, which was equipped with a keypad similar to the one at the gate. I entered the same six-digit pass code and the lock clicked open. Once inside, we found the furniture had all been moved to the middle of the room and was covered with sheets. The place seemed stuffy and had that old house smell mixed with a new paint smell, which was confusing to the senses.

"It just needs some fresh air," Raquel said. "Let's open some windows."

While she did that, I opened the sliding glass door and stepped out onto the lanai. From there, the view overlooked the ocean, now windswept and dotted with countless whitecaps in every direction.

Raquel called to me, "Mike, come look at this!"

I headed to the bedroom where I found her sitting on an old-style canopy bed draped on all sides with mosquito netting.

"Isn't this beautiful?"

I pulled back the netting and climbed in. Playfully, Raquel backed away until I grabbed her and pulled her close.

She looked into my eyes and we prepared to kiss.

Just then, we heard the sound of footsteps coming up the stairs. As we hurried to climb off the bed we both became tangled in the mosquito netting. She and I pulled and turned until we finally managed to unravel ourselves—and just in time. We tried to appear composed as Kekoa came to the door.

He looked around the room. "Wow, you guys totally scored."

Not quite.

Raquel asked him, "What's your cottage like?"

"Not as nice as this, but it has a fireplace and lots of kitchen stuff."

"Great."

He looked at me. "Kaui and I are going to start bringing some of groceries up here to your kitchen."

"Good. I'll be there to help in just a bit."

Later, while putting the groceries away, I found the keys to the two ATVs and gave them to Kaui and Kekoa. "Be sure to wear helmets," I told them. "If one of you winds up in the hospital our cover will be blown."

Kaui put on a fake smile. "Thanks for your concern."

On the way back to the cottage, I stopped at the car and grabbed my Colt from under the seat and brought it up to the bedroom. Raquel was busy hanging our clothes in the closet, so I slid the gun under a bed pillow to keep it out of sight until I found a better hiding place. From my bag, I removed my Sig .22 along with the boxes of ammo and hid all that in the top drawer of the bedside table.

After everything was put away, Raquel and I grabbed our sunglasses and went downstairs to explore the property. We walked together, hand in hand, down a dirt road that led from the old barn to the ocean. There were wild flowers growing everywhere along with countless palms, ferns, and tropical plants.

Before long, we reached the windy shoreline. There, we walked along a rocky trail until we arrived at a gate at the front of our cottage. We went through the gate and entered the yard where Raquel spotted an old rope hammock tied between two coconut palms.

"I love hammocks," she said.

I helped her climb on and then sat on the grass beside her, giving the hammock a push.

"I think I could get used to this," she told me.

"Me, too."

She looked over at me. "Do you really think I'm pretty?"

I gave the hammock another light push. "If I tell you, you might turn into a vain, egotistical snob."

"Earlier you told me I was beautiful."

"Then you already know."

She gave me a playful slap on the head, which I guess I deserved.

For the next half-hour, Raquel and I talked about all sorts of things, but not about Cronus, or planetary rovers, or about anything to do with what had happened back in Florida. We were enjoying the peace and solitude we'd found here, and enjoying each other's company as well.

After sunset, Raquel and I went to the twin's cottage and helped prepare things a cookout on the patio. The wind had calmed and the clouds were turning from gold to a beautiful violet color.

Under Raquel's close supervision, I grilled some juicy steaks and spicy jumbo shrimp, which came out great. Kaui made local-style steamed rice to go with it. The four of us relaxed on cushioned patio chairs, enjoying our food as the night sky put on a show.

Raquel found a bottle of Chablis and we shared a glass while looking up at the first stars. In the southwestern sky I spotted Venus, the evening star, but chose not to point it out. Before long, a nearly full moon rose up out of the east. The completely full moon, I knew, would occur during my fishing trip tomorrow morning—along with a total lunar eclipse.

I let Raquel know that I'd be up early in the morning and that I expected to be back from my trip by around one p.m. I was looking forward to meeting Chuck and his son and to being out at sea once as well.

After we'd all finished our meals, the twins helped Raquel clean up while I stayed on the patio and relaxed with my feet on an ottoman.

Before long, Raquel returned and sat back down in the chair beside mine. She'd brought a woven blanket from inside and covered herself with it. We held hands and relaxed silently in the cool of the evening, listening to the sound of waves landing on the shore while crickets chirped all around us.

"Sometimes I like it when you shut up," she told me, smiling.

I smiled back. "I was just waiting for my cue."

She leaned closer and asked in a low voice, "Do you remember the first time we met?"

"I do," I replied. "I'd come over to the twin's place with Chinese food and you happened to be there. I gave you my meal and told you I'd already eaten—though I was starving."

"So, you lied to me right off the bat?"

I smiled and continued, "That night, you wore your hair pulled back and you took off your glasses right after I arrived. You were wearing a turtleneck sweater and baggy grey pants that looked like pajamas—"

"Those *were* pajamas. I was staying at the twin's and sleeping on their couch because—"

"Because your apartment was being fumigated."

She looked at me. "I'm surprised you remember all that."

I made no reply and went back to listening to crickets.

After a moment, she leaned toward me again and whispered, "Thank you."

"For the Chinese food?"

"No, for remembering."

On the patio table, the twins had managed to get a small twelve-volt TV working using an extension cord from one of the special outlets inside the house.

Kekoa looked over at me. "Good thing we have a wind turbine, huh?"

"Yeah. Otherwise you'd be watching TV by candlelight."

Raquel suppressed a grin, then looked at me. "I think I'll go lie down."

That was the cue I was waiting for.

Chapter 38

Tonight, I was going undercover.

I followed Raquel to our cottage. Once upstairs, I excused myself and headed to the bathroom where I took a moment to brush my teeth, fix my hair, and practice my best sexy expression in the mirror. I took off my shirt but kept my shorts on.

Despite what women say, every man knows the first 'encounter' can make or break a relationship. Talk about pressure. I wasn't nervous, but I could feel my heart starting to beat in a funny way.

As I stepped out of the bathroom, I saw Raquel had turned off the lights and had lit a scented candle, which she'd placed on the bedside table. A golden glow emitted from the flame and flickered nicely across the walls and ceiling of the room.

Without a word, she stepped over to me and I took her into my arms. As I ran my hands through her long hair, I detected the faint scent of her perfume. It was lovely. As we began to kiss our bodies drew closer. After a while, I moved my hand under her shirt and felt the smooth warm skin of her back and shoulders.

Suddenly she pulled away. She stood and looked at me for a few seconds and I wasn't sure what to expect. To my surprise, she pulled off her shirt and tossed it to the floor. She posed for me for a moment, allowing me to admire her as the soft light of the candle illuminated her sleek body, her dark hair, and her beautiful skin. She hesitated for another moment, then slowly unbuttoned her shorts and slid them, one inch at a time, over her hips until they finally fell to her feet. I took her into my arms once again.

As I held her close, I felt her tremble and could tell she was nervous. She looked up at me and we began to kiss while our hands ran over each other's necks, backs, and shoulders.

She pulled away from me once again and stepped over to the bed. There, she drew the mosquito netting aside and pulled the sheets down, then crawled onto the bed and positioned herself, waiting for me.

I remembered to use my sexy expression as I took off my watch and set it on the bedside table. I'd read an article once about how it's supposed to be a turn-on for women when a man undresses slowly. That may be true, but I've found I have only one speed. I dropped my shorts and pulled the netting aside.

I climbed onto the bed. While Raquel repositioned herself, her hand happened to slide under one of the pillows. As bad luck would have it, this was the same pillow where I'd hidden my gun. She grabbed the weapon and looked at it, then dropped it and pushed it away.

"What's *that* doing here?"

You'd think she'd found an atom bomb. Wasting no time, I grabbed the gun and placed it into the top drawer of the bedside table, alongside my .22. I then turned to her and smiled as if nothing had happened.

She held out her hand. "That's yours? What are you doing with that thing?"

"I forgot that I put it there."

"I hate guns."

I needed to sound like the good guy here, so I told her, "I hate guns too. But lately I feel like we need some kind of protection." I looked her in the eye. "I'm just thinking of you and the twins."

She thought about it. "Well…just promise you'll never use it."

"Okay, I promise." You'll never use it.

After that, I scooted close and pulled one of the sheets over my hip. I wove my fingers gently through her hair, which reached all the way to her tiny waist. I could tell she was still ruffled from the handgun incident, so I proceeded carefully.

I felt the warm sea air as it flowed through the open window and mixed with the flowery scent of the burning candle. From outside I could hear the faint sound of waves as they rolled gently upon the shore.

Before long, our lips fell together again and I felt the energy between us return. This was exciting, but after a few minutes I felt it was time to move into unexplored territory. I repositioned myself, and soon after that our relationship entered a new phase.

After we'd finished, I rested my head on top of her and listened to her heartbeat. My normal senses and functions began to come back as blood flow slowly returned to my brain.

Raquel let out a faint laugh.

"What?"

"We're both so out of breath—and we're soaked."

"I didn't sweat at all."

"Then why are you all wet?"

"That's from you sweating on me," I replied. "C'mon, let's rinse off before we pass out."

Our legs were still shaking. Nonetheless, we managed to make it to the shower. After soaping each other and rinsing off, we headed back to the bed where we tossed the soaked sheets to the floor and passed out.

Chapter 39

Sunday, April 25, 2032

My watch alarm went off at 3:30 a.m. I slid silently out of bed. I stood and glanced over at Raquel, who looked like an angel sound asleep. I smiled to myself. Somehow, I felt more happy and excited about life than I had in a long while. At the same time I was aware that when everything seems to be coming your way, you might be in the wrong lane.

Cool air drifted through the open window, chilling my skin. I slapped on my watch and went to the closet where I quietly sifted through my clothes. I decided on cargo shorts and a white t-shirt along with my windbreaker and the ball cap I'd borrowed. I cautiously removed my Colt Mustang from the drawer in the bedside table and wrapped it in a t-shirt, then grabbed my wallet, my sunglasses, plus a bottle of water from the fridge and slipped out the door.

After stopping for coffee, I drove straight to Kahului Harbor where I met up with Chuck and his son. The three of us transferred the boat into the water and made some final preparations. While the motors warmed up, we mounted and readied the outriggers and checked the lights, radio, and gauges. Finally, we placed four heavy rods and reels into their mounts, fastening each with a lanyard.

Before long, we were sailing slowly toward the mouth of the harbor. The light of the full moon sliced through the blackened sky, casting my shadow against the white deck. The temperature was cool and the water was remarkably calm. It felt good to be at sea once again, and I was looking forward to taking my mind off Raquel and Malia and Cronus and…everything.

I took a moment to study some of the boat's features and the tackle. I saw the transom had a small door on the starboard side. There were two gaffs stored along the starboard side of the deck as well as a short wooden club in a storage bin at the stern. I studied the club for a moment and was reminded of the dream I'd had a few nights earlier. I made a mental note not to bring a shark onboard.

Chuck's son, Chas, opened a large pouch containing an assortment of large jet lures. "Go ahead and choose," he told me.

After studying the selection, I picked out a pair of bright orange lures and a silver one and handed them to Chas, who nodded in approval. As he began attaching those to the lines on the port side, I spotted a worn-looking weathered lure strung together using a chrome-plated steel head. It had lurid-looking grey eyes and razor-sharp hooks hidden under a tattered black rubber skirt.

Chas noticed my last selection and gave me a nod. "You know how to pick 'em, Mike. That one's got some history behind it."

"Good. Let's hope history repeats itself."

Once we had all the lines in the water, I pulled a few bills from my wallet and handed them to Chas. "Here's a little something," I said to him.

"Thanks." He slid the bills into his pocket and asked, "So, what kind of work do you do, Mike?"

I used my standard lie. "I'm in the corporate security and data protection business."

His dad heard that and turned to me. "I bet that's a busy business," he said. "Every day I read about another corporation losing all of its secrets to spies and computer hackers." He added, "I'm always glad when they nail one of those jerks."

It's sad for me to think how the spy profession has developed such a negative public image. In truth, not all spies are jerks. It's the ninety-nine percent of them that give the rest of us a bad name.

As we continued into deeper seas, I looked up and saw the edge of the moon had already begun to dim from the shadow of the Earth. I pointed this out to Chuck and Chas. The three of us watched as the shadow crept slowly across the lunar surface until the moon was fully eclipsed.

I noticed the sea now appeared black as ink. For a moment, I had an eerie feeling and a chill ran up my spine. Somehow, I felt as though a page had turned and a new chapter—a dark chapter—had now begun.

After some time, the eclipse passed and the setting moon finally fell behind the West Maui Mountains. After that, we saw the first light of dawn on the horizon. As we watched, the sky slowly turned a deep and conspicuous crimson hue.

Chas looked over at me. "Red sky at night, sailor's delight. Red sky in morning—"

"Sailors take warning," I said, completing the ancient rhyme. We watched quietly as the color of blood covered the eastern sky until the sun finally peeked over the clouds.

Right then, the VHF radio broke the silence with an announcement:

This is US Coast Guard Station Maui…An urgent marine weather message has been issued by the National Weather Service…Small craft advisory is now in effect for all Maui County windward and leeward waters until further notice…This is US Coast Guard Station Maui…Out.

Chuck turned to his son. "So, what do we do?"

Chas thought for a few seconds. "It looks like clear skies," he said. "But we'd better not risk it. Let's head back to the harbor."

His dad shook his head. "We're having all the luck today, aren't we?"

"Yeah. When it rains it pours," Chas replied.

And he was right about that.

Chapter 40

Raquel felt exhilarated with the morning sun to her back and the cool wind in her hair. She held on to Kekoa as he raced to keep up with his brother. He pushed the throttle further as he steered the ATV around a curve and then through a deep puddle.

"Hey, I'm getting wet!" she told Kekoa while trying to speak over the sound of the motor.

He eased off the throttle. "Is that better?"

"I guess so," she said, wiping her face. "Just don't go too fast. I don't have a helmet or goggles, remember?"

He continued slowly until they'd reached the security gate near Hana Highway. There, they began to turn around.

Raquel tapped Kekoa on his shoulder. "Hold on a sec. Is that place open?"

Up ahead was a dilapidated wooden building decorated with bamboo and old palm leaves. A sign on the highway read 'Island-Style Surf School & Rentals.'

"I want to see if they rent stand-up paddleboards," she said. "Let's find out."

They parked their ATVs to the side of the dirt road and walked around the gate and to the building. On the front porch they encountered a young man, thin and tanned, wearing grey shorts and a t-shirt with the business logo printed on back. He introduced himself as Ian.

"You guys are early birds," Ian said. "I just opened."

Raquel pointed to a wide, thick board with padding. "That one's a stand-up paddleboard, right? Do you rent those?"

"Yeah. Have you paddled before?"

"Just once."

"Well, that's a great board for beginners," he said to her. "You can try it out right over there if you like." He pointed to a small but pretty beach cove, Hoolawa Bay, which was only a few hundred feet up the road. "It looks like you might have the place all to yourself."

Raquel thought for a moment. "Maybe I'll come back later. I don't have a bathing suit with me."

"We have some nice bathing suits in the shop."

"My size?"

Ian looked her over. "Yeah, we've got lots of tiny ones."

The twins followed Raquel into the small shop, leaving Ian outside to finish setting up.

As Raquel began combing through a rack of bikinis, Kekoa asked her, "Are you sure Mike would be okay with this?"

She shrugged. "We can all rent boards if you want to come."

"Kaui and I don't paddle," he replied. "Besides, we can't leave the ATVs parked on the road."

"I'll be fine," she said. She lowered her voice and explained, "I'll pay for the bathing suit and the board rental with cash, so that won't be a problem. Besides, I think Mike is more worried about you two, especially after that news report."

Just as Ian entered the store, Kekoa told Raquel, "So, we'll come back and pick you up at what, nine o'clock?"

"Make it 9:30—and thanks."

The twins exited while Raquel picked out a bikini and placed it on the counter along with a beach towel. "I'll take these," she told Ian, "and the board rental." She removed her wallet from her pocket.

"Okay then." He tapped at his register for a moment. "That'll be…two-hundred eighty-five dollars, please." He smiled and added, "I gave you a discount."

"Thank you." She pulled out a few bills. As she did so, Ian looked at her open wallet and happened to catch a glimpse of her citizen card.

After the transaction was completed he pointed to a small, curtained closet. "You can change in there if you want."

Raquel went in and removed her clothes and changed into the bikini. She looked at herself in the dirty mirror, admiring her thin body and pretty legs, then giggled at her own silliness and stepped out of the dressing room.

She folded her jeans and t-shirt neatly and asked, "Do you have somewhere I can keep these while I'm paddling?"

Ian's eyes locked onto her body. "Wow. I like how that looks on you."

"Do you have somewhere I can keep these?" she repeated.

"Oh yeah, of course." He took the items and placed them below the counter. "Oh, one more thing," he said. "I'll need to hold onto your citizen card while you're out there. Company policy."

"I don't have my card with me. Is that okay?"

He let that roll around in his head for a moment. "Yeah, it's all right. You look like the kind of person I can trust." After that, he followed her outside where he helped her select a paddle and offered to carry the board down to the beach.

Raquel followed Ian to the cove where he set the board near the water's edge. There, Raquel removed her sandals and fastened the leash strap to her ankle, then looked out at the aqua-blue cove as it sparkled in the rays of the early morning sun, silently inviting her to enter.

"Anything else?" Ian asked while taking another look at her.

"No, but thanks, Ian." She lifted the board by the center handgrip and carried it into the water where she began to paddle out into the cove.

Back at the shop, Ian checked that no one was around and then took Raquel's clothes from under the counter. He put his nose to her t-shirt and breathed in her subtle scent. After that, he carefully unfolded her jeans and removed the wallet from one of her back pockets. Tucked inside was her citizen card. He glanced at it for a second, then placed it onto the copy machine behind him and pressed SCAN.

"Company policy," he said to himself.

After that, he carefully returned the wallet with the card to the back pocket, refolded the jeans, and placed them as they were below the counter along with her t-shirt.

Out of curiosity, he decided to type her name into his computer's search engine. *Raquel Richards*, he thought as he looked at the letters on the screen. *Sexy name.*

He then pressed ENTER.

Chapter 41

Lucas Richter's cell phone buzzed. He saw the incoming call was from Derrick Haut and answered it. "What have you got?"

"Well, besides a headache I think I have a possible lead."

"Okay…"

Haut explained, "I'm monitoring everything I can think of over here. I have IP trackers going like I'd told you about, and a hit just came in."

"Did we find them?"

"Not exactly, but what I found is better than nothing. According to my radar, someone in Maui, Hawaii just did an internet search on the name Raquel Richards."

"Perfect. Can you tell who it came from?"

"Actually, yes. I have an IP address and an Internet Protocol number. From what my geolocation software tells me it's registered to a business by the name of Island-Style Surf School & Rentals."

"Excellent. Our team is in Maui already. We've just been waiting for Brennan or one of them to slip up."

"Well, they just did."

"Can you find me an exact location, like a street address?"

"I'm way ahead of you," Haut said. "I just did a simple search and came up with the geographic location. The place is located on State Road 360 in the town of Haiku. The address is 6272 Hana Highway."

Richter scribbled the information down. "Got it."

"So…do I keep the search going, or what?"

Richter thought for a moment. "Actually, I need you to pack your stuff right away. You and I are going on a trip."

"Now? Where are we headed?"

"Washington, D.C. I have a meeting scheduled there this afternoon and I need you to be there, just in case."

"In case of what?"

"I'll explain everything when we arrive in D.C. We're taking the Gulfstream, so the flight will be short, probably under an hour. I'll pick you up in thirty minutes, so be ready to go."

"Thirty minutes?"

"That's right. By the way, pack some clothes that look like something I'd wear. You might need to impersonate me." He then ended the call.

Impersonate him? Haut thought. *What am I getting myself into?* He plugged his phone and tablet into their chargers and began packing.

Chapter 42

Ellis Lacorde pulled over and parked outside Island-Style Surf School & Rentals. He removed his handgun from its hiding place and slid it into his left pant pocket before stepping out of the car. He looked around and saw no other cars around and no other businesses or buildings in either direction.

Perfect, Lacorde thought. He put on his gloves and walked to the shop.

Inside, Ian was seated behind the counter reading a magazine. He looked up at Lacorde as he entered. "Aloha. Can I help you?"

Lacorde smiled and stepped over to the counter. "Maybe you can. A lady friend of mine by the name of Raquel Richards mentioned she was planning to stop by here. She's a tiny thing. Have you seen her?"

Ian studied Lacorde for a few seconds. "Yeah. She rented a board about an hour ago." He pointed to the window. "She's right down there paddling in the cove."

Lacorde glanced out the window. "Excellent."

"If you want to join her, I have boards for rent—"

"No, thanks. I'm more of a swimmer."

"No problem. Is there anything you might need? Sunscreen? Maybe a beach towel?"

Lacorde reached into his pocket and gripped his gun. Using his thumb he flipped the safety lever to the fire position. "A towel, perhaps."

Ian grabbed a beach towel from behind the counter and began to click at the register. "Will this be on a credit card?"

"That depends. Do you accept Smith & Wesson?"

"Excuse me?"

Lacorde pulled out the gun and pointed it at Ian's face. He waited a few seconds to savor the moment, then pulled the trigger.

As the shot exploded, Ian fell back, crashing onto the printer station behind him. He then slid off and dropped to the floor, dead.

Lacorde glanced behind the counter at Ian's now lifeless body. With a grin, he took the towel from the counter and headed out, flipping the Open sign to Closed and locking the door behind him. Seeing no one around he walked to his car where he hid the gun. He then removed all his clothing and placed the items onto the back seat. After that, he wrapped the beach towel around his waist and pressed a number on his cell.

Safire answered. "Where are you at?"

"I'm close to the girl," Lacorde said. "She's by herself."

"I'll come help you."

"No. I'll take care of it. Just wait for me where I told you. After that—"

"What do you plan to do?"

"I'll handle this, all right? After I find out from the girl where they're staying I'll meet you at the parking lot at Twin Falls. From there we'll go after Brennan and the two brothers."

"Perhaps you should try to capture the girl," Safire suggested. "Richter wants Brennan alive, so why not use the girl as bait?"

Lacorde made no reply.

She added, "He's coming here, you know."

"Who's coming?"

"Richter."

Lacorde was surprised at that. "Is he out of his mind? Why would he risk coming all the way here?"

"All I know is that he plans to extract some kind of information from Brennan."

Lacorde let out a breath. "He's getting out of hand."

"If this is too difficult for you, Ellis, perhaps I should—"

"Enough!" he shouted. "I'll take care of it." He ended the call and stopped himself from crushing the phone in his hand. *What am I getting myself into?* he thought.

He locked the car and headed for the beach, the grin now gone from his face.

Chapter 43

Ellis Lacorde looked out over the tranquil water of the cove as it glistened before him. He checked his watch. 8:47 a.m. *It was going to be a long day,* he thought, *but so far, so good.*

He dropped his towel to the sand and stood unclothed at the water's edge. He watched young Raquel Richards as she paddled along the far end of the lagoon. He rehearsed in his mind what he would say to her, then strode into the water and began swimming out to the center of the cove.

After swimming out about one-hundred yards, Lacorde noticed Raquel had changed direction and their paths would soon cross. Moments later, as she approached, he called to her, "It's beautiful here, isn't it?"

Raquel stopped paddling and looked over at Lacorde. "Yeah. It's incredible."

While treading water, Lacorde told her, "The water is so clear. My wife and kids would love this place. I've gotta bring them down here to see this."

"Where are they?"

He smiled and joked, "They're probably still asleep."

Raquel smiled politely.

Lacorde continued, "Actually, my wife hates the hotel we're at and she wants me to find somewhere else for us to stay. Are there any decent places in this area?"

"Not really," Raquel replied. "My friends and I are visitors and we're staying at an oceanfront property located over there.'" She pointed in the general direction of the Haiku house. "It's a private residence though."

"Must be nice."

She ignored that and told him, "There aren't too many hotels in this part of the island."

"Oh, well." He swam a few strokes, positioning himself closer to the front of her board. "You're probably here with your husband or boyfriend, right? He should be out here with you."

"He would be," she answered, "but he was invited to go deep sea fishing on the North Shore today." She turned and looked out at the open ocean. "He's out there somewhere."

Lacorde moved even closer. "I'd love to squeeze in a fishing trip while I'm here. What boat is he on?"

Raquel hesitated, noticing only now that Lacorde was naked. She turned her head away. "I have no idea."

Lacorde scanned the shore, checking again to be sure there was no one watching. He then grabbed the front of her board and pushed it forcefully, causing Raquel to lose her balance and fall forward. She let go of her paddle and tumbled headfirst into the water. Lacorde took a deep breath and dove under. Wasting no time, he grabbed her by the back of her hair and wrapped his legs around her small torso and squeezed hard—forcing the air from her lungs.

In horror, she tried desperately to writhe and squirm from his grip.

Using his powerful arms, he took hold of her head and twisted it sharply. Raquel's thin arms swung about and her legs kicked for a moment, then stopped as she gurgled a silent cry for help.

Lacorde held her under until he was certain she was dead. Finally, he let go and swam to the surface where he gasped for air, feeling exhausted and light-headed from the brief struggle. While catching his breath he glanced at his watch. It was nine o'clock on the dot.

After he'd regained his strength he swam straight for shore. Once there, he toweled himself off while he looked back out at the water. In the distance, he spotted Raquel's paddleboard. Just then, a gust of cold wind blew over the cove and chilled his body as he watched the board drifting aimlessly, alone in the midst of the cove.

A wide grin slowly returned to his face.

Chapter 44

C huck continued in the direction of Kahului Harbor while Chas and I reset the lines.

Suddenly, a cold wind came from the north and I felt an icy chill run up my spine. I turned into the wind to see a dark ominous-looking cloud formation in the distance. I glanced at my watch. It was exactly nine o'clock.

I told Chas, "Looks like trouble on the horizon." I directed his attention to the storm clouds.

He looked for a moment and I could tell he was concerned. "We need to start bringing the lines in," he said. "The sooner we get to the harbor the better."

Before I could agree with that, the starboard side forward line popped from the outrigger and the reel began to empty its line into the sea.

"That's yours!" Chas told me.

Quickly, I positioned myself behind the reel and adjusted the drag knob behind the crank. The reel clicked away as the powerful fish began pulling precious feet of line out further and further.

Chuck eased back the throttle levers while Chas began bringing the other lines in.

The fish put up a fight and began to bring the line from the stern to the port side. I managed to turn the crank handle a few turns while Chuck did a good job of positioning the boat, keeping the line behind us. The spool grew smaller while I adjusted the drag further. Eventually, I was able to start turning the crank. Before long, my arms began to ache while beads of sweat mixed with sunscreen ran into my eyes.

While I worked the reel, Chas stood at the stern and watched the battle with a gaff in his hand. Suddenly, the fish surfaced. "It looks like an Ahi," Chas announced. "A big one."

I rubbed some of the sweat from my eyes and began to tell him, "Go ahead and open the door on the…" Just then, I saw it. A large grey fin emerged from behind the Ahi. Before I could think or react, the creature darted forward and lunged, mouth wide open. With a quick and fluid movement, it engulfed half of the Ahi in its rows of teeth, then disappeared into the deep. After that, I saw nothing but a splash and some bubbles in the blood red water.

Chas looked at me, and we were both stunned.

He and I stood there for a moment, watching what was left of my fish skipping over the surface of the water.

Chuck turned and looked at us. "What happened?"

"I hate to tell you this," I replied, "but a shark just snipped the thing in half."

He put the motors in neutral and stepped back to the deck. "You'd better reel in what's left before he comes back for seconds."

Following his advice, I reeled in the carcass as fast as I could and dropped it into the boat, splashing blood and entrails across the deck. After removing the lure, the three of us took a moment to study the bite pattern.

"That was a big daddy," Chuck said. "Probably a ten footer."

I figured the Ahi was probably over seventy pounds. Before it was downsized, that is.

After Chas and I had slid the fish into the icebox, the radio came on again, repeating the small craft advisory. This was followed by some chatter back and forth. The entire communication was broken up by static and radio interference, but Chuck thought it sounded like someone was trying to report a drowning.

Before we reached the harbor at Kahului the sun had disappeared behind dark clouds. At the same time a light drizzle had begun to fall.

"Sorry we had to cut it short," Chas told me. He held out the bills I'd given him earlier. "No charge for today."

"Keep it," I insisted. "It's gas money. Besides, this will probably be the only time I'll be able to say I caught half a fish."

Chas grinned at that and put the money back in his pocket.

After we'd pulled to the dock and tied up, Chuck looked again at the black clouds forming over our heads. "This looks scary," he said.

I nodded in agreement. "This is the calm before the storm."

Chapter 45

The limo came to an abrupt stop in front of Washington D.C.'s Sofitel Hotel. Within seconds a valet arrived and opened the door for Derrick Haut. Lucas Richter had already climbed out, so the valet went to the rear of the vehicle and began to unload the luggage from the trunk.

The two men were dressed in fine business suits and overcoats. As they entered the hotel lobby, Haut turned to Richter and asked, "I appreciate you bringing me along, Lucas, but I still don't understand what we're doing here. What's our plan, anyway?"

Richter stopped walking and explained in a low voice, "I think Brennan is in Maui, and I'm heading there."

Haut looked around. "Well, it's a good thing we're here in Washington—or is that part of the plan?"

"I'm only here for one reason," Richter said. "I need to establish a credible alibi. I had the plane return to Florida to make it appear that I'd stayed here for a meeting with—"

"Let me guess—a politician?"

"Right. Our good friend, Representative James Trench." Richter looked around for a moment, then lowered his voice and continued, "Trench is the ranking member on the Subcommittee on Space and Aeronautics."

"That great, Lucas."

"But I won't actually be meeting with him."

Haut gave him a look. "I hope you don't expect *me* to do that. Is that why you dragged me here?"

"Of course not. Trench will be in California for the next few days, so our meeting tomorrow won't be taking place. I'll blame it on a scheduling mix-up and head to Maui on a charter while you stay here in D.C." He added, "I'll try to be back by Tuesday."

"Tuesday? What am I supposed to do until then?"

"You'll be occupying my room so it looks like I'm here."

"What?"

"Just look at this as an opportunity to relax, Derrick. Read a book. Order room service a few times. Just try not to be seen up close and remember to avoid video cameras and—"

"So, this is my prison?"

Richter ignored that and continued, "It would be a good idea to use the hotel wake-up service. No matter what, don't use your own cell phone or credit card for *anything*."

Haut out his hand. "Do you have any cash?"

Richter exhaled loudly. He pulled a few big bills from his wallet and handed them to Haut. "For the sake of phone records, be sure to make some calls to Cronus from the room. But only call numbers you know won't be answered. If you *must* leave the room, try to dress as I would."

"By overdressing, you mean?"

Richter exhaled again. "Basically, Derrick, use your smarts and don't leave a trail of any kind—except that of Lucas Richter, understand?"

Haut, having no choice, agreed.

Richter looked around. "I need to figure out a simple way to mark my presence here."

"I noticed a fire hydrant outside."

Richter ignored that. "Stand by the elevator and wait to follow me to the room," he said. "And watch out for that camera." He pointed to a small surveillance camera behind the check-in desk. He then headed there.

The desk clerk, a middle-aged woman, smiled and greeted Richter as he approached, "Welcome to the Sofitel, sir. Will you be checking in?"

"Yes." He removed his citizen card from his wallet and handed it to the clerk. "I'm Lucas Richter of Cronus Aerospace. I'd like to speak with the manager if that's possible."

"I'm the manager. Is there a problem?"

"I'm afraid there is. I called here twice to check my reservation. Both times the phone disconnected."

"I'm terribly sorry about that sir," the manager said. "You can fill out a complaint form if you like and I'll check into the problem." She opened a complaint form on a tablet and slid it in front of Richter. "For your trouble, may I offer you a room upgrade? At no additional cost, of course."

"That would be fine."

After completing the check-in, Richter followed the valet to the room, a deluxe suite located on the top floor overlooking Lafayette Square.

After the valet had left, Haut came to the room. He looked around at the plush accommodations. "A penthouse suite. Nice work with the upgrade, Lucas."

Richter nodded. "This will be your home until Tuesday. Try to enjoy it." He turned and headed to the door.

"You're leaving?"

"I have a plane to catch, remember?"

"And you plan to travel all the way to Hawaii unnoticed?"

"I have another jet waiting thirty minutes from here," Richter replied. "As you know, chartered aircraft aren't required to keep a roster of their passengers. We'll be in Maui by 9: 30 p.m., Hawaii Time."

"Who's 'we?'"

Richter cleared his throat. "Ellis's brothers, Luis and Max, will be traveling with me. Plus a trusted associate of theirs."

"Those hoodlums? I thought they were in jail."

"Not anymore." Richter looked into Haut's eyes. "Let's just make sure the two of *us* stay out of jail, Derrick. We can't afford any screw-ups."

Haut shook his head. "This whole thing keeps getting worse every time I turn around—and now I find out we're teaming up with Lacorde's idiot brothers? Do you even know what you're doing?"

Richter turned and stepped over to the window. "I know what I'm doing, Derrick. You'll see." He looked down at the famous landmark and statue below. "In his time, many considered Lafayette to be a traitor, a conspirator, and a criminal."

"You and I are not defenders of liberty," Haut told him. "We're basically thieves trying to steal a planetary rover and bring it to Earth—while at the same time killing everyone you and Lacorde think—"

"Enough!" Richter shouted. "You don't understand, Derrick. It's not just a planetary rover we're talking about—"

"Oh, excuse me; it's another 'Rita,' right? A magical mystery machine sent by aliens. Oh, and the key to all the technology of the universe, right?"

Richter stared out the window. "We both need to be on the same page, Derrick, or this will never work."

"The same page? Look, Lucas, this whole thing is spinning out of control, and we—"

"Maybe *you're* out of control!" Richter shouted. He then looked at Haut and warned him, "Before I leave this room, Derrick, I need to know that I can trust you." He stepped away from the window and stood in front of Haut. "If you don't have the backbone for this, just say so right now."

Haut made no reply.

Richter stepped closer and continued, "I just need you to cover for me for a couple of days in case I need an alibi. After everything you and I have been through, is that too much to ask?"

"I'm fine with that, Lucas, I just think—"

"By the time I return there will be nothing to stop us from bringing to Earth that…what did you call it? An alien magic…?"

"A magical mystery machine."

"Right. Well, there will be nothing to stop us from bringing it here from Venus. Once we have it in our possession and unveil all its secrets, you and I will be in position to change the world." He looked closely at Haut. "Is that too much to hope for?"

Haut hesitated for a moment, then replied, "No, I suppose it's not."

"Are we together on this?"

Haut hesitated, then nodded.

The two shook hands. Then, without another word, Richter exited the room.

After the door shut, Haut shook his head and said in a low voice, "I hope you know what you're doing, Lucas." He noticed his hands were shaking and whispered to himself, "More so, I hope I know what *I'm* doing."

Chapter 46

From the cove, Lacorde drove the short distance to Twin Falls where Safire was waiting for him. He parked next to her car and stepped out. With his door open, he dropped his wet towel to the ground, then removed his clothes from the back seat and began to dress himself.

Safire turned and saw his large naked body as he bent over. She quickly looked away.

After he'd finished dressing, Lacorde went to the passenger side of Safire's car and climbed in.

"Was that necessary?" she asked.

"Dressing myself? Why? Would you prefer seeing me in the nude?"

"You should learn to be more civilized."

Lacorde ignored that and informed her, "The girl is dead."

"You fool!" she snapped. "What good did it do to kill her?"

Lacorde looked into the mirror on his sun visor and straightened his hair.

Safire went on, "Use your head. The girl could have been used to capture Brennan. Now you have ruined it. You forget it is Brennan that we—"

"The girl told me everything," Lacorde interjected, "including where Brennan is right now *and* the location where they're staying." He gave her a look and added, "It would have been more foolish to let her live."

After that, he turned his attention to the in-dash tablet and began studying a local map, searching for harbors and boat launches in the area.

"What are you looking for?"

After tapping the touch-screen a few more times he replied, "Brennan is on a fishing boat right now, somewhere right out there." He pointed to a map of Maui's north shore. "According to this, there's only one harbor on this part of the island, Kahului Harbor, and that's where I'm heading right now." He turned to Safire and grinned. "I'll be waiting for him when he arrives."

"And what about the twin brothers—?"

"That's where you earn your paycheck, sweetheart." Lacorde tapped again at the screen, changing the map to satellite view. "The girl told me they're staying at a residential home right here." He pointed to a spot on the map.

While Safire studied the screen, she mentioned, "Never call me 'sweetheart' again, or I will kill you." She then zoomed in on the road and the structures around the area that Lacorde had pointed out.

Lacorde cleared his throat. "Kaui and Kekoa Hamilton should be there."

Safire studied the map further. "What is this building near the highway?"

Lacorde recognized it. "That's a small surf shop," he replied. "The guy who worked there ID'd the girl to me after she'd rented a surfboard."

"You spoke with him?"

"Don't worry about him," Lacorde said. "He's been taken care of."

Safire shot him a glance. "I hope you left no evidence behind."

He thought for a moment. "Nothing at the scene, but I have my gun, plus some gloves and a towel in my car."

"You are so stupid! Dispose of all that."

"But what about—?"

"There are two handguns in a bag under your seat. Take one of them."

Lacorde noticed a light drizzle had begun and droplets were accumulating on the windshield. He reached under his seat and grabbed the bag. Inside, he found a pair of chrome-plated handcuffs with keys as well as two identical handguns with extra clips. He also found a wallet which he opened, revealing a gold-plated FBI badge. "FBI, huh? Are you an agent?"

Safire glared at him again. "Try not to be such an idiot, Ellis. It is annoying."

"Where'd you find the badge?"

"It's from a dead man, okay? Do I ask you stupid questions?"

Ignoring that, he picked up one of the handguns and studied it, noticing that the end of the barrel had been threaded for a silencer. "What is this, a .22?"

"Those are Walther P22's," she replied. "I saved your life with a gun identical to those. Perhaps you remember?"

He recalled that Safire had once expertly dropped a security guard from eighty feet away while firing from inside her car. He slid the gun and one of the clips into his pocket.

As he climbed out of the car, Safire mentioned, "I hope you know not to use that on Brennan. Richter wants him alive."

"That much I know." He looked back at her and added, "The gun is just for persuasion,"—he smiled and gave her a wink—"sweetheart." He closed the door and laughed to himself as he walked back to his car.

Lacorde started his car and left for Kahului Harbor while Safire headed off in the opposite direction. After driving only a short distance, she turned left at the surf shop and soon arrived at the security gate. She studied the entry keypad for a moment, then placed the vehicle in drive, hit the accelerator, and drove forward into the gate—ripping the electric latch and opener mechanisms off their mounting brackets. The gate flung open as she drove through.

Thick clouds had gathered overhead, darkening the sky while a heavy dampness began to fall over the northern shoreline. The light drizzle continued as Safire proceeded along the gravel road. Before long she arrived at the cottages where she holstered her weapon under her jacket and placed the handcuffs and FBI badge in her pocket. She then stepped out of the vehicle and took a moment to study her surroundings. It was quiet and there was no sign of anyone around. She looked and noticed that the garage door had been left open and there were tracks left behind from the ATVs.

She headed first to the largest cottage. At the top of the stairs, she knocked on the door. After waiting a moment, she braced herself against the handrail and used both legs to kick the door open.

Once inside she immediately began searching. In the bedroom closet she found a bag with several passports and wallets. As she looked them over she heard the sound of a motorized vehicle in the distance. She stood and stepped over to an open window where she listened carefully, immediately recognizing the distinct sound of an ATV.

With the bag in hand, Safire darted downstairs to her car where she quickly jumped in and headed in the direction of the ATV. As she rounded a curve, she spotted Kekoa ahead of her on his Honda.

Safire sounded her horn, and Kekoa looked back to see he was being pursued. He also saw the driver was holding a badge out her window and waving for him to stop.

He considered fleeing. Instead, however, he slowed and pulled off to the side of the road.

Safire skidded to a stop and jumped out of the car. Immediately, she raised her weapon and walked directly toward Kekoa.

"FBI," she called out, still holding the badge. "Put your hands behind your head and step away from the vehicle."

Kekoa climbed off the ATV.

With her gun aimed at his head she asked, "What is your name?"

"Kekoa Hamilton."

"Thank goodness." She lowered her gun and put on a smile. "Your friend Mike Brennan sent me here to find you."

"Why did he—?"

"Just do what I say. Understand?"

Kekoa nodded and asked, "Where's Mike?"

"No questions!" She retrieved the handcuff set from her jacket pocket and tossed them to Kekoa. "Attach one side to your wrist. Quickly!"

He looked at the handcuffs. "Why do I need these?"

"Just do what I say. There's no time to explain."

Kekoa fastened the cuff as she'd instructed.

"Now, turn your back to me and put both hands behind yourself. I need you to remain handcuffed until we rendezvous with the others." She assured him, "This is for your protection."

"Protection from whom?"

"Please. Just do what I say and turn around."

As Kekoa did so, Safire stepped forward cautiously and secured the cuffs. She then opened the trunk of her car and moved her rifle and gear bag from there to the rear seat. "Step backward now," she ordered, "and don't make any sudden moves."

"Backward? What are you—?"

"No questions!"

Kekoa took a few steps backward while Safire returned her weapon to its holster. When he was close to the rear of the vehicle, she moved to where they faced each other. Only then did Kekoa recognize her facial features from Mike's security video.

"You! You're Safire, aren't you?"

Before he could think of what to do, she thrust her knee into his groin. At the same time, she rammed the palm of her hand under his chin. His jaw slammed shut as he tumbled backward into the truck.

He was stunned for a second, and in pain, but still managed to struggle as Safire attempted to shut the trunk lid. Using both legs, he pushed her back, causing her to fall to the ground. Before he could pull himself out of the trunk, however, he saw that she'd rolled and jumped back to her feet. In a blur of motion she darted at him, spinning in the air and then kicking him solidly in the chest with the heel of her boot. The wind was knocked from his lungs as he landed inside the trunk once again. Before he could fight, she pulled her gun and pointed it at his face.

"Stay where you are," she told him, "or I will shoot you in the head and leave you here in the road."

Kekoa looked into Safire's cold eyes and could tell she meant it. Slowly, he pulled his legs inside and she slammed the trunk lid shut. Seconds later, Safire climbed behind the wheel and began driving.

In his dark prison, Kekoa began to tremble as feelings of confinement and fear came over him. He thought of his brother, Kaui, and of his friends, Mike and Raquel.

Soon, he felt a warm tear roll down from his eye.

Chapter 47

After we'd loaded the boat onto the trailer, I decided to take Chas up on his invitation to meet at his place and help clean and divvy up what we'd caught. I resisted the urge to point out that part of it had already been divvied.

He gave me his address in Sprecklesville, which I knew was close to Paia. Once in my car, I took a swig of warm water from the bottle I'd left, then voiced Chas's address to the vehicle's GPS and started out of the parking area. As I approached the highway I glanced into my rear-view mirror and saw my face was pink with sunburn. I also noticed a green sedan had pulled out of a space and was now behind me. My rear window was too covered with salt and drizzle to see the driver.

The GPS was telling me to turn left onto Kahului Beach Road, so I put on my blinker and pulled up to the stop bar in the proper turn lane. The car behind me, which I could now tell was a Buick, signaled left as well.

Once traffic was clear, I pulled forward and started left, then made a quick right. As I accelerated, I checked my mirrors and saw the mystery car had turned right as well.

I was being followed.

Without hesitation, I reached under my seat and pulled out my handgun. With one eye on the road ahead and the other on the mirror, I flipped the safety lever to the fire position. Up ahead, a traffic light had just turned green.

After following traffic through the light, I swerved into the left lane, almost colliding into the front end of another SUV as I cut in. Just ahead was another traffic light where the road split. In my mirror I saw that my friend had changed lanes as well and was only a few cars behind me.

He and I were going for a ride. I knew right then this was not going to end well for one of us.

The light at the split was green. I waited until I'd reached the middle of the intersection and stopped. To my right, a line of cars was approaching. Just as they got close, I hit the gas and veered in front of them. The cars all screeched to a halt while I turned right onto Waiehu Beach Road, my tires spinning on the wet pavement.

Through all that, not one single person tooted their horn. I love Maui.

Anyway, I headed as fast as I could up the two-lane road, though I was limited to the speed of the traffic ahead of me. I could see the green Buick about eight cars behind. After passing a few suburban neighborhoods, I took a right where the road ended at Kahekili Highway. There were no cars ahead of me at that point, so I floored it for a while before I checked behind me.

Nothing.

The drizzle had turned to rain as I entered the rural village of Waihee, where I slowed down.

After Waihee, the road became narrow and more winding as it began to carve its way alongside a steep volcanic slope. I continued carefully, all the while with one eye out for my friend.

The road took me increasing higher until I found myself far above sea level. From that elevation I could look out across the ocean and see much of the north shore, including the faint misty outline of Haiku in the far distance. I thought of Raquel and the twins and hoped whoever was following me hadn't found them first.

Soon, I came up behind an old gasoline-powered pickup truck. Its driver, an elderly fellow, appeared to be in no particular hurry. I slowed down and followed him around the next sharp curve. Just after the curve, he and I stopped where the road narrowed into a single lane with no shoulder on either side. To the left of us was a near vertical rock wall rising upward. To our right was a sheer cliff, which dropped into the wooded gulch below. At this section of road, traffic in each direction would have to wait in queue before proceeding one at a time. I noticed my wipers had sped up as the rain began coming down harder. With all the precipitation and thick cloud cover visibility was becoming a problem, though I had other things to worry about.

Suddenly, I spotted the green sedan as it rounded the curve behind me. Traffic was still stopped and I realized that I was about to be sandwiched between him and the truck ahead of me. I was a sitting duck.

At the same time, an oncoming car came out of the single lane and passed by us. As the old man in the pickup began to pull forward, I made the decision to pass him. I hit the accelerator and swung around the left side of the truck. While doing this, I happened to glanced at my mirror with one eye. In that split second, my rear wiper swept my back window just as the Buick driver's wiper swept his windshield. I recognized his face at once.

Ellis Lacorde.

I focused ahead as I squeezed my vehicle between the wall and the pickup. My left side mirror struck a protrusion in the rock wall and swung into my side window. The window shattered loudly as a shower of glass fragments exploded into my face. I spit out a mouthful of sharp shards as I pulled ahead of the small pickup and raced away.

In my center mirror I caught another glimpse of Lacorde. He'd reached his arm outside his window and was aiming a handgun. I quickly crouched down in my seat and heard the sound of small caliber shots being fired. One of the bullets hit my rear window, shattering it.

My heart was pounding. I took a deep breath as the road widened again into two lanes. There, the second line of cars were waiting in queue. The drivers were yelling and blowing their horns at me while I waved at them to stay back.

By the time I hit the next curve I was traveling at a high speed. My vehicle slid sideways on the wet surface while I maneuvered through the hairpin turn. I glanced back and saw the Buick's tires smoke as Lacorde forced the small pickup off the road. The old truck slid over the edge and rolled downward, ripping out small trees as it plunged into the deep ravine.

I came out of the curve and began heading up a steep incline. Just then, I heard the sound of another bullet as it hit my car's front right fender. I kept the pedal to the floor. Ahead, the road disappeared into another blind turn.

As I entered the curve the rear end of my vehicle lost traction on the rain-soaked roadway. All at once I lost control and began to spin. My front bumper dragged along the wall at the inside of the curve, throwing red volcanic dirt over the asphalt. Finally, I came to a stop as my rear bumper crashed into an old wooden guardrail on the outside of the curve. I looked around and realized I was perilously close to the edge of a sheer cliff. In the distance, I spotted Lacorde, who had made it through the single lane section and was heading my way.

An idea came to me. I pulled away from the guardrail and forward about fifty feet on the far side of the curve, out of Lacorde's line of sight. Behind me, I could see my rear bumper had knocked the guardrail loose from its supports on the outside of the curve. Also, the wet red mud was now covering much of the roadway, making it even slicker.

I placed the gear selector into reverse. My left foot was pressed firmly on the brakes while my right foot was ready to hit the accelerator. I fixed my eyes on the center mirror and lowered the passenger-side window.

I watched and listened.

After a long tense moment I heard the sound of Lacorde's car approaching. Its tires began to screech across the wet, muddy pavement as it entered the sharp turn. In that same moment, I hit the accelerator and waited about two seconds while my tires smoked. I then released the brakes and held the wheel firmly. Once the tires gripped, my vehicle shot backward. I held my breath as I headed directly toward the guardrail.

I was gaining speed and saw the edge of the cliff approaching fast. My hands clinched the steering wheel while my entire life passed before my eyes. At the last second I spotted the nose of Lacorde's car pulling around the corner. As I'd hoped, my rear bumper plowed straight into him.

The collision crushed Lacorde's front end and the car was launched backward. In my mirror, I saw his airbag deploy into his face as the rear of his vehicle crashed through the wooden guardrail.

I slammed on the brakes. Fortunately for me, I came to a stop just before the edge of the cliff. Lacorde, however, wasn't so fortunate. After carefully placing the shifter into drive, I pulled forward and parked on the shoulder.

My hands were trembling as I took a deep breath and wiped a few small fragments of glass out of my eye. After that, I stepped out of the car and stood on the roadside for a moment to calm myself and let my pounding heart slow down. The cool rain felt and refreshing and I was soon able to pull myself together.

As I stood there, two couples pulled their cars to the shoulder and parked, apparently curious to find out what happened.

The driver of one of the cars seemed to be a concerned citizen. As he got out of his car he looked at me and asked, "Hey—did you just run that green car off the road?"

Well, that sounded accusing, plus I didn't like his tone, so I didn't bother to reply.

The couple in the second car stayed put while the concerned citizen walked over to the broken guardrail and stepped close to the edge of the steep cliff side. As he glanced down, a look of shock came over his face and he reared back. "Oh my... Oh my...!" He turned to me and pointed over the side. "Look! Quick!"

I knew this had to be good. I walked over to the edge and looked down, only to discover that Lacorde's car had fallen just ten feet or so and was stuck in the top of a large tree. While I looked, Lacorde managed to push the airbag out of his way. He then reached his arm out the side window and, to my utter surprise, quickly fired three rounds from his handgun.

One of the bullets hit me in my right shoulder. Almost at once I fell to the ground. For a moment, everything went black and I found it hard to breathe. As I lay on the ground gasping, the concerned citizen ran to his rental car where he jumped in and sped away.

As my breathing returned to normal, I looked at my shoulder and saw a hole in my new shirt. From the hole, blood was oozing. I held pressure over the site for a moment before I climbed to my feet.

Just then, an idea came to me. Before I could talk myself out of it, I ran to the edge and leaped off. As I fell the ten feet, I saw that Lacorde still had his gun pointed out the window. My feet landed hard onto the windshield. All at once, the reinforced glass collapsed inward, shattering while remaining as one fragmented sheet. Before Lacorde could fire a shot, the top edge of the windshield fell sharply into his neck.

At about the same time, my right foot slid across the sheet of broken glass and landed hard under his chin, snapping his head back. Like *way* back.

During this, I slipped and fell. At once I felt some of the glass splinters bury into my knees. I looked at Lacorde and saw his chin was pointing straight up. His gun was missing, apparently having dropped from his hand during all the fun. In his shirt pocket I spotted what appeared to be a cell phone.

I reached in and grabbed the phone. In that same instant I felt the car move beneath me. One of the tree limbs began to give way and the vehicle started to fall.

Quickly, I leaped off the vehicle and grabbed onto a large branch. Severe pain shot out of my neck and shoulder. Nonetheless, I held on tightly.

I glanced down and watched the car as it fell out of the tree with Lacorde still seat-belted inside. Parts of the vehicle flew everywhere as it tumbled and crashed down the face of the high cliff. Near the bottom, the car landed solidly onto a rocky ledge where it exploded into a ball of orange and yellow fire before rolling into the ocean.

They say it's not the fall that kills you; it's the sudden stop at the end.

Oh, and the explosion.

I guess the slit throat and broken neck didn't help either.

Chapter 48

After witnessing Ellis Lacorde's failed attempt at a high-speed vertical landing, I knew I needed to make a quick exit. I used my left arm to pull myself up from the tree branch and managed to swing my feet onto another limb.

I steadied myself, then looked up and saw the man and woman from the second car. Both of them were standing near the edge and looking at me like I was some kind of nutcase.

With my left hand I grabbed a plank hanging down from the broken guardrail and used it to brace myself. I then stepped from one small ledge to another until I'd reached the edge of the roadside. The woman from the car stepped well out of the way while the man basically stood there. Though it was raining, it seemed to me he didn't want to get himself dirty. In fact, he waited until I'd crawled almost to the top before asking, "Are you all right?"

I didn't feel like answering Mr. Helpful, but I did reach out my filthy left hand and let him pull me over the edge. Once I was standing on the roadway itself, I made sure to give him a good pat on the shoulder while I caught my breath.

He shook his head. "I can't believe you jumped off like that."

Well, I couldn't believe it either, but I was glad I did. The look on Lacorde's face alone was worth it—not to mention the brief fireworks show that followed.

Mr. Helpful, being a man who understood priorities, quickly found some tall, wet grass to wipe the mud from his hands. Once he was sure his hands were nice and clean he looked and spotted my bullet wound.

"Hey, is your shoulder okay?" he asked. "I think you're bleeding."

I ignored his observation and staggered over to my car. Using my water bottle I rinsed the dirt and blood from my hands. After that, I grabbed the t-shirt from the front seat and shook the glass shards from it.

While I did this, Helpful seemed to take notice of my gun which was now sitting in plain view. He and his wife looked at each other, then ran to their car and took off in a big hurry.

Now who's the nutcase?

I held my hand over the wound and tried to think of something other than the pain. This was bad. Nonetheless, I felt lucky to be alive. From what I could figure, Lacorde's bullet had hit me at a sharp upward angle just above my right lung—missing a major artery there by about an inch. I couldn't feel an exit wound, so I assumed the small slug stopped at my collarbone.

Not a bad shot. I mean, considering the situation.

After a full minute, I let off applying pressure to the wound and tore the t-shirt in two. I then folded one part into a small square and placed it over the bullet hole as a bandage. I wrapped the other half around my neck and under my right arm to hold the bandage in place.

When I was finished with that, I carefully shook the glass from my jacket and slipped it on. Then, using my left hand, I flipped the passenger-side mirror back into position and shut the door. On the right front fender, I noticed a bullet hole.

Another decent shot, I thought. He must have taken shooting lessons.

On that topic, I glanced at my Colt and wondered if I'd be able to handle a gun right now. I was rid of Ellis Lacorde, of course, but a thought came to me. I realized that Lacorde may have come here with a partner.

Safire.

Immediately, my thoughts went to Raquel, Kaui, and Kekoa. I jumped into the SUV and headed in the direction of Haiku.

Going back the way I came, I soon came upon the same group of angry drivers I'd encountered when I sped through the one-way section. Several of them were trying to help rescue the driver of the pickup truck that Lacorde had forced off the road. I grabbed my gun and hid it under my seat.

I shook out my ball cap and pulled it low as I came to a stop. A man in the crowd gave me a good look and whistled to one of the other drivers, an older fellow wearing a hooded rain jacket. The two spoke for a few seconds before they turned and stared back at me.

The older guy, who seemed to be in charge of things, began to approach me. As he got close, he held up a police badge. "Hello sir. I'm a retired Maui police officer." He glanced at my smashed-up car for a moment before he continued, "I need to ask you a few questions while we wait for the emergency vehicles to arrive."

"Okay."

"Were you being chased by the person driving the green Buick?"

"What a maniac!" I replied. "That jerk smashed into the back of my car and almost ran me off a cliff!"

He checked my citizen card and asked, "Are you injured in any way?"

Does being shot count? "I think my shoulder is hurt," I told him. "I'm heading to the emergency room to have it checked out."

He frowned at that. "The paramedics are on the way, sir. Just wait here." He looked over my car again and added, "The police will need to ask you a few questions, too."

"I can talk to the police while I'm at the emergency room. Right?"

He looked me in the eye for a moment. As a retired cop, he'd surely heard more than his share of B.S. over the years. I hoped his instincts had become rusty.

"Can I look at your injury?" he asked.

I told him, "When that nut job rear-ended me, it felt like I pulled a tendon. There's no visible injury, but it would be a good idea to have a doctor check it, just to be sure."

The rain was dripping off the bill of his hood. "I think I'd better call the police."

Uh oh.

"I'll tell them to meet you at the emergency room. Just don't leave the hospital until you've spoken with an officer about all this, understand?"

"Yes sir," I lied.

He waved me past the stopped cars and I was on my way. I hadn't gotten far before a long line of ambulances and rescue vehicles hurried past me with their lights blazing and sirens blaring. I wondered how long it would be until someone noticed the broken guardrail and, on the ocean floor below, the charbroiled remnants of a Buick sedan.

As I continued along the rain soaked roads, I went back to thinking. How did Lacorde find out where I was? I had no reason to suspect Chuck or Chas. Who else besides Raquel and the twins knew where I would be today?

Malia.

Could it be? Perhaps she had innocently mentioned the wrong information to the wrong person, which could have led all the way from here to Lacorde's ears.

I thought about calling her, but I knew someone like Safire might be monitoring her phone. My instincts told me to wait until I had more facts.

A dark cloud now seemed to cover the entire island, and a feeling of darkness was coming over me as well. The more I pondered the situation, the worse I felt. I wasn't losing hope—not by a long shot. Nevertheless, I felt I needed to get to the Haiku house as soon as possible. I prayed it wasn't too late.

In the meantime, I'd try to think positive thoughts and keep my chin up.

Chapter 49

Believe me, it isn't easy trying to ignore the feeling of pain when you have a fresh gunshot wound. Besides that, my knees hurt and my whole right arm was throbbing. I felt a tingling sensation in my hands too, so I loosened my grip on the steering wheel a bit. I assured myself that these things were all part of the job and are nothing to worry about. The problem with that is I can tell when I'm lying.

I soon entered the village of Waihee where I slowed down. The rain was still pouring steadily and my left side was becoming soaked. I set the heater to eighty degrees. It wasn't going to make a big difference with two of my windows smashed out, but I figured it was better than nothing.

I heard a phone ring. With all that was going on I'd almost forgotten I had Lacorde's cell in my pocket. I thought for a moment and then answered, "Yeah?"

There was a brief pause before a female voice asked, "Who is this? Who am I speaking with?"

I knew it had to be her. "This is Mike Brennan. I assume this is Safire calling. Am I correct?"

No answer.

I told her, "Your partner Ellis Lacorde is in custody. He told us you'd be calling."

"If Lacorde is with you, Mr. Brennan, let me talk to him. Put him on the phone."

"He's already had his one obligatory phone call," I told her, "which I guess wasn't to you. Right now he's being questioned by other agents, so let's you and I talk for a bit."

"I think you are lying to me, Mike Brennan."

She was right about that. "Think what you like," I said. "I just want to make you an offer."

"Is that so? How amusing. And what do you have to offer me?"

"I'm here with a team of Federal Agents, Safire, and our job is to bring you in. If you surrender now, without any trouble, I can—"

"I think not, Mr. Brennan. In fact, I think you are alone."

Well, she was right about that, too. "Again, you can think what you like, Safire. I'm just trying to help you."

"You say you are with a group of agents. If that is true, let me talk with one of them."

"The other agents are with Lacorde," I said. "Right now, I'm the only one you're going to talk to. I'm also the only one who can offer you a deal."

"There will be no deal."

"Ellis Lacorde spilled his guts and told us practically everything."

She laughed at that one, which actually was kind of funny. "Ellis Lacorde is just a stupid man," she said. "You probably killed him and took his phone."

This wasn't going as well as I'd hoped.

She continued, "I think I will make *you* a deal, Mr. Brennan, so listen carefully: From the sound of it, you are driving somewhere. I want you to drive to the little cove near the home where you have been hiding."

"Why? So you can snipe me or one of my agents—?"

"If I wanted to 'snipe' you," she said, "you would be dead already."

"What's at the cove?"

She laughed again. "I do not want to spoil the surprise. But I do want you to know that I have your young friend Kekoa Hamilton here with me."

I felt my heart stop.

"Perhaps you would like to speak with him?"

I pounded my left fist on the steering wheel. "Put him on the phone."

There was a long pause followed by some muffled sounds. After that, a voice came on the line. "Mike? Is that you?"

I recognized his voice at once. "Yeah. Hey, are you all right?"

"Not exactly. Safire has me handcuffed in the trunk of her car."

Cripes. "Do you know if Kaui and Raquel are safe?"

"I don't know," he replied. "I don't even know where they are." He then lowered his voice to a whisper and told me, "Raquel went paddle boarding this morning." He then asked, "Where are you at?"

"I'm coming for you, Kekoa—and I'm going to kill Safire while I'm at it."

I heard muffled sounds once again and Safire soon came back on the phone. "You are confused, Mr. Brennan," she said. "It is I who am going to kill *you*."

"I don't think so."

She ignored that and told me, "Perhaps I will offer you a deal. If you surrender yourself to me now, without any trouble, I will allow your friend Kekoa to live."

I made no reply.

"Do we have a deal—or do I kill your friend?"

I wasn't about to make any kind of deal with a snake like her, so I asked, "Where are the others?"

She laughed at that and told me, "I will call you back with instructions on the deal. If you are smart, Mr. Brennan, you will not misplace that phone—"

"If you're smart, Safire, you'll free Kekoa right now and turn yourself in to the—"

She ended the call right there.

I slammed the steering wheel again and let out a long, loud yell. I felt my heart beating hard again and I wanted nothing other than to find this woman and strangle her to the ground.

I took a breath and glanced down at the speedometer, which told me I was traveling at seventy miles per hour. I let off the accelerator and allowed the car to slow down. I needed to get to Haiku quickly, but I couldn't risk being pulled over—especially with a fresh bullet hole in my fender and another in my shoulder. I've noticed the cops here like to ask a lot of questions.

Thankfully, traffic was light. I made it quickly through Kahului and Paia. Ten minutes later, I was close to the Haiku property. As I came up over the last hill, I was surprised to see emergency vehicles of every type, including a Coroner's van, parked along the road near the cove. Lights were flashing from the vehicles while cops in yellow rain jackets were standing in the road directing traffic.

Safire, I thought.

One of the cops, a heavyset stolid-looking fellow, raised his hand and signaled me to stop. He glanced over my vehicle as he approached.

"Good afternoon," he said. "Your car looks pretty smashed up."

Well, he hasn't seen Lacorde's Buick.

"Were you in an accident?"

I quickly thought up a lie. "No officer, I found my car like this. I think it was vandalized."

"And when did this happen?"

"Just this afternoon. It was parked near Mom's Fish House, and—"

"Did you report it?"

See what I mean about the cops here? "I'm calling the rental company as soon as I get home," I said, like that was going to happen. "I just want the car out of the rain before the interior becomes ruined."

"They'll want a police report," he informed me. He then waved his flashlight over the car while I was working on a story for the bullet hole and the smashed rear bumper.

A few cars had lined up behind me, but the cop didn't seem to be in much of a hurry. He asked, "Where are you headed?"

"Home. I have a rental place up ahead to the left."

He studied me for a moment before he waved his flashlight. "Move along."

I did as he said. After a few hundred feet, I turned left at the entrance road to the Haiku house and parked off to the side. I needed to find out what had happened at the cove, so I got out and walked back that way.

A chilling wind was blowing from the north while the rain continued to fall steadily. As I approached the surf shop I saw it was being guarded by a cop and there was a length of bright yellow crime scene tape draped around the building's perimeter. I pulled my cap down low and approached the young officer.

"What happened here?" I asked.

He looked me over for a second. "There's a police investigation going on, sir."

Well, that much was obvious. "What are they investigating? Did something happen?"

He didn't seem comfortable with my questions. "Are you a reporter?"

Apparently, he'd been instructed not to talk with the press. "No. I live up the street and my family is worried."

He glanced around for a second and then let me know, "The person that ran this surf shop was found shot to death. Did you know him?"

I shook my head and was glad to hear that it wasn't Raquel or Kaui.

He gestured to the beach where a group of police investigators had gathered. Off to the right was a small group of onlookers. "Another body was found washed up on the beach," he told me. "The detectives are trying to determine if the two deaths are connected."

At that, my heart stopped.

I turned away and walked over to where the onlookers were gathered and sat on the wet sand. The cold wind and rain had chilled me to the bone and my hands were shaking. I watched the police investigators as they discussed things. I could see the victim had been covered with a dark sheet. I also noticed a second sheet covering something closer to the water's edge.

One of the investigators lifted the second sheet, causing a few of the onlookers to gasp. Another cop produced a camera from under his poncho and began taking pictures. I heard someone near me whisper, "It's just a surfboard."

The cop with the camera then looked over at the group of observers. To my surprise, he pointed the camera at us and began taking pictures.

I held my head low and made sure the bill of my hat was pulled down.

Just then, another investigator pulled the sheet from atop the victim, exposing the body. At that, everyone in the group let out a loud gasp. Everyone except me, that is. I recognized the victim at once.

Raquel Richards.

My heart felt pierced. I looked at her pallid body lying there in the sand. I could see her neck was contorted and her mouth hung open, as though she'd left this world crying for help. A drop of rain ran into my eye, and I wiped it away with a trembling finger.

I took one last look at her tiny, lifeless body as she lay there in the cold sand. I touched the raindrop to my lips and sent a subtle kiss in her direction. I whispered, "I'm so sorry."

A woman sitting nearby seemed to have overheard what I'd said and began looking at me with suspicious eyes. I realized, too, that the investigator with the camera was watching me as well.

I stood and walked away. My mind was in a daze as I staggered past the surf shop. The young cop there asked, "Hey, Mister, are you all right?"

I nodded to him in an affirmative way and continued walking. Halfway to my car, I stepped into the woods where I bent down and vomited. As my stomach wrenched, I felt a sharp pain deep in my right shoulder. My bullet wound had apparently reopened. I pressed my hand over the entry site while I hobbled the remaining distance to my car.

I climbed in and sat. For a long while I thought about Raquel Richards, who was so young and innocent, who was so beautiful and full of life, and who loved me.

And I loved her, too.

I then thought about my gun, which I remembered was hidden under my seat. God, I knew, had forsaken me, and I now found myself in the grasp of darkness itself. All hope was gone, and for a brief moment I felt the weight of the world upon my shoulders. To me, it seemed as though all the world's iniquity, shame, and guilt had fallen heavily upon my soul.

I put the gun to my head.

Chapter 50

I decided to count down from five before pulling the trigger. And I would have. But I thought about it and realized five seconds wasn't long enough. I changed it to ten. As soon as I began counting, however, I heard the distinct sound of one of the Honda ATVs in the distance. I lowered the gun and leaned out the window to listen. The sound was coming from the gravel road leading to the house and I knew it had to be Kaui. I looked down at the gun for a moment, then flipped on the safety and slid it back under my seat.

I quickly rinsed the bile residue from my mouth with a swig of bottled water and spit it out the window. I then started the car and headed straight for the house.

When I arrived at the property gate I saw the lock-latch was ripped out and the gate had been forced open. I continued driving while listening for the sound of Kaui's Honda. I was thinking about what to do next when I came upon both of the ATVs, which were parked off to the side of the dirt road. I looked around and saw no one.

I stopped the car and stepped out. A voice came from behind, startling me.

"Mike?"

I spun around to see Kaui stepping out from behind a thick tree. He appeared to be okay, thank God.

"Sorry to scare you," he said. "I pulled over when I saw Kekoa's ATV. When I heard your car coming I hid until I could see who it was."

I walked over and gave him a hug. "I'm glad to see you're okay."

He pulled away cautiously and looked at me. "What is it? What's wrong?"

I couldn't bear to tell him, at least not yet. "We need to get out of here," I said, "and as soon as possible. After that, I'll explain everything."

"Where's Kekoa? Did he pick up Raquel?"

I climbed into the car and told him firmly, "Just get in."

I could tell he was becoming upset with me. He opened the door and brushed some of the glass off the passenger seat. As he sat, he slammed his door and shook his head in frustration. He then looked at me and demanded, "Can't you just tell me if they're all right or not?"

I turned to him, and he seemed to detect the anguish on my face. "We need to rescue your brother," I said, "but first, we need to stop at the house." After I'd shifted into forward gear and began driving I added, "Once we're out of here I'll tell you *everything*, I promise."

I sensed Kaui was both grieved and confused. Despite that, he managed to notice that I'd winced when I reached for the gear selector.

"What happened to your arm?"

"My arm is fine," I replied, "but there might be a bullet in my shoulder."

"You're *shot?*"

"It's a long story. I'll tell you about it—"

"So, I guess that was a bullet hole I saw in the fender?"

I nodded as I continued driving.

We soon arrived at the house. I asked Kaui to wait in the car while I went up to my cottage. When I'd reached the top of the stairs, I found my front door had been kicked open. This looked like the work of Safire. I went in and headed straight to my room.

I checked the closet first and found my bag was gone, along with all my passports and wallets. My tablet was gone too.

I opened the top drawer of the bedside table and was surprised to find my .22 handgun still there, hidden under my jeans. I grabbed the gun and a box of ammo. As I began to leave, I glanced in the mirror and realized my shorts were stained with fish blood, which might look suspicious to a cop. My knees were covered with dried blood too. Wasting no time I changed into the jeans. Before leaving, I stopped at the refrigerator and grabbed two bottled waters, then rushed down to the car and climbed in.

"What did we need to come here for?" Kaui asked.

"Because I thought we might need this." I handed him the gun.

He looked at it for a few seconds. "Uh, okay."

I backed the car out and began heading down the gravel road. "Now we just need to get past the police."

"What police?"

"At the surf shop on the main road," I said. "There are cop cars and emergency vehicles all over the place. We need to get through there without being stopped."

"What are they doing there?"

"The guy that worked at the surf shop was killed."

"Ian?" Kaui seemed shocked. "We just met him this morning," he said. "Raquel rented a paddleboard from him."

I made no reply to that.

Kaui thought for a moment. "What about Raquel? Is she okay?"

I looked directly at Kaui. "Let's just get past the police first. I'll explain everything after that, okay?"

He turned away and let out a moan of frustration.

Minutes later, we passed through the open gate near the end of the gravel road. I could tell from Kaui's expression he was angry. I knew this wouldn't go over well with the cops who were already suspicious about my smashed up car. "Just try to appear calm," I told him. Using a more gentle voice, I added, "I appreciate your patience with me."

He took a deep breath and I saw his face relax a bit.

At Hana Highway I turned right. Just ahead, several cars were lined up waiting to be waved through by the police. I got in line. I saw that the same cop who'd stopped me earlier was still at it. One by one, he looked over each car and spoke to the drivers before allowing them through. When it came my turn, he looked up and down the driver's side before he approached me. Just as before, he didn't seem too happy.

"It's you again," he said. He seemed to study me for a moment. "I'll need you to pull over to the side—"

Just then, one of the other officers called to him.

He signaled back and then told me, "Wait right here and stay in the car." He stepped away and began conferring with his colleague.

Well, I'm a busy person. I didn't have time to wait around for more questions, which could become sticky. The cop had his back to us, so I eased off the brake pedal and allowed the car to begin rolling forward."

"What are you doing?" Kaui asked. "Are you crazy?"

I ignored that reasonable question and continued moving. Once I'd proceeded far enough, I pressed down the accelerator and sped away.

Kaui spun in his seat and looked behind. "I can't believe you just did that. They'll send a patrol car after us."

"Don't worry," I told him. "I'll find a place to hide as soon as I have the chance."

A mile or so later, I spotted a big cemetery on the right. After checking my mirror, I turned into the entrance of Valley Isle Memorial Park. I headed quickly up the hill and turned into a parking area which was, ironically, a dead end. There, I pulled into a space where I knew we'd be out of sight. It occurred to me that a cemetery was probably a poor choice of locations for what I was about to explain to Kaui, but it would have to do.

From our position we could look down and see the highway, knowing at the same time it would be difficult for anyone to spot us. We sat and watched the passing cars for a while before Kaui finally turned to me. "Now, can you please tell me what's going on?"

I wasn't sure how to put this, so I started from the beginning. "Ellis Lacorde and his partner, Safire, have somehow managed to find us."

"What?"

"They're here in Maui."

He let out a breath. "Is that how you got shot?"

I nodded at that and looked at him. "Safire has captured your brother."

He was stunned. After a few seconds he asked, "Do you know if he's okay?"

"When I spoke with him on the phone he sounded frightened. Aside from that, he seemed all right."

He shook his head. "Oh my God…"

I added, "Safire agreed to release him in exchange for me."

"You spoke with her? What phone did you use?"

"Lacorde's." I removed the phone from my pocket and handed it to him.

He looked it over. "How did you come up with this?"

"I took it from his body."

He looked at me. "Did you *kill* him?"

Did I ever. I nodded subtly.

He processed that for a moment and asked, "What about Raquel? Where's she at?"

I leaned back in my seat and drew a long sigh.

"Something's happened, right? She's why all the cops are back there, right?"

I nodded again and finally told him, "Raquel was murdered. By the time I got here, her body had already been found on the beach."

At that, Kaui closed his eyes and hung his head low for a moment. After that, his lungs emptied out and his face fell to his hands while tears poured out.

As he wept, I closed my eyes. Right about then, I felt the grasp around me tighten.

Chapter 51

After we'd allowed ourselves a few minutes to mourn, Kaui and I pulled ourselves together. From the cemetery parking lot, we looked down at Hana Highway. I hadn't spotted any police cars yet, although I did happen to see the Coroner's van pass by. I chose not to point it out. Right now, it was more important for us to think about the living.

I told Kaui the details of my phone conversation with Safire and his brother.

After that, he asked me, "Are you really trading places with Kekoa—or do you have another plan?"

I saw Kaui's eyes were still red and swollen. "I'll do whatever it takes," I said, "but I don't think we should trust Safire to keep her end of any deal. No matter what she says, she'll never let Kekoa go free."

He nodded in agreement. "He'd go straight to the police and identify her."

I explained, "The FBI's file on Safire was mostly guesswork, but they seemed certain about one thing: she is first and foremost a sniper. In fact, I suspect she intends to use her shooting skills on your brother after she has me as a hostage."

He considered that. "What if we're able to figure out a way to rescue Kekoa and then come back for you?"

"Forget about that," I told him. "Once you have Kekoa, I need the two of you to head straight to the police. Do you understand me?"

"Why don't we just go to the police right now?"

"We can if you want to," I said. "But bringing the police in might be dangerous for Kekoa. Besides, we don't know where she's hiding. And even if we did, she's not the type who'd ever surrender to anyone."

We sat in silence for a minute. Finally, I looked over at Kaui and told him, "I'm sorry about what's happened to your brother."

"It's not your fault, Mike."

"I'm sorry about Raquel, too," I said. "Everything's gone wrong. I was supposed to protect all of you, and I...I should have stayed with Raquel."

"You can't let yourself feel responsible," he said to me. "We don't even know what happened or how Lacorde and Safire found us. Besides, we never invited Raquel to come here in the first place. She just showed up. You had no control of that."

I let out a long sigh. "Nonetheless, I'm sorry."

He looked at me in a way that acknowledged what I'd said, and then suggested, "Let's get out of this cemetery and go figure out how to rescue Kekoa."

I agreed.

I started the car and headed down to the main road. Just after I'd entered the highway, I noticed a police car in my mirror.

Kaui was oblivious to the situation. He asked me, "Do you mind if I take a look at Lacorde's phone?"

"Hold on a minute. We've got a cop on our tail."

He checked his side mirror and saw the car gaining quickly. "Uh oh."

I kept my speed down, but I knew our vehicle looked conspicuous, to say the least. The rear bumper was smashed, two windows were shot out, and my side mirror was missing. It occurred to me one or both of the taillights might be broken, too.

Kaui brought up a good question. "What's our story if we're pulled over?"

Before I could answer, the police car's bright lights came on and started flashing behind us. I slowed down further and prepared to pull over. All at once, the cop swerved around us and sped by. Needless to say, we both breathed a sigh of relief.

After that, I took Lacorde's phone from my pocket and held it out for Kaui. "See if you find anything interesting on this thing."

He took the phone and asked, "Do you think Safire came here with anyone besides Ellis Lacorde?"

"Probably. I mean it would be difficult for her to execute a hostage trade all by herself, wouldn't it?"

He made no reply and continued inspecting the phone. Perhaps *execute* had been a poor word choice.

As we entered the town of Kahului, I turned onto the airport entrance.

Kaui looked up from the phone. "Where are you going?"

"I'm dumping this car before we're pulled over."

"At the airport?"

"I'll drop you off at one of the car rental places. From there I'll head to the airport parking area and abandon this thing. After that, I'll take the shuttle back and we'll pick up a new vehicle."

"Why drop me off?"

"Because I'm worried someone at the airport might recognize you. Your face has been on TV, remember?"

He nodded subtly and went back to searching Lacorde's phone for clues.

A few minutes later, I turned left into a rental office and let Kaui out near a covered waiting area. After that, I drove the short distance to the airport, noticing that the rain had reduced again to a steady drizzle.

Once parked, I grabbed both guns from under the seats and tucked them into my jacket pockets. I left the car and headed straight to the bus stop where I waited for the next shuttle to the rental offices.

An older couple sat waiting in the same spot. They looked at me for a moment and began whispering back and forth. I had no idea what the latest news broadcasts had to say, but I began to wonder if Cronus had come up with a better photo of me.

While waiting, I noticed an airport security guard. He was dressed in heavy raingear and riding a Segway patrol vehicle. His helmet had a built-in video camera, and he seemed to be aiming it in my direction. From the corner of my eye I watched as he spoke into his microphone before continuing on his way.

In my mind, I quickly put together an escape route, just in case. Maybe it was my own paranoia, but I *was* concealing two unregistered handguns while on federally secured property. In my line of work, a mild case of paranoia can be an asset.

The shuttle finally arrived and took me straight to the rental office. As I stepped off the bus, I saw Kaui and could tell he was anxious to tell me something.

"You're not going to believe this," he said to me. "It looks like Lacorde had been using the phone's GPS since he arrived in Hawaii."

I shrugged. "So?"

He had a smug look on his face. "*So*, that means we can tell everywhere he'd been and for how long. In fact, I found a clue that might lead us to where Safire is keeping Kekoa."

I gave him a pat on the shoulder. "Good job."

He explained, "I know where Ellis went after he received a phone call last night. It was the same caller who spoke to you today."

"Safire."

"Right. So, after receiving the call from her, Lacorde drove out to a secluded area in the foothills of the West Maui Mountains. He was there for over two hours." He pointed to the screen and explained, "In satellite view, it looks like the location is a wooded area above an old macadamia plantation. As you can see, there are few buildings around other than an old water storage tank and a small cabin."

I looked as he zoomed in and pointed out the structures for me.

Kaui adjusted the image once again. "Do you notice all the canals?" he asked. He held the phone so I could see the miles of irrigation canals running along the foot of the mountain. "Those are the Waihee Canals, built in the early 1900s."

"Interesting. Let's look at the road leading to the cabin again."

He tapped at the screen until I could see a narrow dirt road snaking its way back and forth from the highway up to the cabin.

I asked, "This is where Lacorde drove to?"

"That's the spot."

"Good. This is probably where the exchange will take place."

Kaui looked at me. "Why don't we skip the exchange and just go in and rescue Kekoa?"

I thought about that. "I would, but I don't know how to do that without putting your brother at risk." I told him, "Let's go inside and rent a car. We'll discuss this further while we're driving."

GREG MARION

The woman at the rental center counter had offered me a Buick sedan, which I declined, figuring the police might be looking for one of those. Instead, I decided on a Nissan SUV. Hopefully it would be less drafty than the last vehicle.

As we drove away in our new rental I told Kaui, "We need to stop somewhere and pick up a few things. After that, we'll check out the cabin." I added, "I'd like to know what I'm walking into before Safire starts calling the shots."

Another poor choice of words.

I wanted to avoid being seen in public, so I stopped at a drug store in Kahului that featured a number of outdoor vending machines. From one of the machines I bought a pack of ibuprofen capsules. From another I purchased two Snickers bars.

While I was busy with that, Kaui bought a Mountain Mist for himself and a sports drink for me. He also bought a second Mountain Mist and let me know, "This one's for Kekoa."

"Good idea." I swallowed four of the pain pills and guzzled down half of my sports drink. I told Kaui, "When this is over I'll buy each of you your own Mountain Mist vending machine."

He looked over at me and let out a loud belch. We both managed a smile.

After that, we went back to the car where I pulled out my Colt .380 and handed it to him. "That's a powerful gun," I told him. "Much more powerful than the other one I showed you."

"Why do you have two different guns?"

"Because one is powerful, but loud. The other is less potent but quiet, especially when you use the suppressor. I'll show you how to use both guns later."

He nodded.

I took a big bite of my Snickers. With my mouth full I told him, "Let's look at the satellite image of the cabin again." I pointed to the in-dash tablet.

He tapped away at the screen and voiced his selections until the desired image appeared. The map showed an aerial view of the winding dirt road connecting from Kahekili Highway to the old cabin in the mountains.

"Look at this," I told him, pointing to a paved road just north of the cabin.

Kaui zoomed in on it. "It's called Mahaili Road."

I studied the image for a moment. "It looks like it comes close to some of the switchbacks on the dirt road that leads up to the cabin." I pointed to a spot where the two roads were close. "That looks like a footpath."

He looked closely and nodded.

I told him, "I'm guessing Safire will have one or two helpers, though I'm sure the exchange itself will be no more than a charade. They'll either recapture Kekoa or have Safire put her sniper skills to use before he reaches the highway."

He processed that and then asked, "If you were a sniper, Mike, where would you position yourself?"

"Good question." I looked at the map. "There are four switchbacks between the highway and the cabin. The first one is too close to the highway and too short from one end to the other for a decent shot."

"How about the next one?"

"The second switchback is longer," I replied, "and has a footpath connecting to Malaihi Road. That's probably the best sniper spot."

"What about the other two switchbacks?"

"The third is too short while the forth has a bend in the middle. As you know, bullets don't handle curves well."

He nodded.

"Also, the third and fourth are too close to the cabin. They'll want me to believe your brother was freed, so they wouldn't want me to hear a rifle shot right after the exchange, would they?" I took the last bite of my Snickers bar.

Just then, Lacorde's phone rang.

Chapter 52

I gave Kaui a signal to be silent while I answered Lacorde's cell, "This is Mike Brennan."

"Mr. Brennan," Safire said, "tell me your exact location."

I found the sound of her voice irritating. I looked out at the weather, which was dark and cloudy with wind and rain. "I'm at the beach right now, working on my tan. Where are you?"

"I am pointing a gun at your friend's knee, Mr. Brennan. If you joke again, I will pull the trigger. Do you understand this clearly?"

"Why don't you just release him and we can all go home?"

"I think not," she replied. "So, one last time, tell me your location."

I thought for a moment and let her know, "I'm parked at the Maui Mall in Kahului on East Kaahumanu Avenue."

"And your friend, Kaui Hamilton, he is there with you, correct?"

"I can't find Kaui anywhere," I told her, "I assumed you'd killed him—like you killed Raquel."

She let out a laugh. "You assume too much. I had nothing to do with the girl."

"I'm sure."

"Yes. And I am sure Kaui Hamilton is there with you."

"Well he's not here. Are you able to understand that?"

She paused for a moment and then began to explain, "I'm wearing boots, Mr. Brennan, leather boots with—"

"I'm sure they're quite fashionable, Safire."

"Yes, they are," she replied. "Listen carefully while I demonstrate my fashionable boots to your friend."

I heard a muffled sound, which was followed by the sound of Kekoa screaming. I listened in horror as Safire continued kicking him.

"Wait!" I yelled. "Stop!"

I looked over at Kaui, who had a horrified look on his face.

After a few seconds, Safire came back on the phone, "Perhaps now you will be more cautious how you speak to me." She asked, "Are you able to understand that?"

I took a deep breath. "Got it."

"You are learning. Now, tell me what type of car you are driving."

I looked over at Kaui, who was obviously troubled. I let Safire know, "I'm in a maroon Nissan SUV."

"Good. Now drive to Vineyard and Market Street in the town of Wailuku. You will park in the lot along the tall bushes to the north. That way, Mr. Brennan, I can keep an eye on you. Are you able to understand that?"

"Yeah."

"Wait there until I call again. If you do anything stupid, I will kill all of you."
She ended the call.

I put the phone down and turned to Kaui.

"What happened?" he asked. "What did she do to Kekoa?"

"She kicked him. I could hear him screaming."

He shook his head. "Well, maybe you should've talked to her nicer."

"Sorry."

"Tell that to my brother."

I let out a sigh. "Look, Kaui, you have to understand that someone like Safire
thinks *tactically*. She suspects you're with me, so she's trying to cause division."

Kaui looked down at the gun I'd given him. "I want to be the one who kills
her," he said. "After I've shot her, I'm going to kick her head in."

Well, I was okay with that. "She wants me to drive to a parking lot in Wailuku
and wait for her next call."

"Why there?" Kaui asked.

"Supposedly so she can keep an eye on us. Instead, let's go check out the paved
road we saw on the map, the one near the cabin."

"Malaihi Road?"

"Right."

"What if Safire doesn't see us in the parking lot?"

"It's a bluff," I replied. "She'd never give away her general location."

"You gave her *our* location—and what kind of car we're driving."

"So I did, but keep in mind that Safire's the one doing the fishing, and she's just
using your brother Kekoa as bait."

"And what are you?"

I thought for a moment. "I guess I'm the catch of the day."

Chapter 53

I returned Lacorde's phone to my pocket and told Kaui, "I'm going back to the drug store. Need anything?"

"What are you going there for?"

"We'll need another phone in case we become separated."

"You don't have to go inside," he said. "They have pay-per-minute cheapo phones right in the vending machine. While you're at it, get an extra phone for Kekoa."

"Good thinking."

From the car, I headed through the cool drizzle to the row of machines. Sure enough, the machine sold phones. Unfortunately there was only one left. I bought it and placed it in my pocket with Lacorde's. As I started back to the car an idea came to me. I spun around, pulled my cap down low, and went straight into the store.

There were quite a few shoppers inside, but no one gave me a second glance. I went through the aisles and soon found what I was looking for. Rain gear. I picked out two heavy-duty ponchos, each with a dark green camouflage design. In the next aisle, I searched through shelves of oddball items: light bulbs, car fresheners, and hardware until I found it—shoe polish. I grabbed a tin of lo-gloss black and headed for the checkout.

I placed my items on the counter and noticed a display of pay-per-minute cell phones hanging on a rack. I selected the most expensive one and paid for everything in cash. As I began to leave, I spotted a security guard, a big guy, standing near the exit door.

The guard looked at me and held his hand up. "Hold it a sec." He pointed to my pocket and asked me, "You got something in there, pal?"

I pulled out the two phones for him to see. "One is mine," I said, "and the other is from the vending machine outside. I bought it right before I entered the store."

The guard inspected the vending machine phone as well as the contents of my bag and my receipt. He handed the phone back to me and commented, "Two phones, huh? You must be one busy guy."

"Yeah. Too many girlfriends."

He laughed at that and waved me by.

Once in the car, I gave the bag to Kaui and told him, "Go ahead and set up the new phones—and be sure to put them on silent mode." While he started on that, I used the tablet to look at a satellite view of the Wailuku parking lot.

Kaui glanced at the screen. "I thought we weren't going there."

"We're not. But we need to be familiar with the location, just in case."

"In case of what?"

"In case Safire calls to check if we're there. She could ask for some kind of landmark or something—probably while using the same map and street view as this."

He nodded at that. "What's with the black shoe polish and ponchos?"

"The shoe polish is for your face," I told him. "During the exchange, I figured you could hide in the woods near the footpath. With the camouflage poncho and face paint you'd be almost invisible."

"So, what would I do once I'm there? What's our plan?"

I explained, "First, we'll drive out there and scope out the place. If everything checks out I'll leave you there with two of the cell phones and both handguns. Your job will be to hide in the woods and hope Safire shows up." I gave him a look and added, "In that event, you'll know what to do."

"What if she doesn't show?"

"In that case, keep in mind that your brother will probably be given my car to drive out with, but—"

"But they won't allow him to reach the main road."

I nodded at that and went on, "So if you haven't seen Safire, you'll need to wave him down and get him out of the car. The two of you can then escape on foot." I warned him, "Just don't try to drive out unless you're *sure* Safire is dead. Okay?"

"Okay. But what if we're wrong about the location? Like, what if the exchange takes place somewhere else?"

"If that happens, I'll text you and have you contact the police. You can also text me on Safire's status if you have the chance."

"Once Kekoa and I escape, then what?"

"Once you're both in the clear, you'll need to call the police."

"We can't leave you there," he said. "The police would probably—"

"The important thing is that we save your brother. Just call 9-1-1 and turn yourselves in. After that, the cops will come for me, understand?"

He made no reply, so I reiterated, "Whatever happens, *do not* try to come after me yourselves, or this whole thing will be—"

"All right," he said. "We won't."

"Good."

The clock showed it was after six. I pressed a button on the steering wheel and asked the computer, "What time is sunset?"

After a second or two, it answered, *"Tonight's sunset will occur at 6:46 p.m. Hawaii time."*

I started the car, then pulled out and started toward Malaihi Road. On the way, I took a moment to call Malia's cell. It rang a few times before going to voicemail. I left a message for her to call Kaui's new number. After that, I deleted the call data from the phone.

By the time we reached Wailuku the drizzle had turned to driving rain. Puddles were beginning to form on the sides of the streets. At Kahekili Highway, I turned right and proceeded slowly. After about two-hundred feet we spotted a dirt road on the mountain side. The entrance was gated and locked with a heavy chain.

I continued further and soon saw a second dirt road. This was gated too, but had been left unlocked. I pointed this out to Kaui.

"That has to be the one that leads up to the cabin," he said.

I agreed.

After that, I went another two-hundred feet and turned left onto Malaihi Road, which was a steep incline. We proceeded slowly to where a narrow dirt road forked to the right. I turned there and drove under some low hanging branches and through a small creek overflowing with rainwater. I parked at the end.

We both climbed out and began to put on our ponchos. As I pulled mine over my head, I noticed a pocket inside the front. I showed this to Kaui and told him, "Both guns can go right there."

He gave me a nod.

I reminded him, "Make sure to keep their safety levers on."

"Got it."

From that spot the two of us walked back the way we came. Within minutes, we arrived again at the fork at Malaihi Road. I whispered to Kaui, "If you hear someone coming, hide as fast as you can. Okay?"

Kaui nodded in reply.

We headed up the paved road a short distance. In a low voice I told Kaui, "The foot trail should be up here on the left."

Kaui walked further. After about fifty feet he stopped and signaled me, directing my attention to an opening in the woods. Sure enough, it was the narrow trail we were looking for.

I glanced around. At the side of the road I spotted a small wooden log which someone had stood upright. I pointed to it and whispered, "Looks like a marker."

Kaui nodded in agreement. "Hopefully it was Safire."

He and I entered the trail. After about eighty feet or so, we came to a dirt road. We knew this led uphill to the cabin. I looked at the straightaway between switchbacks and whispered, "This would be the perfect place for a sniper to—"

"To die."

"Yeah."

Kaui soon decided on a spot where he'd hide while waiting for Safire. Together we collected some branches and trimmings, which we piled at the spot for extra camouflage.

"Are you sure you're okay with all this?" I asked him.

"I'll be fine," he replied. "It's *you* I'm worried about."

"Me? I'll be in a warm, cozy cabin while you're out here in the rain."

Kaui managed a grin. "I think my chances are better than yours."

I couldn't argue with that.

Once we'd finished, the two of us headed back to where our vehicle was parked. When we arrived, Kaui pulled out one of the handguns, the small Sig Sauer .22, and looked it over.

I pointed to a cypress about twenty feet away. "See if you can hit that tree."

Kaui flipped the safety off and raised the weapon with one hand. He aimed for a few seconds and squeezed the trigger. Thanks to the small caliber and the suppressor there was little sound. He did miss the target though.

"Rats."

"Try gripping with both hands," I said. "And take your time."

He took my advice and carefully lined up the sights before firing—this time hitting the target dead center.

I noticed a grin.

"Try again," I said, "only this time without using the sights."

"Like, by feel?"

"Right. When you have Safire in range it'll be dark and you won't be able to use the sights."

"Good point."

He practiced that for a few minutes until he had the hang of it. He then asked, "What about the other gun?" He pulled the Colt .380 from his poncho and handed it to me.

I took the gun and explained, "Unlike the Sig, this one is loud and powerful. Because of that we can't take any practice shots, but I can show you a few things you should know." It was painful to move my right arm, but I demonstrated as best I could the proper way to hold it for firing. I also instructed him in operating the laser sight as well as how to eject the clip and reload it.

Kaui had no trouble understanding any of this. In fact, he didn't seem to have any problem with the prospect of killing someone either.

He asked, "What kind of gun do you think Safire will be using?"

"She'll be using a sniper rifle," I replied. "Besides that, she'll probably be carrying a handgun as well."

"Is handling a sniper rifle like using one of these?"

"Why do you ask?"

He shrugged.

I gave him a serious look. "Look, once Safire is eliminated your only job will be to recue your brother and get out of here. Right?"

"I'm only asking in case I need to use it for something…unforeseen."

I told him, "Using a sniper rifle is different than using a handgun. For one thing, they're *extremely* powerful and designed for long-range accuracy, where handguns are more for close-ups."

"So they have scopes, right?"

"Usually. Safire would probably have a digital night scope. If so, there would be a small switch to turn it on or off, and maybe a cap over the lens."

"How do I load it?"

"Her gun would already be loaded," I said, "but it would have a lever you can rotate and pull back if you needed to load the barrel for some reason. There would also be a bullet case on the bottom with a release lever." I added, "Each bullet is over four inches long."

He whistled.

"Yeah. They recoil like a cannon and can knock you to the ground if you're not prepared. Plus the sound-level will blow your eardrums out."

By the time Kaui earned his merit badge it was almost dark. We got in the car and headed back to Malaihi Road. On the way there I gave Kaui a few words of advice. "Tonight," I said, "you'll need to stay focused." I looked him in the eye. "When the time comes, show Safire the same mercy and kindness she'd show you."

He nodded.

As we arrived at Malaihi Road, Kaui grabbed the cell phones and his tin of shoe polish. He stepped out into the rain and then turned to me. "We're going to make it through tonight—you included. Right?"

"Right," I lied.

He looked at me as if it would be the last time we'd ever see each other. With no further ado, he shut the door and walked straight to the trail and disappeared into the woods.

Though we'd been presented with few alternatives, my heart still felt uneasy about all this. I let out a long sigh as I drove off, leaving my young friend alone to tend to his mission.

To kill a killer.

Chapter 54

Safire turned her gaze to a rusted lantern resting on a shelf inside the small cabin. A brilliant flame glowed from its mantle, sending golden light dancing across the walls of the cabin. That, along with the rhythmic sound of falling rain on the steel roof was soothing to her. Suddenly, the sound was drowned out by the roar of an approaching vehicle, a jeep, as it splashed along the narrow unpaved road before screeching to a stop just outside. She stood from her wooden chair, sending a large black cockroach scurrying about. Before opening the door, she glanced over at her young captive who lay handcuffed in the far corner. She then stepped outside onto the small covered deck.

Lucas Richter was there. He climbed out of the jeep, followed by his three hired guards. Each of the guards grabbed a gear bag from the rear of the vehicle and carried them to the deck.

Richter first glanced at Safire and then at the dilapidated old structure. He frowned. "This is it?"

Safire made no reply, but continued studying the unfamiliar faces accompanying Richter. Like her, the three men were wearing black military jackets. The biggest of them opened his gear bag and pulled out an assault rifle, which Safire recognized as a Heckler & Koch G36. He unfolded its stock and snapped the magazines in place, jungle-style. He looked over at Safire and grinned.

Richter make quick introductions. "Safire, meet Luis and Max." He gestured to two of the men. "These are Ellis's brothers."

She seemed startled by that.

Richter noticed her reaction before pointing to the third guard. "This is Diego, a trusted associate of theirs." He glanced around. "Where is Ellis?"

Safire locked eyes with Richter. "Perhaps you and I should talk."

He shrugged. "Just tell me where he is."

Luis, the biggest one, stepped forward. "Answer the question, lady. Where's my brother?" He began to raise his rifle.

Richter held his hand out to stop Luis, noticing that Safire had already drawn her weapon.

"Ellis Lacorde is gone," she announced. "Mike Brennan claims to have captured him this afternoon—but I do not believe him."

"Captured?" Luis asked. "Well, why are we just standing here? Let's go after him."

"First, we need Brennan," Safire told him. "Do you understand?"

"So we just sit here and do nothing?"

"Ellis is most likely dead," she informed him. "Brennan has your brother's phone in his possession. He also claims to be a government agent—though I believe he is a common spy." She then turned to Richter. "I believe Ellis was killed by Brennan."

Richter's expression hardened. "Who is Brennan working with?"

"I'm convinced he is alone," she replied. She pointed inside the cabin. "All he wants is to rescue *him*." She went inside and motioned for the others to follow.

Before entering the cabin, Richter instructed Diego, "I need you and Max to secure the area and set up perimeter sensors at two-hundred feet. Understand?"

Diego acknowledged that, then grabbed one of the gear bags and headed off.

Richter joined Safire and Luis inside. They looked down at Kekoa and saw his hands were cuffed behind his back and his ankles were bound together. As Kekoa stared up at them, they noticed his swollen face was covered with dried blood and his pants appeared to be soaked with urine. In the damp air, they could detect the pungent smell of stale vomit coming from his hair and shirt.

"Who is this?" Luis asked.

Safire looked over at Richter. "Your guard asks too many questions."

"Excuse me, lady," Luis snapped, "my brother is missing." He glared at her. "And you were the last person to—"

"Your brother was reckless and stupid," she snapped back. "He is probably dead as a result!"

Luis stepped forward. In an instant, Safire positioned herself into a martial arts stance.

"Knock it off!" Richter shouted. "Both of you!" He turned to Luis. "Go outside and cool off."

Luis's face was red with anger. He stared at Safire before he exited the cabin, slamming the door behind him.

Aside from the sound of rain landing on the metal roof, it was quiet. Richter asked, "What makes you think Brennan is a spy?"

She gestured to her captive on the floor. "*He* told me."

Richter crouched down beside Kekoa. He saw there were dozens of ants crawling on Kekoa's face and hair, attracted by the dried blood and vomit. He leaned close and asked, "Do you know who I am, Kekoa?"

Kekoa opened one eye and cleared his throat. "You're Lucas Richter."

"That's right. Now tell me, who does Mike Brennan actually work for?"

Kekoa's lips quivered. "I…I don't know. He never told us any—"

"He *must* have told you!"

"He didn't, I swear."

Richter leaned closer. "You and your brother designed the mainframe for the control room. Right?"

Kaui nodded.

"Who placed the transmitter inside that mainframe, Kekoa? Was it Brennan?"

He shrugged. "I don't know."

"Tell me," Richter warned, "or I'll kick your head in right here."

Kekoa began to tremble uncontrollably. Finally, he admitted, "Mike said he put it there."

"Okay, good." Richter patted Kekoa on his shoulder. "Now tell me who *you* work for."

Kekoa looked up from the floor. "I work for Cronus Aero—"

"Don't lie to me!" Richter yelled. "I know you and your brother are spies—just like Brennan."

"I'm not!" Kekoa cried. "I'm not a spy and neither is Kaui. I'm telling the truth." He began weeping while his body convulsed from the combined trauma of terror, cold, and pain.

Richter stood and turned to Safire. "Brennan has Lacorde's phone, right?"

She nodded.

"Let's give him a ring."

Chapter 55

The windows had fogged and the air inside the car was starting to feel damp and cool. Using the in-dash tablet, I found a breaking article in the Maui News: *Two Dead in Haiku. Killer at Large.* The reporter explained that the body of a local merchant had been found with a fatal gunshot wound. At the same time, the body of a young woman was discovered only a few hundred feet away. Authorities believed that the victim's neck had been broken. I turned off the tablet.

Just then, Lacorde's phone rang.

I answered, "This is Brennan."

"I'm glad I've finally tracked you down, Mike."

I thought I recognized the caller's voice. "Is this Lucas Richter?"

"Yes, it is. I hope you're not too surprised."

"I guess I shouldn't be. This whole thing stinks like one of your harebrained operations."

There was a short pause before Richter replied, "I'm flattered, really. Now tell me, Mike, where is our friend Ellis Lacorde?"

"He's your friend, Lucas, not mine."

"Where is he?"

"He's in custody, as you—"

"Let's not play games, Brennan. Just answer my questions with none of your nonsense. If you can do that I'll allow your friend Kekoa to live."

"You always were a schmuck."

Richter ignored that and explained, "The boy has lost a lot of blood. He's still breathing, but we don't have much time."

"Well, if you surrender now—"

"Stop wasting time, Brennan. Right now you're the one who needs to surrender. That's the deal if you want Kekoa to live. Should we break his legs while you think about it?"

"Just let him go," I said. "He and his brother stumbled into this mess by accident, Lucas. They don't know anything—but *I* sure do."

"Like what, for example?"

"I can tell you all about Rita. How's that? I know everything, Lucas, including where it's kept and who's in charge of it." I figured that had him drooling. Just to be sure, I tossed my ace card out there. "How about that rover you found on Venus? Would you like to know where *that* came from?"

There was a long pause and I figured he may have wet himself. Finally, he replied, "Okay. Let's say I'm interested. What do you—?"

"If you allow Kekoa to go free I'll tell you everything."

He seemed to think about that. "I'm sure you're full of it," he said, "but okay. Kekoa goes free. You can watch him drive away in your car."

Perfect. "Where do we meet?"

"Where are you right now?"

"I'm still parked where your idiot girlfriend told me to park."

Richter made a grunt. "I wouldn't push her buttons if I were you, Brennan. And she's not my—"

"Yeah, yeah, I got it."

"Start driving," he told me. "From North Market Street go to Kahekili Highway. When you see Waiehu Beach Road on the right, pull over."

"Then what?"

"Then you'll wait for my call, that's what." He let me know, "Make sure you're alone, Brennan, and don't try anything cute." Right there he ended the call.

I thought for a moment and decided to try something cute. I sent Kaui a text message:

EXCHANGE IS A GO. HEADING THERE NOW. STICK WITH PLAN. FYI…IT IS RICHTER.

I pressed *send* and took a deep breath as I pulled out of the parking lot.

From the corner of his eye, Lucas Richter noticed that Safire had pulled her handgun from her holster. His eyes darted around the room for a moment before he asked, "What are you doing with that?"

Safire ignored his question as she ejected the clip. After inspecting the cartridges, she slammed the clip back into place and returned the gun to her holster. She then grabbed her rifle case and stepped outside.

Richter heaved a sigh and went out to the deck where he joined Luis and Safire. From there he could see that Max and Diego were patrolling the grounds. Using his phone, he checked the perimeter sensors and saw they were operational. He said to Safire, "If anyone steps within two-hundred feet of this shack, we'll know about it."

She gave him a look. "Send one of your guards down to the entrance gate—just in case."

He thought about that and turned to Luis. "Go take Diego's position," he said. "Have him go down the hill and stakeout the gate. After Brennan arrives, no one enters—"

"And no one leaves," Safire said, completing his statement.

Luis glared at her for a second before he marched off.

Safire grabbed her rifle case and told Richter, "Call me when you have sent the boy my way." She then pulled up her hood and stepped hastily from the deck.

Richter stood and watched as Safire disappeared into the woods. After that, he pulled out his phone and entered the number for Lacorde's cell. He took a deep breath and pressed *call*.

Chapter 56

Kaui sat motionless in the darkness, waiting patiently for his moment while large drops of cold rainwater fell around him from the canopy of leaves and branches above. Under his camouflage poncho he was mostly dry. Between that and the black shoe polish on his face he felt almost invisible.

In his right hand he held the Colt .380. He ran his fingers over the texture of the gun's grip and felt the knurled face of the trigger. His hands were steady, though his heart was pounding. In his mind, he'd carefully acted out every possible scenario he might encounter. He understood that one small mistake could cost his life—and Kekoa's and Mike's as well.

His thoughts were interrupted as he felt a large insect, a giant centipede, crawl slowly over his ankle. Just as he began to reach down to crush the creature he noticed a shadow moving in the distance. He froze and watched the silhouette of a figure marching down the hill toward the main road before disappearing into the woods below.

Kaui's thoughts then returned to the centipede. He reached down to his right ankle, but now felt nothing. Frantically, he patted his legs and felt the ground under his poncho, but the huge insect was nowhere to be found.

Suddenly, the sound of approaching footsteps came to his ears. At once he felt his heart quicken. He turned his eyes to his left. As he looked, a shadowy image appeared from the trail. He could make out the faint outline of a woman. She walked purposefully with quick calculating steps. As she stepped closer, Kaui could see she was carrying a rifle case.

At the same moment, he saw an automobile's headlights slice through the darkness. Quickly, the woman knelt down behind the branches and foliage, mere inches from Kaui's feet. He remained motionless, drawing slow shallow breaths.

He listened as the approaching car traveled back and forth up the hill through the switchbacks. As the vehicle came into view, Kaui turned his eyes and recognized the maroon Nissan SUV. It was Mike Brennan.

For a brief moment, the headlights shone through the narrow wooded area where he and the woman were hiding. A ray of light fell upon the woman's face and Kaui recognized at once who it was.

Safire.

He sat in silence as Mike drove past. After that, it became dark and quiet once again. He gripped the gun in his hand and mentally prepared himself while waiting for his eyes to adjust.

A sudden gust of wind blew, bringing down heavy drops of rain from the leaves above. As the drops fell, they landed onto his plastic poncho. This made a strange and unnatural sound. Hearing this, Safire leaped to her feet. She drew a handgun from her jacket and turned in his direction.

Kaui sat frozen as she cocked her head and listened intently. In the distance, a low rumble of thunder came and went. Kaui felt his lower lip tremble and his lungs began to burn as he held his breath. He made no movement except to slowly and carefully slide his gun's safety lever into the fire position.

Safire looked around and kicked at the branches piled around Kaui. Seeing nothing, she lowered her weapon and relaxed her stance. In the meantime, Kaui considered his next move. Carefully, he wrapped his finger around the trigger, then raised the weapon and aimed it at her chest. As he prepared to fire, he heard a faint buzzing sound. Safire turned and reached into her pocket. He paused as she pulled out her phone, which was vibrating.

Safire answered the call. After listening for a few seconds, she told the caller, "Good. Just call me when the boy leaves the cabin." After ending the call, she grabbed her rifle case and moved to the edge of the trail where she opened the gun case and bent down to prepare her weapon.

Kaui's heart was pounding even harder now as he contemplated what to do. He heard Safire's phone vibrating again and knew he was running out of time.

Safire answered and listened for a moment and muttered a brief reply before ending the call. After that, she positioned herself against a thick tree and made a few final adjustments to her rifle.

Seconds later, Kaui spotted the vehicle's lights again and knew the exchange had been made. He began to raise his weapon slowly out from under the poncho. As he did, he realized the centipede had returned and was now crawling up his leg. Ignoring that, he raised the weapon higher and focused his attention on the target.

As he aimed, the huge centipede crawled through his shorts, then up onto his waist. Without warning, it bit into his skin with its sharp scissor-like forcipules while injecting its painful venom. Kaui cringed in agony and stifled a cry. Quickly, he reached down and grabbed at the writhing creature with his left hand and tossed it into the bushes before it could attack again.

From the corner of his eye, he noticed lights and could hear the vehicle approaching. Seconds later, it rounded the turn and was heading toward them.

Safire lowered her eye into the scope.

Seeing this, Kaui took aim and pulled the trigger.

Nothing. The trigger was locked.

In a panic, Kaui shook the gun frantically before realizing he'd slid the safety lever into the wrong position. He jumped to his feet and flipped the lever into the fire position. As Safire was about to take her shot, he raised his gun and yelled loudly.

At the sound of his cry, Safire took her eye from the target and spun around. Kaui pulled the trigger while charging toward her. The shot missed, but Safire was startled. She dropped her rifle to the ground and began to pedal backward. She then stumbled onto the dirt road where she fell into a wide puddle.

Kaui stopped in his tracks as the headlights from the SUV shone on him. He hesitated for a second and looked up at the vehicle. He could see his brother at the wheel. In that same second, Safire drew her handgun and prepared to fire.

Kaui saw this and fired first. The bullet struck the right side of Safire's chest. She gasped as her head curled downward and her lungs emptied. Without taking aim, she pulled the trigger and fired one shot.

The bullet struck the mud at Kaui's feet. Undaunted, he stepped forward and fired again. This time, the shot exploded the right side of her head, sending specks of flesh everywhere.

Kaui wiped a piece of skull bone from his cheek. He then pulled down his poncho hood and rushed forward to the oncoming vehicle, waving his arms.

Kekoa slowed down to look. Despite the poncho and black shoe polish, he recognized his brother at once. Immediately, he came to a stop and climbed out of the vehicle.

After they'd shared a few heartfelt words, Kekoa looked over at the body lying in the puddle.

"Safire?"

Kaui nodded. "She got in the way of a bullet."

The two stepped over to where her body lay. As Kaui grabbed the gun from her dead hand, his brother looked at her closely, noticing the fatal head wound. Part of him was tempted to kick her as she had done to him. Instead, he turned away.

Kaui tossed Safire's rifle, along with her handgun and gun case onto the back seat. He glanced over at Kekoa. "Let's go. I'll take the wheel."

They both jumped in and prepared to head off. Before leaving, however, Kaui pulled forward, rolling the left front tire directly over Safire's upper body, pressing her deeper into the puddle of mud. He turned to Kekoa, who nodded in silent approval. After that, Kaui placed the gear lever into forward and started down the hill.

With the pedal to the floor, Kaui splashed through a long puddle and headed into a sharp left curve—although too fast. As the tires lost traction, he slammed on the brakes and spun the wheel to the left. Almost at once the vehicle went into a spin. The right rear fender slammed into a thick tree and the passenger-side airbag deployed just as Kekoa's head struck the side window. Kaui was tossed from the driver's seat up onto the center console.

The vehicle's onboard computer began an announcement. "Airbag deployed. Calling emergency—"

"Shut up!" Kaui yelled as he scrambled back into his seat. "Give me four-wheel drive, now!"

On the dash, the *4WD* symbol lit and Kaui again hit the accelerator. All four tires dug in and the vehicle pulled away from the tree and back onto the trail, leaving its rear bumper cover behind.

Kaui glanced over at his brother, who was untangling himself from the side airbag. "Are you all right?"

"Just drive," he replied. "And try to stay on the road."

At the bottom of the hill, Diego had seen the vehicle's lights spin around and had heard the sound of the crash. After that, he saw it moving again and gaining speed. He began to realize something had gone wrong with the plan.

While the twins rounded the last hairpin turn, their vehicle slid sideways in the road while its tires spun through the mud. Seeing this, Diego stepped behind a nearby tree and raised his assault rifle into position. As the car emerged from the curve, the bright headlights beamed into Diego's eyes, temporarily blinding him.

Kekoa caught a glimpse of Diego up ahead. "Look right there," he yelled. "Someone's behind that tree."

Kaui saw the glare reflecting in Diego's eyes and noticed the rifle aimed in their direction. "Get down!"

They both crouched low in their seats as Diego fired three shots in rapid succession. Two bullets struck the rear of the vehicle, just above the battery compartment. Using his left hand, Kaui grabbed the .380 and held it out the window. Diego dove to the side as Kaui emptied the remaining ammo. Then, just in time, he slammed on the brakes. The vehicle slid along the wet surface, stopping just inches from the tree.

One of Kaui's shots had grazed Diego's right arm, causing him to drop his assault rifle into the bushes. Diego cried in pain, then looked up at the twins before he turned and darted down a trail.

Kaui and Kekoa jumped out. "Look for his rifle," Kaui told his brother. He then grabbed his Sig .22 from his poncho and ran down the trail in pursuit.

After entering the woods, Kaui lost sight of Diego. He slowed his steps and crouched low to listen. After a few seconds, he heard the sound of heavy breathing. Slowly, he stood and looked around. At the same time, Diego pulled out his cell, not realizing the light from the phone's screen would give away his position.

Kaui could see his opponent had his back to him. Without a sound, he turned on the gun's laser sighting and aimed the red beam at Diego's head. Kaui's hand shook slightly as he prepared to fire. Diego caught a glimpse of the red light as it flashed across a nearby bush. He spun around just as Kaui fired three silenced shots. One of the bullets hit Diego's throat. Instantly, he dropped the phone and raised his hand to his neck, gasping for air. Without hesitation, Kaui stepped forward and fired a final shot at point blank.

After this, he picked up Diego's phone and held it to his ear. A male voice on the other end asked, "What was that? Hello? …Diego?"

Kaui replied with a deep voice, "It's all right. The boy is dead." At that, he ended the call and ran back to the car. After he and his brother had jumped in, he started the engine. "Hang on," he told Kekoa. "We're not out of the woods yet."

"Are you okay?"

Kaui reversed to the road, then threw the shifter into drive. "I will be once I'm out of here." He noticed Kekoa was holding Diego's assault rifle. "I see you found our friend's little gun."

"Yeah. So what happened to our 'friend,' anyway?"

They passed through the open gate. "He had a meeting to attend."

"A meeting?"

Kaui turned onto the highway and hit the gas. After putting some distance behind them he looked over at his brother. "He went to meet his maker."

Chapter 57

The rain began pouring down even harder, making it difficult to drive. After reaching Wailuku Town, Kaui turned onto a narrow side street and parked. He and Kekoa leaned back for a moment to catch their breath.

From the center console, Kaui grabbed the bottle of Mountain Mist and the Snickers bar and passed them to his brother. "Here, Brah, I saved these for you."

Kekoa wiped some of the air-bag residue from his face and guzzled down half of the drink. He then opened the candy wrapper and took a bite while Kaui pulled out his phone.

"Who you calling?" Kekoa asked.

"Uh…9-1-1?"

"But what about Mike? We need to go back for him."

Kaui gave him a look. "We're not going anywhere, Kekoa. Mike specifically instructed me to call the police as soon as you were out of there. He'll kill us if we—"

"No, they'll kill *him*," Kekoa protested. "We have to go back. As soon as they find out Safire and that guy are dead, they'll know I've escaped—if they haven't figured it out already. By the time the police find the place, Mike will have been killed and Lucas Richter will be long gone."

Kaui considered that. "How many of them are left?"

"Besides Richter, there was a big guy named Luis and his brother. That's all."

"Well, that's one more than us."

Kekoa held up Diego's assault weapon. "But now we have this thing—plus a sniper rifle." He looked Kaui in the eye. "Let's head back. If things get too dangerous we'll call the cops. All right?"

Kaui thought for a moment, then let out a breath and looked over at Kekoa. "All right, let's go before I change my mind."

They tapped fists together. As Kaui started the car and prepared to pull out, Kekoa asked, "Where's Raquel, anyway?"

Kaui froze.

"She's okay, right?"

Kaui moved the gear selector back into park and leaned back in his seat. As he thought about how to reply, he glanced through his side window at the foreboding black sky.

Somehow, the night had just become darker.

Chapter 58

I could tell by the way the cabin was shaking that the wind had picked up. The rain, too, as the soft sound of droplets tinkling on the steel roof had been replaced by a loud metallic rumble.

Lucas Richter was here. He and I were giving each other a cold stare, I guess to see who would blink first. He blinked and then told me, "I have a few questions, Brennan. First, I want you to tell me where you've stored the data you stole from the control room."

"I don't know what you're talking about."

He grabbed me by the hair and pulled my head back. "Talk, or Luis here will break your jaw."

I glanced over at Luis Lacorde. He was a big guy, and he looked like he could knock the lungs out of an ape. He put his big face in front of mine and added, "While you're at it, tell me what you've done with my brother."

I told Luis, "Richter's girlfriend, Safire, told me she killed Ellis." I leaned back in my wooden chair, which I was tied to, and added, "Truth is, she plans to kill both of you too."

Richter looked over at Luis and I hoped they'd start arguing between each other. Instead, Richter pointed his thumb at me and told Luis, "Break something."

As soon as Luis stepped forward I looked up and spit a mouthful of saliva into his face. I'd been saving it.

Luis reared away and wiped the spit from his angry eyes. In a rage, he stepped forward again and popped me in the jab. As the blow landed, I drew my tongue back and rolled my face. Nonetheless, I heard something crack. I hate when that happens.

During the fun, part of a tooth snapped off and rolled to the back of my mouth. I gasped for air, which caused it to drop into my windpipe. I quickly realized I couldn't breathe.

I raised my head and coughed as hard as I could. After a few tries, the fragment dislodged and a mist of blood and phlegm shot out at Luis and Richter. After taking a few breaths I looked at my captors, who now had blood and goo spattered on their faces.

I managed a laugh.

Luis, for some reason, didn't think that was funny. He wiped his face and pointed his fat finger at me. "You're going to wind up like your puny girlfriend."

I gave him the eye. "And you're going to wind up like your idiot brother."

"Where is he?"

"Try looking in the ocean just off highway 340," I said. "He'll be the one in the green Buick."

Luis stepped forward as if to kill me. Before he could get his hands on me, Richter raised his hand, signaling him to back off. I assumed the whole killing part would have to wait until later, which was okay with me. That would give me extra time to piss them off even further.

It was Richter's turn now. For his act, he pulled out a small folding knife and opened it. "You've done a good job of taunting us, Brennan—"

"I'm just getting started."

He smiled politely. "I'm sure. But fun time is over." Using the knife, he cut the makeshift dressing from my shoulder and took a moment to study the bullet wound. "My, my, what happened here?" he asked. "You're just having a bad day, aren't you, Brennan?"

Well, I sure was—but I decided to keep that to myself.

Richter pressed the tip of the knife blade slowly into the bullet hole, reopening the wound. From behind, Luis grabbed my hair, jerking my head back while I cringed.

Richter reminded me, "You told me you have information about the planetary rover we found—"

"Yeah. The one on Venus. Take that knife out of me and I'll tell you what I know."

He withdrew the blade.

After a short breather, I told him, "If you look close enough at the images you'll see a small oval symbol on the side of the rover."

"What symbol?"

"The symbol of *Wright Aerospace.*"

He appeared more stupefied than usual.

I continued, "The people at Wright are sneakier than you realize. After the Praxis II accident, which we know wasn't an accident at all, Wright began staggering their missions."

"What are you saying?"

"The supposed mission rockets they send up are actually just test probes or satellites. Their satellite launches are, in reality—"

"The actual mission," Richter said, completing my explanation. He seemed to be deep in thought for a moment and then asked, "What about Rita? I'm curious to hear what you have to say about that."

I closed my eyes and made no reply.

After waiting for a moment, Luis jerked back on my hair. "Answer the man now, Brennan, or I'll snap your neck."

"Go ahead. But then you'll never know where it is."

Richter, schmuck that he is, reinserted the blade deep into my bullet wound and gave it a twist, sending a shock wave across my shoulder. "You're going to tell me, Brennan. I can do this all night."

Between gasps I managed to say, "You…don't…have…all…night!"

He released the pressure on the blade. "Why not? I'm in no hurry."

I took a breath. "This place will be surrounded soon, if it isn't already."

He let out a laugh. "No one knows we're here, Brennan, so don't even—"

"Then where's Safire?" I asked. "Shouldn't she be back by now? Huh?"

He and Luis looked at each other. Neither spoke, but I saw Richter make a gesture to the door. As Luis began to leave, Richter asked for his knife. From a sheath on his hip, Luis removed a huge combat knife and handed it to Richter. The long polished blade glistened in the faint light.

After Luis had gone, Richter came over and tapped the blade of the big knife over my shoulder a few times. "Okay Brennan, no more games. You'll either tell me everything right now or I'll slit your throat."

Upon my arrival, I had remembered to use my ring to activate the recorder on the ICD thing in my ear. That way, every word this idiot spoke would wind up on tape. "I'll take the third option."

"Which is…?"

"I'll ask *you* a question. If you answer it—and no bull—I'll answer yours. Deal?"

Richter shrugged. "Okay. Ask away."

"Good. The Praxis II rocket and the sabotage at Wright—"

"That was us. I organized it."

"Okay, but someone in a high position at Cronus must have come up with the idea, right?"

Richter nodded. "Right."

I continued, "And the four dead control room team members. That must have been—"

"That must have been me."

Geez. "So what about Derrick Haut? How does he fit into all this?"

"Haut has been involved all along," he replied. "But that's enough questions from you. I think it's my turn."

"Ask away."

"First, tell me where you've stored the data from the—"

"Piss off."

He seemed confused by that and repeated himself, "I want you to tell me where—"

"Didn't you hear me? I said, 'Piss off.'"

He let out a breath, then stepped behind me kicked the back of my chair. This sent my head crashing into the corner. After that, he grabbed me by the hair and jerked my head back. I saw his face was red with anger as he held the huge razor-sharp blade under my jaw. "Answer me!" he yelled.

I made no reply.

"Answer me—or I'll cut your head off right here!"

I noticed his hand was trembling. "Go ahead," I told him. "I'm ready to die." And I was.

Chapter 59

Storm warnings and flash-flood advisories had been announced island-wide. Wind-driven rain had brought down countless tree branches while mud and rocks poured down from the hillsides. Across the island, people closed their windows, brought in their pets, and stayed indoors.

Kaui and Kekoa drove past the open gate leading to the cabin, and then past Malaihi Road. A quarter mile later they turned left through a flowing stream of rainwater onto Akakuu Street where they found a small abandoned warehouse. The property was surrounded on three sides by a six-foot chain-link fence.

Kaui looked around. "It should be here," he said. "On the map it shows a dirt road going up the mountain from behind this warehouse. Once we find that, we should be able to connect to the top of Malaihi Road without being seen."

They pulled closer to the building. From there, Kekoa spotted a double gate built into the fence at the back of the property. "That must be the entrance, but I think it's locked."

Kaui flipped on the high beams and looked. "It's just a padlock," he said. "It'll pop right open."

"Are you sure?"

"Of course I'm sure." He hit the gas and aimed for the center of the gate.

Kekoa crouched down in his seat as the car collided into the gate. Rather than popping open as his brother had expected, the gate doors wrapped across the front of the vehicle, forcing them to stop.

Kaui cursed the lock, then backed up until the fence fell from the front end. At that point the two of them climbed out. In the driving rain, they lifted the gate section over the hood and up onto the roof. "That's good enough!" Kaui yelled. "Let's go!"

Once they'd climbed back in, he pulled forward. The gate doors slid off the roof, landing behind them. After that, they started up the narrow mud-soaked road.

The SUV bounced along over rocks and fallen branches while Kekoa hung on to the dashboard. He looked over at Kaui. "Pretty strong padlock, huh? They really build those—"

"Shut Up." Kaui slowed down and turned off the lights.

The onboard computer made an announcement: *The driving lights have been turned off.*

"You shut up, too," Kaui told it. He then turned to Kekoa and grinned.

As they crept along slowly in the darkness, low branches swayed in the wind and brushed across the car's roof and fenders. In the meantime, Kekoa kept an eye on the GPS. Once they were within a few hundred feet of Malaihi Road, he told Kaui, "Stop here."

"Is this it?"

"I think so. The top of the road should be just ahead. From there, the cabin is about ninety yards or so through the woods."

Kaui looked at the satellite map of the area and pointed to the narrow system of canals. "This old irrigation channel runs for miles along the foot of the mountain."

Kekoa zoomed in on the canal. "Can we get to the cabin through it?"

Kaui shook his head. "It's probably overflowing at this point. Besides, we'd never get close to the cabin without being shot at."

"Okay. So, what's the plan?"

Kaui thought for a moment. "You know how in shooter games you always have the advantage if you gain the high ground?"

"Yeah."

"Well, what if we go up there?" He pointed to a water tower located high on the steep hill above the canal.

They looked at each other for a moment before Kaui announced, "I'll grab the sniper rifle."

The downpour and the strong winds had finally begun to subside. To the east, the full moon had begun breaking through the distant clouds, its luminous glow reflecting over the face of the sea.

The twins hiked up the hill until they'd reached the tall cylindrical water tower. About thirty feet in front of it they found a large round rock which they felt would suffice as a lookout point. There, they took their position.

Using the rifle's night-vision scope, Kaui scanned the area below. "There's the cabin," he whispered, "right below us."

"Do you see anyone down there?"

He looked over the cabin itself, noticing only a trace of light from around the door. To the left of the cabin he spotted a guard. "There's a guy right there," he whispered, "just north of the cabin."

Kekoa took the weapon to see for himself. Right away, he spotted the guard and saw he was carrying an assault rifle. As the guard turned, he noticed he was wearing heavy goggles. He ducked behind the rock. "Get down!"

Kaui cowered behind the large rock. "What is it?"

"I think he has night-vision goggles."

"Did you see anything else?"

"Besides the big assault rifle? No."

"Can we pick him off from here?"

Kekoa considered that. "I guess so, but there might be more guards besides him."

"Right. Let's call 9-1-1 first, before we start shooting. Head for the water tower—and stay low."

The two walked quickly while crouching until they'd reached the tall tower. There, Kaui pulled out his vending machine cell phone and dialed 9-1-1. After a few seconds, the phone buzzed an alert notice: *No cellular reception available.* He showed his brother the notice.

Kekoa nodded. "We're probably too far up in the mountains for cell phones."

"Then it's up to us," Kaui said. "Time could be running out for Mike." At the front of the water tower, he noticed a large gate-valve. Next to that was a ladder leading to the top.

Following Kaui's line of sight, Kekoa looked up. "Do you want to climb up there?"

He seemed to think about it. "If we have to, yeah. But for now I think we're better off behind the rock."

Keeping low and quiet, they returned to their vantage point. There, Kaui handed the rifle to his brother. "You take the first shot."

"Why me?"

"Because it's your turn."

Reluctantly, Kekoa took the weapon and carefully positioned it over the top of the rock. After a few seconds, he had the guard in his sights.

Kaui whispered a warning, "That thing fires *huge* bullets—four inches long—so hold on tight."

On that advice, Kekoa pressed the stock firmly against his shoulder and aimed the crosshairs at the guard's chest. He pulled the trigger. A loud fiery blast roared from the muzzle. When the echo from the explosion had faded, Kekoa opened his eyes. He peered through the scope and saw the guard lying on the ground. He turned to his brother. "I just killed a person for the first time."

Kaui looked below. The guard appeared to be curled up and holding his hand over his groin. "I think you shot him in the crotch, Dude."

Kekoa raised the weapon again, this time unfolding the bipod and resting it on top of the rock.

"Aim higher," Kaui suggested. "The scope might be off."

Kekoa made the adjustment and pulled the trigger. This time he saw the guard's head explode.

"Now he's dead."

"You sure?"

"Pretty sure."

Kaui took the rifle and scanned the area, looking for any movement or signs, but saw nothing.

"So…what do we do now?" Kekoa asked.

"I could fire a shot at the cabin."

Kekoa shook his head. "If Richter realizes someone's out here with a rifle, he might kill Mike right there."

Kaui went back to thinking. Suddenly, an idea came to him. "I think there might be another way to create a diversion." He pointed to the water tower. "I don't know if there's any water in that tank, but there's a big discharge valve right on the front of it."

"So?"

"So, if we're lucky, the water will blast out and run down this hill all the way to the cabin. That should draw Richter's attention without causing him to panic."

"Okay, but what about the canal right below us?"

"It's already full from the storm," Kaui said. "The water would overflow and go straight to the cabin."

"And when Richter steps out to have a look—"

"Bang."

The twins ran up to the water tower. At the front of it was a six-inch gate valve topped with a round handwheel. Wrapped around the handwheel was a thick chain fastened with a brass padlock.

"Oh great, another padlock," Kekoa observed. "Got a key?"

"Actually, I do," Kaui replied. He pulled out Safire's P22 and placed the end of the silencer near the top of the lock, then fired. It opened.

"That one's a lot wimpier than the one at the gate—"

"Shut up."

They removed the chain and began rotating the handwheel. After a few turns, it began to spin freely. Soon, a mist of rust-tainted water shot out from the opening. With each turn, the water flowed out faster. By the time the valve was fully opened a huge surge of water was blasting all the way from the tank to the base of their lookout rock thirty feet away.

The twins stood aside and watched. After a minute, they realized the water was rapidly washing away the soil from under the rock. As they looked on, the rock slowly began to roll forward. To their surprise, it rolled over the edge and tumbled down the steep slope.

From atop, the twins heard a huge crash as the boulder landed into the canal below. That was followed by another strange sound. Kaui and Kekoa rushed to the edge and looked down. To their astonishment, they saw the boulder had smashed open the canal wall.

They watched helplessly as a massive flood of water, countless thousands of gallons drawing from the entire canal system, burst out into a giant surge.

And that surge was headed directly for the cabin.

Chapter 60

I could tell Richter's patience had reached its limits, though his sanity had gone past that a while ago. He pressed the sharp blade of the combat knife against my throat. "Tell me!" he yelled. "Where's the copy of the control room data?"

"Just cut my head off and get it over with," I told him. "Or don't you have the guts?"

"I'll give you two seconds to start talking."

"Go to Hell."

"I'm warning you!"

I looked into Richter's eyes and grinned.

His face was red with fury and I could tell he'd had enough. Just as he was about to slice my throat, the door of the cabin burst open. Richter stopped mid-swing and looked up to see Luis. From the look in Luis's eyes, he could tell something was wrong.

"Safire and Diego are dead," Luis announced. "And I just found Max's body."

I let out a laugh, then looked up at Richter. "See? Only two to go!"

"No Mike," he replied. "Just one to go." As he held the blade across my neck he took a moment to add, "It's time for *you* to go to Hell."

Just then, a thunderous sound shook the cabin. I turned to see the lantern spinning about, casting swirling shadows across the walls before falling to the floor. Instantly, everything went dark. Seconds later, the entire cabin launched upward and rolled to its side as a wall of water exploded upon us.

All at once, we were thrown against the ceiling, then onto the walls. The flood tore the building from its foundation and began carrying it along its raging path. Suddenly, the front wall shattered apart. Wooden beams splintered and panels flew in every direction. At the same time, the roof collapsed—trapping the three of us under it.

I could hear Richter beside me screaming in terror. Seconds later, the cabin collided into a tall tree. Instantly, the structure disintegrated into a debris field of planks and splinters. While still tied to my chair, I was tossed into the swirling, downward rush of mud and water. I held my breath while being battered against tree limbs, rocks, and bushes.

From their lookout point, Kaui and Kekoa watched helplessly as the cabin disappeared from their sight.

"What do we do now?" Kekoa asked.

Kaui felt his pockets, remembering only now that he was carrying Safire's cell phone. He pulled it out quickly pressed 9-1-1.

Kekoa looked at him. "Is it working?"

Kaui held up one finger, signaling his brother to wait.

"Do you have a signal?"

"Wait!" Over the roar of the rushing water below, he heard a ring, and then another. After the third ring, it picked up.

"9-1-1. What is the address of the emergency?"

Chapter 61

Normally, the weather people in Hawaii have it easy. But when they warn about *flash-floods*, they aren't kidding.

While being swept along, I felt my wooden chair break apart. I was finally free, which was the good news. That, plus Richter had missed his one chance to hack my head off. The bad news was that I was being knocked into trees, roots, rocks, and whatever else Hawaiian woodlands had to offer. Also, I was just about out of air.

The rush of water hurled me along and I could tell I was gaining speed. To slow myself, I dug my feet into the ground as hard as I could. As I did, I felt pieces of debris and wood planks ramming me in the back. I raised my head out of the cold water and gasped for air. After that, I managed to maneuver myself out of the center of the current. Once to the side, I climbed up on one knee and wiped the mud from my eyes. I was pretty beat up, of course, but at least I'd escaped Richter. I turned and looked upstream. Coming straight at me, I spotted a pair of boots sticking out of the water. The boots appeared to have legs and a body attached to them.

Richter.

Before I could move to the side he collided into me. This caused me to fall backward. After that, we both climbed to our feet and looked at each other. His face was scraped and smeared with blood.

I turned to scramble away and he followed right after me. I sensed we weren't friends any more. This I could tell by the way he was splashing through the mud and water to get to me. Also by the way he'd pulled out his folding knife.

While I looked around for some kind of weapon, Richter opened the blade and continued to close the distance. From the knee-deep water, he grabbed a drifting piece of lumber and hurled it at me. Before I could duck, the board struck the side of my head, knocking me into the water.

He made a dash for me. As I struggled to get back on my feet, I looked and saw the piece of lumber floating away and quickly dove after it. I grabbed the board, then spun around. Richter glanced at the board and stopped just outside my reach. He held the knife for me to see, turning it and waving it around.

He stepped forward. "What's wrong, Brennan? Nothing to say before I slice you up?"

I stepped back. "Go to Hell."

He flipped the knife in the air, catching it by the handle. "C'mon. You can do better than that."

"I'll take a rain check."

He snickered at that, then lunged forward and swung the knife at me. I jumped back but felt the blade slice across my right elbow. He took another step and swung at me again. This time I blocked his attack with the board, but the blade sliced through my right small finger—ripping the skin almost to the bone. Before he could attack again, I stepped way back. As I did, I lost my balance and stumbled into the moving water.

The board fell from my hand and drifted away before I could reach it. With the help of the moonlight I began looking for another weapon. After a few seconds, I noticed something coming downstream. I looked closer and realized it was a human body drifting face down. Judging from the black military jacket, I knew it had to be either Luis Lacorde or Max.

As the body floated behind Richter, I gestured to it. "There goes your buddy," I said. To my surprise, he turned to look—and that was my chance. With everything I had, I sprang up and shoved him from behind. He tumbled over the floating corpse and plunged into the muddy water. During this, the body turned over and I saw it was my buddy Luis. I also saw something else: his gun.

While Richter splashed around to position himself again, I went for Luis's holster. I yanked the gun out. As I did, a measure of mud and sand poured out with it.

Richter came out of the water and saw me chamber a round. Before I could get a shot off, he dove into the water and swam out into the current. I aimed and pulled the trigger. Nothing. I slapped the side of the gun, realizing too late that the firing mechanism was packed with mud.

I wasn't about to let Richter get away, so I dove in after him. Before long, I felt the current becoming more powerful. I managed to grab onto a narrow tree before being pulled further. I looked ahead and saw I had almost been swept over a steep ledge. Grabbing onto trees and branches, I pulled myself back to shallow water.

As I stopped to catch my breath, it occurred to me that Richter had likely gone over the ledge. Just then, I saw a shadow from behind me.

Right then, I was struck on the back of my neck by a powerful blow. Before I could turn to look, a second crushing blow landed onto my right forearm. I was sure I heard a bone snap.

I quickly rolled to my left—just in time to dodge another attack. I looked up to see Richter standing above me. To my right, I spotted a pile of planks and boards that had drifted onto the bank. I grabbed the first board I could reach and swung it at Richter. The board struck his face, and I was startled to see that a protruding nail at the end of it had driven into his right eye.

Richter let out an earsplitting cry, then backpedalled, pulling the board from my hand. I watched in astonishment as he pulled the board with the nail from his head. As he did, his eyeball came out with it.

He looked at me with his one remaining eye and came at me. He swung the nail-end of the board at my head, missing by less than an inch. As he prepared to deliver the death blow, a red laser light flashed across the bushes. He stopped to look. Seconds later, the sound of a gunshot exploded through the damp air.

Richter and I turned to look. In the distance I could see Kaui and Kekoa walking toward us. Kaui was holding a rifle and had his right eye buried into the scope. His first shot had missed so I took advantage of the unexpected distraction. I leaped forward and caught Richter solidly under the jaw with a left uppercut. I felt his teeth crash together before he dropped the board and fell back.

Stunned by the blow, Richter allowed himself to be caught in the rushing current. Before he could help himself, he was drifting toward the ledge. I watched as he grabbed desperately at floating tree limbs and planks. For a moment, he managed to cling onto a protruding rock while being blasted by an onslaught of water, mud, and debris.

In the seconds before his grip weakened, he glanced over at me with a look of terror. Finally, his strength gave out and he was swept over the ledge. A loud cry echoed as he fell downward, his body pummeling along the face of the ravine before plunging into the depths of the dark, rock-strewn gulch below.

Seconds later, the twins arrived at my side. Kekoa grabbed my right wrist to pull me from the water; not realizing the bone there was broken. The pain took my breath away. That, combined with the loss of blood and overall exhaustion caused the walls around me to begin closing in.

Once they'd gotten me to the bank, Kekoa looked me over. "Just hang in there," he told me. "An ambulance is on the way." I wondered, as I lay there in a weakened state, how many other President's Agents had heard those same words.

For the next few minutes, I drifted in and out of consciousness. I recall hearing the sound of my own heartbeat, which became louder to my ears as each minute passed. I also remember shivering from the cold. From time to time I opened my eyes and looked up at the radiant moon in the midst of the sky above.

Slowly, everything around me became darker and quieter. Even the sound of my heartbeat faded to silence. I gazed upward again and could see only a pinpoint of pure white light beaming in the distance. I remember that it was beautiful. I also remember that it called to me, and I was ready to go to it.

Then that went dark as well.

-PART V-

Maui Memorial Medical Center

"In the time of darkest defeat, victory may be nearest."
~William McKinley

Chapter 62

Monday, April 26, 2032

Iawoke feeling like I'd just checked out of club Hell. I managed to crack open one eye and saw everything was blurry. I tried opening the other eye, but found it was covered with something, maybe a bandage. That's when it dawned on me where I was. In a hospital.

My brain felt numb, like I was medicated, and my stomach was nauseated. Nonetheless, I could remember what had happened. To tell the truth, I had expected to wake up hearing angels and harp music.

Soon, a nurse strolled in and began removing the bandage from my eye. When she'd finished, she lifted each of my eyelids and checked my pupils.

Once my vision readjusted, I looked to my right and saw Kaui and Kekoa standing beside the bed, beaming at me. I wanted to say something stupid so they'd know I was okay, but my words came out slurry.

"He's trying to say something," Kaui said to the nurse.

She leaned over the bed. "Hello Mr. Brennan." She wiped my face and continued, "My name is Ashley. I'm your nurse today. This is Maui Memorial Medical Center. Okay?"

I nodded my head so she wouldn't repeat all that.

"Are you feeling all right?"

I glanced over at the twins to see their expression, then back at Ashley and realized she was serious. I shook my head.

"You just had surgery, so you might feel groggy for another few minutes. All right?"

I slurred something in reply. Whatever came out of my mouth must have been a bit off because she and the twins gave me a funny look.

Before long, I felt like I could think more clearly. I was also able to talk. After I'd talked for a while, I sensed that Ashley wanted to have me put to sleep again.

I began to assess myself. First of all, I noticed my nose was bandaged up and stuffed with cotton, so I knew I looked ridiculous. Both my arms were casted and there were tubes and wires running everywhere. My jaw was bandaged and I had a tooth missing, which I remembered swallowing. I made a mental note to ask Ashley to keep an eye out for that.

I saw a big fellow standing near the door of the room. I asked the twins, "Security guard?"

Kaui nodded. "Mr. Van Essen wanted the place secured."

"Craig?"

"Yeah. He stepped out just before you woke up. He said to tell you he'd be back later."

That was a surprise.

It got quiet for a moment. Finally, I looked up at Kekoa. "I want you to know I'm sorry about everything that happened—especially about Raquel."

He patted me on my cast and let me know, "Kaui and I talked about this, Mike. We don't blame you for anything."

It got quiet again. I turned to Kaui and asked, "What happened to Safire, anyway?"

"Dead."

"Are you sure?"

He nodded. "I couldn't be more certain."

"What about Malia?"

"Malia's fine," he replied. "In fact, she'll be here this afternoon, so you might want to freshen up."

I managed a smile.

Just then, Ashley returned to the room. "How are we doing?"

"We have to pee," I told her.

She smiled. "Go right ahead. You have a tube inserted in your thingy. It drains into a bag."

I thought about the mechanics of that for a second, then let loose.

Ashley busied herself by checking my dressings and bandages. While she changed the cotton in my nose, she asked, "Do you think you could drink something?"

"Sure. I'll have a Corona—and grab one for yourself while you're at it. Do you have any limes?"

She gave me a look, like she'd heard that one before. "No beer for you, Mr. Brennan. I'll bring some ice chips instead." Before leaving, she turned and added, "While I'm at it, I'll check to see if your testicles are black." She gave me a quick wink and exited the room.

I looked over at Kekoa. "What did she just say?"

"She's going to find out if your test results are back."

"Oh."

After a few minutes, Ashley returned with a small cup of ice chips. She looked at me and asked, "Do you feel like you need more pain medication?"

"I asked for a Corona earlier and you said 'No.'"

Before she could break out in laughter, one of the doctors entered the room wearing a white lab coat and thick glasses. He seemed to ignore us while studying one of the monitors on the opposite wall.

I asked Ashley, "What kind of surgery did they do on me?"

"Mostly, it was to remove a bullet from your right shoulder."

"A bullet? Really?"

She gave me a look and went on, "They also put some titanium plates on your jaw and your forearm, plus a skin graft to replace missing tissue on your right elbow."

"Where did they take the skin from?"

"Your buttocks."

The twins both snickered at that.

I asked Ashley, "Does this mean I can moon people without pulling my pants down?"

She gave me another look of disapproval. The doctor, however, seemed to like that one. With his back still turned to me, he muttered a few things to the nurse. After that, she signaled the twins to follow her out of the room, which they did. Once the security guard had closed the door, the doc faced me and removed his glasses. "Don't worry, Mr. Brennan; I'm not here to check your prostate."

Daniel Morris.

He looked me over for a moment. "I was told you'd had a close brush with death."

"You heard right. This job is a killer."

Daniel nodded in agreement, then switched into serious mode. "Before I go any further," he said, "allow me to state my deepest regrets over the loss of young Raquel Richards. The President also sends his most sincere condolences."

I let a moment pass before I changed subjects. "So, how is the President?"

Daniel moved a chair beside me and sat. "He is quite well—although he is certainly concerned about you."

"Tell him he can start looking for a new agent. I'm resigning as of right now."

He seemed to ignore that and told me, "The body of Lucas Richter was found this morning."

"He was behind it all," I said. "It was Richter himself who killed the four people in the control room."

"Be sure to include the details of that in your report."

"I also had my ICD in record mode, so everything Richter said is on tape."

He nodded. "Excellent."

"And have someone arrest Derrick Haut. He was up to his gills in this, too."

Daniel looked down and typed a brief message into his phone before turning his attention back to me.

I went on, "Richter told me he'd personally orchestrated the sabotage of Praxis II. He also indicated that someone high up at Cronus had originated the plan."

He managed a weak smile. "You've done quite well."

Well, I didn't think so, but I continued with my explanation, "While exploring Venus, the control room team discovered another rover was already there. Richter seemed to believe it was of the same origin as the one found in Mexico—"

"Are we talking about Rita?"

"Yes. In fact, I think Richter must have been a fanatic on the topic." I paused for a moment, then went out on a limb and asked, "Do you know if Rita actually exists, or is it simply a legend?"

Daniel leaned back in his chair and looked at me. "Yes, Michael, it does indeed exist."

Well, that's interesting to know.

He leaned forward and explained, "Rita's age and origin can only be guessed at, but it is certainly ancient. The machine was in poor condition by the time it was discovered. A President's Agent, like yourself, dug it out of the earth and managed to smuggle it over the border undetected."

"So we stole it."

He let that sail by and continued. "The theorists preach that Kennedy chose to name it Rita, which is Latin for 'arisen.' In truth, the agent himself named it. He chose Rueda, which is a Spanish word for wheel. Over time, the pronunciation degenerated into Rita, which stuck."

Nurse Ashley glanced at me through the glass door while Daniel moved along with his story. "As you may have guessed, the discovery laid the foundation for most of our modern technology. When they began the reverse engineering process, the scientists involved quickly realized there was a vast amount of knowledge to be gained—more than anyone had dreamed. The experts concluded that if too much were introduced to the world too quickly, we would get ahead of ourselves—"

"You mean *destroy* ourselves."

"Correct. Therefore, we've introduced only small bits of its technology at a time. Some of your surgical procedures relied on recently introduced nanotechnology. Over the coming decades we'll see fusion energy, bioware, wireless power, and much more." He added, "All of this must be presented to the world in a careful and calculated way."

"That, I understand."

He checked an incoming message and informed me, "Derrick Haut is in custody."

"Good. Make sure they throw the book at him." Just then, I looked at his hand and noticed a unique ring. Like mine, it had a polished gold inlay on one side and platinum on the other. This, I knew, was designed for only one purpose: to operate an Implanted Communication Devise. Perhaps there was more to Daniel Morris than I'd thought.

He leaned back in his chair again. "Before you consider resignation, Michael, there are a few other things you should understand as well."

"My resignation is not under consideration, Daniel. It's decided."

"Hear me out. There is a unique opportunity ahead, just waiting for you." He placed his chin on his hands and told me, "With the evidence you've collected, you've made it possible for Wright Aerospace to quietly acquire Cronus Space and Communications. This is exactly what the President wanted."

"I'm glad to hear that, but I still quit."

He continued, "Craig Van Essen has made it known that he wants you to be his successor once the President's terms are over."

"Are you serious?"

"Quite. Once in that position, you will have friends in high places. Friends who will remember what you've done here." He looked at me and added, "You will also be in charge of virtually all decisions concerning Rita."

Holy smokes. After that sunk in I told Daniel, "The twins should be involved with Rita's research—whether I resign or not."

He smiled at that and stood from his chair. "You should rest for a while," he said. "However, I'll need your word that you will be continuing as President's Agent before I go." He added, "I strongly recommend you continue."

I never liked being pushed. I looked around the room. There were monitors, IV pumps, and tubes everywhere. I realized I was lucky to be alive. I then thought about Raquel, who wasn't so lucky.

Soon, Daniel Morris began tapping his fingers on the side rail. Finally, he looked down at me and asked, "Tell me Michael, are you in or out?"

-EPILOGUE-

"You cannot escape the responsibility of tomorrow by evading it today."
~Abraham Lincoln

I didn't want to test Daniel's patience. At the same time, I didn't appreciate being pressured into a decision I might live to regret—or die before I had a chance to. The wheels in my head were spinning as I weighed my options.

To be honest, my life choices up to now had been selfish—and look where that has gotten me. I need to turn things around while I still can.

Apparently, Daniel figured I could be easily lured and was trying to tempt me with a devil's deal. At the same time, he was hinting that things might not go well for me if I didn't stay on as the President's Agent. The implications of that alone were more than I cared to ponder. In truth, I had enough classified information stored in my head to turn half the corporate world upside down—and I'd only completed one mission so far.

I tried to avoid eye contact and focused at the monitor on the far wall. I felt angry inside and told Daniel, "This is still *my* life and no one owns me—not even the President." I looked at him and added, "Not even you."

He made no reply.

I closed my eyes and tried to calm my mind. Immediately, my thoughts went to Raquel. I could see her young face and her soft eyes. I could see her smile and hear her laugh. What would she have wanted for me? And where would the two of us have wound up if she hadn't…?

At that moment, I realized the dreams I was holding onto had died, and had died along with the only woman in this world I'd ever really cared about.

Daniel's voice startled me. "Please Michael, I must have an answer. Tell me," he pleaded, "are you in or out?"

I looked up at him. My words, though few, felt heavy on my tongue as I answered him, betraying myself once again. "I'm in."

The End

The Author

Greg Marion is a long time resident of Maui, Hawaii and a licensed RN. He is a graduate of University of Hawaii Maui College and a member of the International Thriller Writers and the International Screenwriters' Association.

Besides reading and writing fiction, his interests include graphic art, water sports, hiking, and travel. Greg and his wife have three grown children.

For more, check out his website at gregmarion.com or his Facebook site at https://www.facebook.com/gregmarionbooks

A note from Greg Marion:

I sincerely hope you've enjoyed reading Red Sky Morning as much as I did writing it. In case you didn't know, things are changing a bit for writers and reader's reviews are becoming increasingly important, especially for newer authors. If you feel inclined, please submit an honest review for this book and others you read.

Aloha, Greg

Acknowledgements

First of all, I would like to thank my wife Rose for her patience, great advice, and words of encouragement while I wrote Red Sky Morning. She also let me know when I screwed up. I guess I should be thankful for that, too.

In addition, I'd like to thank my beta readers including Linda Hewlett and Jeanne Mathews, as well as my friend Jack Foster and my brother Brad Marion, all of whom offered suggestions and helped with figuring out where all the commas, periods, and parenthesis should go. I think we got most of them.

Mahalo to everyone.

www.ingramcontent.com/pod-product-compliance
Lightning Source LLC
Chambersburg PA
CBHW070622130626
46556CB00001B/443